THE GUARD LET GO OF JACK'S HAIR. HIS HEAD dropped and banged against the floor. The light over the Magus's throne went out, and the Rüstov emperor's mechanical eye glowed in the darkness. Light trails followed the eye as the Magus turned away and Jack's vision blurred. He felt dizzy. Somewhere deep inside him, he heard Khalix laughing as the world faded away.

THE END OF INFINITY

BOOK 3

a JACK BLANK ADVENTURE

Matt Myklusch

ALADDIN

NEW YORK LONDON TORONTO SYDNEY NEW DELHI

ALADDIN

An imprint of Simon & Schuster Children's Publishing Division

1230 Avenue of the Americas, New York, NY 10020

First Aladdin paperback edition August 2013

Copyright © 2012 by Matt Myklusch

All rights reserved, including the right of reproduction in whole or in part in any form.

ALADDIN is a trademark of Simon & Schuster, Inc., and related logo is a registered trademark of Simon & Schuster, Inc.

Also available in an Aladdin hardcover edition.

For information about special discounts for bulk purchases, please contact Simon & Schuster Special Sales at 1-866-506-1949 or business@simonandschuster.com.

The Simon & Schuster Speakers Bureau can bring authors to your live event.

For more information or to book an event contact the Simon & Schuster Speakers Bureau at 1-866-248-3049 or visit our website at www.simonspeakers.com.

Designed by Karin Paprocki and Karina Granda

The text of this book was set in Goudy Old Style Regular.

Manufactured in the United States of America 0719 OFF

6 8 10 9 7 5

The Library of Congress has cataloged the hardcover edition as follows:

Myklusch, Matt.

The end of infinity / by Matt Myklusch. — 1st Aladdin hardcover ed.

p. cm. — (A Jack Blank adventure ; bk. 3)

Summary: Ever since Jack Blank learned that he came from the amazing country of the Imagine Nation, he's known that his fate could go down two very different paths—he could either be the greatest hero the world has ever known, or its greatest villain. Now the final battle is here, and it's time for Jack to discover the direction of his destiny.

ISBN 978-1-4169-9567-8 (hc)

[1. Superheroes—Fiction. 2. Adventure and adventurers—Fiction. 3. Virus diseases—Fiction. 4. Identity—Fiction. 5. Fantasy.] I. Title.

PZ7.M994End 2012   [Fic]—dc23   2012000861

ISBN 978-1-4169-9568-5 (pbk)

ISBN 978-1-4169-9569-2 (eBook)

FOR MY DAD,
A REAL-LIFE SUPERHERO

Contents

THE END OF INFINITY

The Emperor's New Clothes

Voices echoed in Jack's ears. The blackness surrounding him began to take shape and light faded in as if someone were sliding a dimmer switch, stopping at a dull amber glow. It took a moment for Jack's eyes to adjust. Once they did, he found himself surrounded by the Rüstov. Judging by the appearance of his captors, he was in the presence of royalty. He had been taken to the emperor's throne room.

The Rüstov's typical architecture and design, represented by a chaotic mess of jury-rigged scrap, was eschewed here in favor of a clean, industrial aesthetic. Smooth steel panels lined the walls, with giant rivets drilled into their edges. Massive I beams filled the chamber, running from the floor all the way up to the ceiling. By Rüstov standards, they were the equivalent of intricately painted frescoes and marble columns—a lavish display of elegance. Fresh-faced nobles dressed in fancy robes stared at Jack in silence. On the far side of the room, a small run of steps led up to a large iron throne. The chair was spun around, facing the other direction, its occupant looking out a window into space. Jack tried to move, but he was held fast by one of the Magus's imperial guards. He struggled against its grip, but he had no strength.

Jack's thoughts were sluggish, like someone had poured cement into his brain. His powers had no effect on the guard, who, like the nobles, was using a host that had very little techno-decay. Standing next to Jack, also locked in the grip of another Rüstov guard, was a man dressed in prison rags. He was clearly terrified.

"What is this?" Jack asked, his voice weak and groggy. "What's going on?"

"Silence!" the guard behind Jack shouted, striking him on the head.

Jack's head throbbed with pain. Lacking the energy even to give the guard a dirty look, he opted to hold his tongue rather than risk another blow. A bluish-white spotlight switched on above the throne, and the chair slowly rotated until Jack was face-to-face with the Magus. The guard holding Jack immediately dropped to one knee and forced him to genuflect before the emperor as well. Jack tried to look up, but the guard pushed his head back down. "Bow your head, meat. You do not look at the Magus."

From his knees, with the Rüstov guard's hand on the back of his head, Jack peered up at the Magus as best he could. Despite his limited vantage point, it was plain to see that the Magus was unlike any Rüstov he had ever encountered before. Rüstov host bodies were typically withered, frail husks that had been sucked dry by their parasites. They were broken shells of people, with veins that had been turned into circuits, bones that had been morphed into rusty metal, and organs that had been transformed into greasy, ramshackle contraptions with dirty gears. Jack had seen the ruinous effects of Rüstov infections firsthand in the many Para-Soldiers he'd fought over the years. The host body that the Magus inhabited exhibited none of the mummified, zombielike features he'd come to expect from the Rüstov. The Magus was in peak physical condition—

a strong, perfect, muscle-bound specimen with almost no sign of infection.

The Magus rose from his seat and walked toward Jack and the other prisoner. The closer he got, the less Jack saw of him. With his head pressed firmly toward the ground, Jack could see only a pair of bare feet advancing along the path, beneath the folds of a snow-white robe. The prisoner next to Jack was whimpering. Jack didn't waste words trying to tell him that everything was going to be all right. He knew better.

Jack heard a loud *pop-hiss* noise, like a knife stabbing a can of soda, and the Magus's body collapsed to the floor. The Rüstov emperor had released his host. Jack had a clear view of the unconscious body until it was dragged out of sight by the greedy hands of other Rüstov royals. He could picture the parasitic nobles fighting over the body as if it were some kind of stylish hand-me-down. As the Magus's former host was pulled away, his white robe stayed behind. Something was stuck beneath it, trying to punch its way out from under the folds of fabric. Jack, who had never seen a Rüstov without its host before, gasped when a scrap-metal scorpion the size of a small dog crawled out into the open. It snapped its claws and curled its tail to strike.

The guard beside Jack let go of the other prisoner, and the guard behind him relaxed his grip on his head. Jack craned his neck up and looked around. The prisoner next to him ran to the exit and banged on the door, unable to open it. Frantic, he ran off in the other direction, but the Rüstov soldiers that lined the perimeter of the room threw him back into the center. The guard behind Jack laughed. He and his fellow Rüstov watched the scene play out like a sporting event. Trapped in the Magus's chamber, the helpless prisoner backed away from the iron scorpion on the ground. His eyes darted back and forth, wide as golf balls. "Help me!" he screamed, looking directly at Jack. "Please!"

Jack was speechless. He was powerless to stop what was about to happen. The doomed man backed away from the hostless Magus and tripped over the steps leading up to the throne. He fell on his rear end and shuffled backward up the steps. The scorpion pounced. It crawled up the man's leg in a flash and skittered over his chest. Jack could tell what was coming next. The scorpion latched onto the man's shoulder with its tail, and then disappeared around his back. There was a noise like a heavy shovel digging into the earth, and Jack cringed as the man cried out in pain. Jack turned away, unable to watch the rest of the transformation. He saw only the Magus's shadow on the wall as his shape went from being that of a man to something else. Something large and terrible. The screaming stopped and the Magus's silhouette relaxed. The Rüstov emperor breathed out a sigh of relief and stretched. Jack turned back toward the Magus as his aides draped his robe over him and tied it off at the waist. The guard pushed Jack's head down again. Jack made no effort to look back up this time around. He had seen enough.

It turned out that the Magus's fresh, smooth-skinned hosts were not completely unblemished after all. Right next to his eye with the Rüstov mark, a large iron horn extended out from his temple, and six swordlike growths fanned out of his back like wings, three to each side. When Jack glimpsed the Magus earlier, he had mistakenly thought those elements were part of his throne. Now he knew differently. They were part of him. The Magus looked like a cyborg version of the devil himself.

The Magus crossed the room and stood over Jack. "Rise," he commanded. The Rüstov guard stood up and pulled Jack onto his feet. Jack did not look at the Magus until he had no other choice. The Rüstov emperor took him by the chin and lifted his head up, forcing him to meet his gaze. The Magus stared at him, studying him. Jack thought he was going to melt under the Rüstov leader's penetrating, heartless eyes. Quite unexpectedly, his lips curled up, forming a thin smile. The Magus gave Jack a light tap on the cheek and rested his hand on Jack's shoulder. "Welcome home, my son."

Jack did his best to sound brave. "I'm not your son."

The Magus frowned and grumbled out a low growl.

Jack dropped to the ground in a heap. A searing hot knife was turning inside his brain. His eye was burning. He pressed his palm against it like he was afraid it might pop out of the socket. Just when he thought he couldn't take it anymore, the pain stopped. Jack rolled over onto his back and struggled to catch his breath. When he finally did, he looked up at the Magus and realized something very scary. The Magus hadn't moved an inch. He had hit Jack with his mind.

Jack tried to get up but decided to give it a few seconds first. He rested on all fours for a moment. The Magus nodded to a guard, who stepped on Jack's back, pushing him down. The guard knelt to Jack's level and grabbed his hair, pulling his head up to face the Rüstov emperor. "I wasn't talking to *you*," the Magus said. "You will speak when spoken to. I will not have this reunion with my son spoiled by your filthy tongue."

Jack was gasping for air. Drool dripped from his lower lip. "What did you just do to me?"

The Magus laughed. "I simply helped your infection along, ever so slightly. Get used to the pain. There's more to come."

Jack's mind was racing. The hopelessness of his situation was starting to sink in. "I can't . . . I can't use my powers."

The Magus smiled with chilling confidence. "Patience . . . you will."

The guard let go of Jack's hair. His head dropped and banged against the floor. The light over the Magus's throne went out, and the Rüstov emperor's mechanical eye glowed in the darkness. Light trails followed the eye as the Magus turned away and Jack's vision blurred. He felt dizzy. Somewhere deep inside him, he heard Khalix laughing as the world faded away.

Ghost in the Machine

Solomon Roka moved through the Rüstov super-dreadnaught *Apocalypse* with the swift, silent purpose of a black ops commando. He was a tall man with a lean, muscular build, short black hair, and three days' worth of stubble on his face. He wore a formfitting black suit lined with flexible circuitry and carried a backpack filled with all the tools of his profession. Roka crept around corners like a thief in the night, and although the time of day in deep space was relative, he was without question a thief. He was there to steal the future of the Rüstov people.

Roka approached a sliding metal door with a small window right at eye level. As he reached out to open it, a green light lit up on its access panel. He froze in place and his heart followed suit. The door was about to open from the other side. Rüstov sentries were coming through. They hadn't seen him yet, but he had only a few seconds before they did.

Roka had no cover in the empty passageway. The door on the opposite end of the hall was too far away, but he ran for it, hugging the shadows as he went. The sound of compressed air being released filled the hallway as the doors began to slide apart behind him. He had time left for only a simple choice: right or left. The lack of an exit in either direction was not a problem. The uncertainty surrounding each option was. Roka made up his mind and activated his Ghost Suit. The circuits covering his body blazed with light, rendering his molecules intangible as he leaped *through* the wall directly to his left. He just hoped he wasn't diving into a situation worse than the one he was trying to escape.

Roka found himself alone when he emerged on the other side of the wall. He stood on the engineering deck of the ship, overlooking the *Apocalypse*'s powerful warp core. He had to get his bearings straight and find his way to the detention block, but first he needed a minute to collect himself and gather his nerves. They were scattered everywhere, which was unusual for him. This kind of operation was Roka's stock in trade, but this was more than just another job. This breakout wasn't about money; his own freedom was on the line this time too. There was something else as well. The *Apocalypse* wasn't just any Rüstov ship. It was the personal flagship of the Rüstov emperor. Roka was quite happy to go on living without ever having the honor of meeting the Rüstov leader.

Getting back to business, Roka activated a holographic map-finder device on his wrist. It emitted a high-frequency sonar pulse that generated blueprints of the ship and projected them into the air in front him. The ship's plans glowed brightly in the darkness, faded down, and returned as each sonic pulse sounded. Roka saw where he needed to go. His objective was three hundred feet below him, straight down.

Roka measured the drop with a laser ruler and took out a length of special evaporating rope. He latched himself to a railing overlooking the ship's engine, jumped over the top, and dove down alongside the white-hot column of pure energy that powered the starship's Infinite Warp Core. Air whistled through Roka's hair as he fell, anchored to the walkway above. He swung his feet out to land as the floor raced toward him. The thin, black rope stretched like a bungee cord, slowing his descent, and then dissolved into smoke as he touched down softly on the ground. The jump would have been perfect if not for the fact that he landed right among a trio of Rüstov Para-Soldiers.

Before the Rüstov even had time to register his presence, Roka flipped down a pair of shades and set off a light grenade to blind his enemies. He grabbed the Para-Soldier closest to him by the wrist, turned, and flipped it over his shoulder. The Rüstov sentry crashed into one of its fellow guards, and Roka detached a small disk from his belt. He slapped it onto the third Para-Soldier's chest. Electric currents poured out of the disk, ripping through the Rüstov's body and permanently disabling it. The first two Para-Soldiers were just getting back up when Roka jumped and threw both feet into them, kicking them back over the edge of the platform. They fell into the warp core's towering column of energy and were vaporized instantly. The whole fight, if it could truly be described as such, lasted all of seven seconds.

The Rüstov threat neutralized, Roka once again activated his Ghost Suit and phased through the wall on his right. He emerged in the detention block and took a deep breath, mentally preparing himself for what would be the hardest part of the mission. Roka walked down the hall, forcing himself to ignore the pleas for help coming from the prisoners who were locked up in the cells to his left and right. It wasn't easy. Roka knew what was in store for them. A long time ago, he'd been a Rüstov prisoner himself. It was absolutely killing him to leave them behind, but there was nothing he could do for them. Not here. Not now. But maybe . . . just maybe, if what he'd been told was true, there was hope for them yet.

At end of the hall, Roka arrived at a locked door. He could see through its foggy laser-proof window well enough to make out a prison lab on the other side. This was it. Roka narrowed the focus on his Ghost Suit to phase only his hand. It flickered like a faded movie projection as he ran it through the lock, shorting out its circuits. The door slid open and Roka entered the lab.

The room was empty, which was good, but Roka still didn't like what he found inside. In the center of the lab was an operating table surrounded by vicious-looking surgical tools and trays of techno-organic hardware. Roka didn't know what kind of sick experiments went on in this room, but it was clear that whatever prisoner had spent time on that operating table wasn't dealing with the standard Rüstov infection.

Next to the table was a stasis pod, large enough to fit a single person inside. Next to that, a holo-screen readout displayed the words "Infection Level: 25%." Roka plugged a CodeBreaker into a data port on the pod's access panel, and the cover rose up like the lid of a coffin. Gas poured out from the inside. As the vapors cleared, Roka noticed a red light flashing on the pod, blinking out the words "Incubation Period Interrupted." He'd set off a silent alarm. Roka frowned and, in a very businesslike manner, knelt down to remove a pair of special suits from his pack. He held one out toward the figure in the pod, who was just waking up. "Put this on. We don't have much time."

A groggy voice called out from inside the pod. "What's going on? Who are you?"

Roka kicked his pack away and stood up, pulling his suit on over his clothes. "I'm Solomon Roka. I'm here to rescue you."

Jack Blank stepped out of the stasis pod and nearly fell over. Roka caught him and propped him up. "Can you walk?" Jack nodded, and Roka thrust a space suit into his arms. "Put this on. Quickly. We need to be gone before the guards show u—"

They moved into the light and Roka stopped talking.

"What is it? What's wrong?" Jack asked.

It took Roka a moment to answer. He was locked in a frozen stare, transfixed by Jack's appearance. "You, uh . . ." Roka shook his head and started sealing up his own suit. "You've got something on your eye, kid."

Jack touched a hand to his face and drew in a sharp breath. He checked his reflection in the stasis pod's glass lid, and sure enough, there it was. A parting gift from the Rüstov. Just a little something to take home with him. The mark of Rüstov infection surrounded Jack's eye like a line drawn with black paint.

CHAPTER

The Great Escape

An explosion tore through the *Apocalypse*'s hull and the inescapable vacuum of space ripped Jack and Roka out of the ship. They shot out into the cosmos wearing the armored space suits Roka had brought with him. Jack went spinning wildly into the void. His eyes went wide as he tried to draw focus on the endless sea of stars around him. He was in space. Deep space, light-years from home. It was almost too much to process. One minute he was sleeping in a metal pod, and the next thing he knew, some complete stranger had pulled him out here. His brain was still playing catch-up. What was he doing in that pod? Where was *here*? If the dying planets and Rüstov warships all around were any indication, it was no place good. Jack's head was full of cobwebs. The only thing he knew for sure was that he had to get far away from this place as fast as possible. Unfortunately, he was completely out of control.

Roka tried to grab Jack's wrist as he went flying through space, but he lost his grip when they ran into a small asteroid belt. A hailstorm of pebble-like fragments pelted Jack's helmet and body, disorienting him. He tried to grab onto some of the larger asteroids and steady himself, but he couldn't get a handle on them. His limbs felt heavy and slow. A watermelon-size meteor struck Jack and sent him tumbling head over heels. He tried not to panic, but he knew precious time was being wasted. The Rüstov weren't going to let him just walk out of here. He had to get himself together. Hardly an easy thing to do when you are flailing helplessly in space. Jack watched an upside-down Solomon Roka use the thrusters in his suit to right himself, and something clicked in Jack's head. His powers . . . the armored space suit was a machine.

Jack opened his mind up to the suit as Roka called to him on a radio in his helmet.

"Use your thrusters! The controls are on your—"

Before Roka could even finish his sentence, Jack engaged his thrusters, spun around, and steadied himself in a right-side-up position. He noticed something off in the distance behind Roka. A wrist cannon on his arm called out to be used, and Jack raised his hand, firing three shots over Roka's shoulder. All three shots hit their marks, blasting holes in the Rüstov Para-Soldiers that were silently coming up behind Roka.

"That's better," Jack said. It felt good, using his powers. It felt even better fighting back against the Rüstov. Jack's head cleared a little. He remembered how he ended up in Rüstov space. He'd been kidnapped by the Rüstov agent Glave after stopping his plot to take over the Imagine Nation. He remembered Glave's men pulling his half-conscious body out of a pile of crystal rubble back on Mount Nevertop. The question was, what had happened after that?

Roka raised an eyebrow, clearly impressed with how Jack had handled the Rüstov soldiers. "I see someone found the suit's blasters. Used this model before?"

Jack shook his head. "I'm just good with machines."

Roka grunted. "You're gonna have to be. We've got company." He pointed toward a battalion of Rüstov space-troopers that was flying out of the *Apocalypse* like hornets from a broken nest. Jack felt a twinge of pain behind his eyebrows, which rapidly grew in intensity. The Magus was angry. He didn't know how he knew that, but he knew it. Jack winced and reached for his temple, touching his hand against the outside of his space helmet. His right eye felt like it was on fire, and he heard a voice:

"Jack, stop this. My father isn't going to let you go. Don't try to be a hero. . . . You're going to get us both killed."

The voice put a layer of frost on Jack's spine. It was Khalix, son of the Magus and heir to the Rüstov empire, talking. Khalix was the alien parasite who had infected Jack years ago, when he was just a baby. He was the dark reflection Jack saw in the mirror whenever he thought about his future as Revile, the unstoppable killing machine of the Rüstov.

"Hey, kid," Roka said, placing a hand on Jack's shoulder. "You okay?"

Jack cleared his throat and shook his head, working to power through the pain and shut Khalix out of his mind. "I'm fine," he said, brushing Roka's hand away. "I've got this."

Jack reached a hand out toward the Rüstov troops that were coming his way. So much of their bodies were made up of machinery. Everything from the microprocessors in their brains to the metal hinges in their knees was his to control. Or so he thought. He tried to lock up the Para-Soldiers' joints and jam their weapons, but nothing happened. Jack looked at his hand as if it were a gun that had just misfired. "Something's wrong."

"You think?" Roka grabbed Jack and pulled him behind a meteor as the Rüstov opened fire. A salvo of laser blasts pounded against the other side of the rock. "Don't move!" Roka yelled as he reached over the top and returned fire without looking where he was shooting. He didn't hit anything, but the kickback from his blasts helped push the meteor away from the Para-Soldiers. Jack leaned around the side and reached his hand out toward the Rüstov attackers. Again, his powers failed him.

"I don't understand. Nothing's happening!" He was

still trying to use his powers against the Rüstov when Roka pulled him out of the line of fire for the second time.

"I said stay down!"

This time Jack did as he was told. He leaned back against the meteor, pulling his arms and legs in close as laser blasts raced past him on all sides. It didn't make any sense . . . his powers worked on the space suit. They *should* have worked on the Rüstov. What was going on?

"In case you haven't noticed, I've grown a lot stronger over the last year," Khalix taunted Jack. "You still have your powers, but I won't stand by and let you use them against my people. We control you, not the other way around. Don't ever forget that."

Jack scowled. "Uh-uh, my powers keep *you* in check. That's the way it's always be—" Jack stopped short, realizing what Khalix had just told him. "Wait a minute . . . a year?! What do you mean, a year?"

Roka scrunched up his face. "Who you talking to, kid?"

Khalix's cackling laughter rang in Jack's ears. His stomach tied itself into a knot and he looked up at Roka with frightened eyes.

A Rüstov laser blast just missed Roka's head, and he

ducked back down behind the meteor. "We can't stay here much longer. We gotta move." Roka looked around at the meteor field and then tapped Jack's shoulder. "There. Follow me." He pushed hard off the meteor with his feet and sailed out toward larger rocks in the distance. Jack burned a few seconds trying to decide if Khalix was lying or not before he finally took off after Roka. He kicked himself for wasting even that much time. Every second counted. He couldn't let Khalix's verbal jabs psyche him out. That was just what the Rüstov prince wanted. At least, Jack hoped that's all there was to it.

Once Jack got going, the asteroids provided excellent cover as he and Roka hopped from stone to stone. Jack got a handle on using his space suit and moved through the field easily, even with the Rüstov space-troopers trailing close behind. The real challenge was staying focused. Jack wanted to believe Khalix was just messing with his head, but he couldn't be sure. He tried to remember yesterday or the day before. Nothing came to mind. He thought about the week before that, or the month even. There was nothing there. No memories. Jack had no idea how long he'd been the Rüstov's prisoner or what they had done to him during that time. Only one thing was certain. Rüstov technology was off-limits for him. Khalix was telling the truth about that. Jack was completely surrounded by Rüstov machinery, and he couldn't "feel" any of it. Giant dreadnought warships filled the sky, blocking out the stars. The massive, cone-shaped battleships were rife with exposed wiring, cable, and tubing that wove its way through every inch of their exteriors. Sharp, spiky antennae jutted out at odd angles all along the hull of each ship, but Jack couldn't make contact with any of them. Bursts of static drowned out any connection he tried to make. His powers couldn't touch the Rüstov fleet.

What Jack's powers could touch and feel were the small metal disks that Roka had left behind on key meteors as he made his way through the field. They snapped onto the surface of each rock, magnetically attracted to the minerals inside. Jack scanned the disks as Roka laid them down and saw that his newfound friend was setting a deadly trap for the Rüstov. Jack and Roka reached the other side of the meteor field and took cover behind a giant rock fragment as the Rüstov steadily advanced.

"End of the line," Roka said as the Para-Soldiers came

in, guns blazing. Jack took aim at the Rüstov, but Roka pushed his hand down. "Let 'em come," he told Jack, holding up a remote control. "I got a little surprise for them." Just as he was about to push the button, a Rüstov laser blast shot the remote out of his hand. Roka stared at his empty hand in silent disbelief. "Okay, that's a problem."

"Don't worry. This one I really do have." Jack held out his hand and activated the electro-disks Roka had planted on the meteors. A net of blue lightning bolts cast itself through the meteor field, catching the entire company of Para-Soldiers in its lines and frying them. The mummified husks of their hosts' infected bodies shook violently, and their cybernetic scrap-metal components blew apart from the electric current. When the bolts finally blinked out, they left behind scores of lifeless Rüstov bodies drifting off into space.

Roka raised an eyebrow. "Good with machines, huh?"

Jack shook his head. "Not as good as I used to be."

A pair of Shardwing starfighters angled on Jack and Roka. Rüstov voices crackled into the open frequencies on their helmet radios. "Halt in the name of the Magus," the voice ordered. "Surrender or be destroyed."

"I hope there's more to your escape plan than this," Jack said, putting his hands up.

"Relax, kid. I do this for a living."

A flash of light ignited behind Jack, and two large plasma blasts tore through space. The Shardwings exploded, and the resulting force sent Jack and Roka flying backward. Jack used his suit's thrusters to stabilize his position and looked up as a new ship appeared on his internal radar. He used his powers to quickly scan the ship's logs and found out it was Roka's ship, the *Harbinger*. Jack breathed a sigh of relief as it swooped in above him and dropped its cloak. The *Harbinger* was a sleek, mid-size warship with a long fuselage and sharp, curved wings that made it look like a bird of prey.

"Nice ship," Jack said. "Is it fast?"

"Is it fast?" Roka repeated. "What kind of question is that?" Jack used his powers to look through the *Harbinger*'s systems, taking note of the ship's powerful twin warp engines. He gave Roka an impressed nod. A cargo bay door opened up on the ship's belly. "Let's go, kid, we're not out of the woods yet."

Jack followed Roka inside the ship, where Roka

immediately sealed the doors, pulled off his helmet, and shouted into the intercom, "Outer bay doors are locked, let's move!"

"Moving," a voice called back as the ship surged into gear. Roka grabbed hold of the cargo bay netting to keep himself standing upright as the ship rocketed away. Jack was knocked clean off his feet, but even if the *Harbinger*'s sudden takeoff hadn't sent him reeling, the voice on the intercom would have done it all by itself.

"Is that who I think it is?" he asked Roka, getting back up on his feet.

Roka didn't answer. He was already running through the ship, presumably headed for the bridge. Jack took off after him. The ship tilted from side to side as they ran, taking hard turns and extreme nosedives.

"What's going on?" Jack shouted.

"They're not letting you go without a fight," Roka said as more Shardwing fighters were scrambling to chase them down. Jack got a good look at them through the ship's windows as he ran. Waves of Rüstov starfighters flew after them in attack formations. Their sharp, irregular shapes made them look like metal splinters that had broken off the larger dreadnought gunships, and they swirled around the *Harbinger* like a swarm of killer bees. "We're in it now, kid," Roka said as he opened up the door to the ship's cockpit. Jack barely heard him. His attention had been completely hijacked by the sight of the ship's pilot:

"Jazen!" Jack yelled, his earlier suspicions confirmed. He ran ahead of Roka. Sure enough, Jazen Knight was at the ship's helm.

"Jack!" Jazen yelled back.

Roka ran in after Jack, motioning for Jazen to let him at the controls. "Up," he ordered, sliding into the chair to trade places with Jazen, who happily sprang out of the seat to wrap his arms around Jack.

"Thank goodness you're safe," Jazen said, clutching him tight. "I can't believe he got you out!"

"I can't believe *you're* here!" Jack replied. "How did you even know where to find me?"

"What are you talking about? We've been getting your SOS signals for a month now."

Jack furrowed his brow. "SOS signals? What?"

"You didn't think we'd just leave you out here, did you?" Jazen let go of Jack and took a good look at him, smiling from ear to ear. He tried not to let it show, but Jack noticed a widening of his android friend's eyes when he saw the Rüstov mark on Jack's face. Jack looked down at his shoes, and Jazen leaned over to catch Jack's eyes. "Hey. It's gonna be okay, Jack. We're gonna get you out of here. We'll deal with the rest later."

Jack ran a hand through his hair and let it drop. "I don't know, Jazen, I—"

"Jack!" a voice called out from overhead.

"Allegra!" Jack shouted. His face lit up as he turned to look at her. She was busy manning one of the *Harbinger*'s guns. The young Valorian girl craned her liquid metal neck around the firing controls to smile down at Jack. Her eyes bugged out at the sight of the scar on his eye, and Jack's smile evaporated.

"No time for hugs and happy reunions!" Roka shouted. "We still have to fight our way out of here. There's two more guns that need gunners, and a lot more unfriendlies out there." Roka pulled the ship into a spiral dive, flying through the asteroid belt with the Shardwings hot on his tail. "Jack, you think you can fire a plasma cannon as well as you work a space suit and rig electric webs?"

Jack nodded. "I'll do my best."

"These two tell me that's pretty good. Get going."

Jack ran to the gun turret on the starboard side of the ship and climbed in. Jazen took the cannon on the port side, and Roka took evasive action as the *Harbinger*'s crew all did their best to outrun and outfight the Rüstov.

Jack went to work blasting away at the enemy fighters. Just like outside with the space suit's wrist cannon, his powers worked fine with the *Harbinger*'s weapons. He'd never used a gun like this before, but after a quick "conversation" with the targeting system and firing controls, he became an instant expert. Jack sat in the gyroscope chair, spinning around at target after target, scoring direct hits. He fired relentlessly and took out every Shardwing that came anywhere near his range.

"Looking good, kid!" Roka shouted across the ship. "I'm starting to see what the Rüstov wanted with you."

Jack grunted. He doubted Roka had any idea. It felt so good to be using his powers to fight back again. It made him feel a little bit more normal. More like himself. Of course, that door swung both ways. It bothered Jack that he couldn't use his powers against the Rüstov. That made him feel much less like himself, and he worried about what that might mean.

Jack held on tight as the ship rolled to the left, dodging a volley of Rüstov missiles. "Hey, Jack!" Jazen called out. "How 'bout you tell these Rüstov fighters to lay off, so we can get out of here?"

Jack felt a sharp pain in his head and heard the voice of the Rüstov prince. "Yes, Jack, tell them. Better yet, tell your friend over there that you'd blow all these fighters up with a single thought if you could . . . but you can't. I won't let you."

Jack shivered as Khalix snickered at him. He'd never get used to hearing that voice in his head. It shook him every time he heard it. Khalix had always been there, but now he had a real voice. A strong voice with an unbearable personality. Jack felt violated. It was like he had an intruder in his brain eavesdropping on every word he said.

"Jack, what's wrong?" Jazen asked.

Jack shook his head. "I'll tell you later." A nearby explosion rocked the ship. "If there *is* a later," he added under his breath.

"Jack, can't you just take these guys out with your powers?" Allegra asked.

"I wish," Jack told Allegra. "Gotta do this the old-fashioned way." Jack spun his chair around to blast five Shardwings in succession.

"I can live with that," Roka said, clearly pleased with Jack's deadly accuracy. "Glad you're on our side, kid."

Jack smirked. Again, Roka couldn't have realized how funny that statement was. If they ever got back home, the subject of which side Jack was on was sure to be a hotly debated topic. The Rüstov had been trying to turn him into their ultimate weapon ever since they kidnapped him. As Jack was thinking about that, he remembered he had no idea how long ago that really was. He thought about what Khalix had told him. He couldn't have been gone that long . . .

"Jazen?" Jack called out, still firing away at the enemy.

"Yeah?" Jazen called back over the ship's radio.

"How long have I been gone?"

"How long have you—?" Jazen stopped himself. "You mean you don't know?"

"How long, Jazen?"

Jazen's only answer was silence. After a few moments, Allegra answered for him. "It's been a year, Jack. They had you for a year."

Allegra's words hung in the air like germs. Jack felt like he was sinking into his chair. His lungs contracted. His chest felt heavy and tight.

"Listen to me, Jack," Jazen said. "It's all right. We're going to move forward from *here*. Right now, let's just focus on getting back home."

Jack frowned. That was easier said than done. A whole year of his life had been lost. Khalix was stronger. His parasite was deciding what he could and couldn't use his powers on now! *What did the Rüstov do to me?* Jack gritted his teeth as he fired plasma blasts into Shardwing fighters.

"Jack?" Allegra asked. "How do you feel? I mean . . . Are you okay? Is everything okay?"

Jack didn't know how to answer that. A Rüstov blast pounded the *Harbinger*, rocking it from side to side. "A few more hits like that and none of us are gonna be okay!" Roka shouted as he struggled to right the ship. "Let's focus, people!"

"Allegra. We'll talk about it later," Jazen said.

Jack grunted in agreement and focused on keeping Khalix quiet and shooting down more Shardwings. It took some concentration, but he did it. He was grateful that he was still able to hit the mute button on the Rüstov prince if he really put his mind to it. The last thing he wanted to hear right now was his "roommate's" smug voice in his head. Jack's shots continued to hit their marks, but no matter how many enemy fighters he, Jazen, or Allegra took out, it wasn't getting any easier. The Shardwings darted through space with incredible dexterity and force, and they just kept coming. "There's too many of them," Allegra said. "What are we still doing here? Can't we just jump to hyperspace already?"

"Don't look at me," Roka said. "Talk to the warp drives. We need to phase first."

"We need to what?" Jack asked.

"Traveling at light speed means flying too fast to steer," Roka explained. "We'd crash into meteor showers, stars . . . even planets if we tried it without phasing."

Still confused, Jack did what Roka suggested and reached out to the ship's engine to get some clarity. He learned that the *Harbinger*'s Ghost Box needed to render the ship intangible before they could safely engage the hyperdrives. The box needed to scan the ship and everything on it so that it could throw everyone's molecules into flux for the jump to light speed, and then properly realign them afterward.

"Shouldn't we be ready to punch it by now?" Jazen asked. "What's the hold up?"

"I am," Jack said. "The scan's taking longer because the ship is having a hard time mapping my body."

"Because of your infection?" Allegra asked. "Just talk to the ship's computer and tell it what the Rüstov did to you."

"I can't," Jack said, scratching his chest uncomfortably. "I don't even know that myself." His chest felt heavy underneath his space suit. Jack would have chalked it up to anxiety, but it hurt when he coughed. He could tell that his infection was advancing.

The *Harbinger* took a direct hit, and the ship was thrown onto its side, heading into a flat spin. Powerful centrifugal forces pinned Jack forward against his gun's firing controls as Roka fought to regain control of the ship. The *Harbinger* leveled off, and Jack felt the pressure ease, but the damage had already been done.

"I've got good news and bad news," Roka announced once he'd gotten the ship back under control. "Which one do you want to hear first?"

"Give me the bad news," Jazen said.

"We just lost the Ghost Box."

"*What?*" Allegra asked.

"It's gone," Roka said. "That last shot fried it. No Ghost Box, no light speed."

"What's the good news?" Jazen asked.

Roka shrugged. "Sorry, I lied about the good news. Anybody got any ideas?"

Silence fell over the cabin as the realization sank in that the ship was trapped in enemy territory. They were hopelessly outnumbered and there was no chance of outrunning the Rüstov Armada without light speed.

"Anyone?" Roka asked again. No one said anything.

"Don't tell me that's it," Jack said. "We're done?"

Roka shrugged. "Unless one of you can fly this bird at light speed manually, we're not going anywhere."

Jack thought about what Roka was suggesting. He left

his gun station and ran to the captain's chair. "Give me the stick."

Roka looked at Jack like he was crazy. "Kid, I was being sarcastic."

"I know you were. I'm not. Let me fly this thing. I'll get us through at light speed."

Roka squinted up at Jack. It took him a second to process that Jack was serious. "I'm not just good with machines," Jack said. "I can talk to them. I can talk to the ship. I can do this."

"No," Roka said, pointing back at Jack's empty gyro-chair. "Get back to your gun. I need you shooting down Shardwings while I figure this thing out."

Jack planted his feet. "There's nothing to figure out. There's no other way out of here. I'm the only chance we've got."

"That's not a chance. That's suicide."

The *Harbinger* sustained another hit, and red lights started flashing throughout the cockpit. "So's staying here," Jazen shouted, talking over the sirens as the ship shook back and forth. "You want to die out there, or you want to die here? We're dead either way."

Jack put a hand on the ship's controls. "There's no time to argue. Please. You have to trust me."

Roka scowled at Jack. "I just met you."

"If Jack says he can do it, he can do it," Allegra said.

"You said you wanted ideas," Jazen reminded Roka.

"I meant *good* ideas," Roka shot back. "You can't navigate light speed manually. No one can. You're talking about flying through a rainstorm without getting wet. It's impossible."

"Nothing's impossible," Jack said. "The only thing faster than the speed of light is the speed of thought. I can save us if you'll just get out of the way and let me do it!"

Roka gave Jack a hurt look. "That is the most ungrateful way to talk to someone who just busted you out of the Magus's personal flagship."

"Just do what he says already!" Allegra screamed.

"Roka!" Jazen shouted as a squadron of Rüstov fighters closed in. More alarms started blaring. "They've got missile lock on us. Get up and let Jack fly!"

Solomon Roka looked back and forth at Jazen and Allegra, then shook his head and unbuckled his seat belt. "This is mutiny, is what this is," he said, getting out of his chair. Roka stepped aside to let Jack sit down in his place. He eyed Jack nervously as he looked over the ship's controls. "I don't suppose you've ever flown one of these before. . . . That's probably too much to hope for, isn't it?"

"Don't worry," Jack said. "I learn fast."

CHAPTER

Jack's Back

Jack found out two things rather quickly. The first was that space was an endless minefield of comets, meteors, planets, stars, satellites, spaceships, and more. The second was that the speed of thought did not necessarily exceed the speed of light. If anything, the two speeds were equal at best. Flying the *Harbinger* through hyperspace by himself was like running across a firing range and trying to dodge the bullets.

Luckily, Jack's powers made dodging the bullets possible, letting him bypass the *Harbinger*'s controls and fly the ship with his mind. His reaction times were amplified by a direct connection with the ship's radar and navigation systems, allowing him to anticipate obstacles and chart a course that was light-years ahead of what he could see with his own eyes. Even so, it was by no means a smooth ride. Navigating light speed in real time took perfect concentration, and Jack was anything but perfect. He bobbed and weaved his way across the universe, narrowly missing head-on collisions by inches and grinding through enough minor scrapes to keep Roka screaming about his ship the entire ride home. By the time the *Harbinger* reached the Milky Way galaxy, the ship was so banged up it could barely stay together.

Jack pulled out of hyperspace as the ship limped into Earth's atmosphere, held together mainly by the sheer force of his will. Landing was not even a consideration. He was just looking for a soft place to crash.

"Hold on tight!" Jack shouted as the *Harbinger* streaked across the sky like a shooting star. The heat of reentry burned away at the ship's protective layers, and it struck the earth like a fireball. It hit the earth hard and kept right on going, charging ahead like a runaway train tearing down the track.

Roka shouted out the obvious command to the ship's computer: "Eject! Eject! Eject!"

The cockpit shot backward and skidded out into marshlands as the rest of the *Harbinger* raced forward, carving a path through a swamp. The ejected capsule skimmed across a hundred yards of shallow, slimy water like an out-of-control airboat. Eventually, it spun out and settled into the muck, where it sank a few feet and hit bottom. Roka popped the hatch, and Jack and the others climbed out unscathed. The rest of the *Harbinger* was anything but. Roka's ship didn't stop until it crashed through a fence and into a small cinder-block shed, effectively demolishing the structure. The resulting explosion left Roka's ship somewhat intact, but the front end was on fire and the hull was riddled with holes big and small. Roka put both hands on his head as he stared out at the flaming wreck of the *Harbinger*. He looked like his dog had just died.

"My ship . . ."

Jack walked up alongside Roka and took in the fiery view with him. "Sorry, Roka. I did the best I could."

Roka stared in silence for a few moments, then finally

answered. "I thought you said you control machines. You couldn't bring us in any softer than that?"

"I control *working* machines," Jack said. "I can't make them not be broken. Look on the bright side. We're alive, aren't we?"

Roka rubbed his thick, stubbly beard as he considered Jack's logic. "You got us out kid, I'll give you that. But still . . ." Roka lifted a hand toward the *Harbinger* and dropped it to his side with a heavy sigh.

"The important thing is we made it back in one piece," Jazen said. "That's all that matters."

"Maybe to you," Roka said. "Where am I going to get the credits to fix this? I'm not even getting paid for this job."

"Where the heck are we, anyway?" Allegra asked.

Jazen looked around. "I don't know. It looks familiar, though."

Jack agreed, taking special note of the tall, fluttering reeds in the marsh that reminded him of his childhood. Sparks were shooting off the broken fence that the *Harbinger* ran through, and there was an oddly shaped building off in the distance surrounded by construction vehicles. Jack's powers picked up on the work they were doing. They were adding a new floor onto the building's roof. He shook his head in disbelief. "No way. It can't be."

"What in the name of Dixon Ticonderoga is going on here?" a booming voice called out. The next thing Jack knew, his old school's head disciplinarian, H. Ross Calhoun, came bounding across the swamp wearing knee-high mud boots over his suit pants. Jack couldn't believe it. He was right back where he started: St. Barnaby's Home for the Hopeless, Abandoned, Forgotten, and Lost.

When Calhoun saw the blazing starship that had just crashed into his orderly little world, he put his hands on his head, striking a pose much like the one Roka had taken up a moment earlier. "My generator . . . My beautiful new generator!" Calhoun hung his head, looking defeated by life. "This can't be," he said, tugging at his hair. "We haven't had anything like this happen since—"

Calhoun stopped short as he looked up and laid eyes on Jack. "No," he said, turning white. "No, no, no! Not *you*! What are you doing back here?"

"Hey, Mr. Calhoun," Jack said. "Nice to see you, too."

"Don't get smart with me, boy," Calhoun shot back,

sticking a finger in Jack's face. A switch had been flipped. The distraught headmaster was gone, and the hardened tyrant masquerading as an educator was back. "You're not supposed to be here. You were supposed to be gone . . . for good!" Calhoun curled his fingers, looking very much like he wished he were closing them around Jack's throat. "You're going to pay for this. You just ruined my brand-new power generator *and* my electric fence!"

"Really?" Jazen asked with a mischievous grin. "How do you like that? Déjà vu all over again, huh, Jack?"

"And you!" Calhoun said, spinning around to face Jazen. "What are you doing bringing this boy back here to cause trouble?"

Jazen patted Calhoun on the shoulder, leaving mud stains on his suit. "Sorry for the inconvenience, sir. Couldn't be helped. Don't worry. The bureau will take care of everything."

"The bureau?"

"The Bureau of Bureaucratic Operations. Just send the bill to me. My office will cover all the damages."

Calhoun puffed up his chest. "I should say you will! There wouldn't even be any damages if you had done your job in the first place." He pointed an accusing finger at Jack. "That *child* is not supposed to be here! You said he was getting deported. You said if he was lucky, he'd never see me again!"

Jack shook his head. "You can call me a lot of things, but I don't think 'lucky' is one of them." He looked around at the orphanage of his childhood, barely able to comprehend all the ways his life had changed since he'd left this place. *Another lifetime,* Jack thought. He was a different person back when he'd lived at St. Barnaby's. Back then he had no friends, and his biggest problem was a bully named Rex Staples. Today he had far worse things to worry about.

Calhoun let out an exasperated sigh and looked around. He chewed on the inside of his cheek a moment, then shot a hand to his brow and leaned forward to take a closer look at the flaming wreckage. "Is that a spaceship?" he asked, just now noticing the *Harbinger.*

"It was," Roka said. "Will it be again? That's the question." He pulled a fire extinguisher out of the scuttled cockpit and went to tend to the flames. Calhoun followed him a few steps to get a closer look at the burning ship. His head snapped around to stare at Allegra, whose gleaming silver skin reflected the light of the fire as she passed him by. Calhoun's jaw fell open as the reality of the situation began to dawn on him. Jazen stepped forward and gently pushed his mouth shut.

"There. That's better."

As the *Harbinger* burned, a glint of light reflected off a broken corner of the ship, and Jack froze. Something about it triggered a memory for him. Not a full memory. Just a flash. A fleeting moment. He stumbled as the flashback hit and grabbed on to Jazen for support. The light gleaming on the ship became the shining tip of the Magus's iron horn. Jack saw it in his mind's eye, and the unexpected jolt of that vision nearly knocked him to the ground.

"Jack, what is it?" Jazen asked, but Jack wasn't there. For a few terrible seconds, he was right back in the Magus's throne room. The world shook and he was transported to a Rüstov prison lab. He was strapped to an operating table, struggling to get free. He heard the *cling-clang* of surgical tools rattling on trays he couldn't see. He was staring at a holo-screen with his eyes taped open. He saw the Rüstov Armada on the march. The extent of their forces was almost impossible to compre-hend. Images of explosions and war—real-life footage from the Rüstov's many conflicts and conquests—played in an endless loop before Jack. A cavalcade of death and destruction paraded around his brain. What were these images? Where were they coming from? Why wouldn't they—

"Stop!" Allegra pleaded. "Jack, please stop. You're going to hurt yourself!"

Jack blinked his eyes open and saw that Allegra had wrapped her silvery metal arms around him several times. He was fighting hard to break free, but she had bound him too tight to move. Jack looked around. He was dripping with sweat. He stopped struggling and took a deep breath.

"What just happened?" he asked.

Allegra loosened her grip and let Jack go. "You had a seizure," Jazen told him.

Jack stretched his arms out and looked around. He was back in New Jersey. Everything seemed okay again, but he knew it wasn't. Jack shook his head. "That wasn't a seizure. It was a memory." *And maybe something else as well,* Jack thought but didn't say.

"That's some memory," Allegra said. "What was it?"

Jack's whole body shuddered. He rubbed his head. "Last year, I think."

Allegra put her hand on his shoulder. "What did they do to you?"

Jack took Allegra's hand. "I can't say for sure. I have a bad feeling we're gonna find out, though." Jack noticed Calhoun studying him with a cockeyed expression. Jack was grateful for his silence, if nothing else. He'd just caught a glimpse of the yearlong nightmare he'd endured, and he didn't need to hear Calhoun ranting and raving while he tried to figure out what he'd been through. Jack's eyes turned back to Jazen and Allegra. He may not have had any friends when he was an orphan in Calhoun's care, but today things were different. He had friends—real friends—and he needed them now more than ever. Jack reached out to Jazen and Allegra and pulled them in close for a hug. It was the first chance he'd gotten to do so since the breakout. The escape was hairy enough all by itself, and the ride home demanded such incredible focus that Jack didn't even speak to anyone the whole trip. There wasn't time to take comfort in his friends' arms before, but Jack needed them now.

"I can't believe it's been a year," Jack said when he finally let go. His eyes were welling with tears. "All that time, and you didn't give up. Thank you."

"*You* didn't give up," Jazen said. "We didn't know what to do or even where to look until we got your messages."

Jack looked up. *The messages again* . . . "I don't understand. What messages?"

Allegra cocked her head sideways. "You know. You sent out distress calls telling us where you were. You led us right to you. I couldn't believe you were able to contact us without the Rüstov finding out. How did you do it?"

Jack squinted at Jazen and Allegra. "What are you guys talking about?"

"You don't remember?" Jazen asked.

Jack shook his head. "I don't remember anything." As soon as he said it, he shrugged, making an allowance for the flashback that had just hit him like a bag of anvils. "Well, hardly anything. It's coming back, but . . ."

"It's okay," Jazen said, patting his shoulder. "Give it time. It'll come. In the meantime, we can fill in the gaps. You sent out an SOS that reached the Calculan Planetary

49

Conglomerate. That's where you were. Calculan space . . . or what was formerly Calculan space. The Rüstov took it over years ago. Luckily we had access to a famous space-pirate who was used to operating in Rüstov territory."

"Ah-hem," Roka said, clearing his throat loudly as he returned from putting out the fires on his ship. "I prefer 'adventurer' or 'entrepreneur,' if it's not too much trouble. I'm more of an unconventional businessman, really. I provide a unique and valuable service."

"Raiding transports?" Jazen asked.

"Raiding *Rüstov* transports," Roka replied. "I go in and free host-body prisoners."

"For a price," Jazen said.

"A very high price," Roka agreed. "I do good work and I expect to be compensated for my time. Nothing wrong with that, and there's nothing illegal about what I do, either."

"Why were you in jail, then?" Allegra asked.

"That's a separate issue," Roka said. "The whole situation was completely unwarranted. Not counting the warrant for my arrest, of course." He turned to Jack to explain. "I tend to operate without licenses or permits. Apparently,

50

that's a big no-no in the Calculan sector. After my last job, I was arrested and sentenced to nine hundred and forty-two years in prison by Calculan authorities."

"That's a long time," Jack said.

"I thought so," Roka agreed. "But I was the only one with the proper experience—and the only one crazy enough—to go in and get you, so the Calculans lifted my sentence in return for bringing you back. And here we are."

"Here we are, all right." Jack rubbed his eyes, trying to process everything he'd just seen, heard, and remembered. It was overwhelming.

"For a guy who just got his life back, you don't seem very happy," Roka observed.

"That's the thing," Jack said. "I'm not so sure I did. I appreciate everything you guys did for me, all of you. And I really am sorry about your ship, Roka, but we've got a bigger problem here. It's not just that I don't remember sending out a call for help. I don't even think I could have. I can't use my powers on anything Rüstov right now. Khalix won't let me."

"Who's Khalix?" Roka asked.

"The Rüstov prince," Allegra explained.

Jack tapped his temple. "He's in here with me. All the time now. How could I have taken control of a communications array and sent out an SOS without him knowing? I don't think those messages came from me."

"Who did they come from, then?" Jazen asked.

Jack turned up his palms. To him, the answer was obvious. The question was why.

"WHAT THE DEVIL ARE YOU ALL TALKING ABOUT?" Calhoun shouted, startling Jack. "Powers? Space-pirates? Who are the Rüstov? Wait, don't answer that!" He held up a hand and looked away. "I can't believe I'm having this conversation with you!" Calhoun rubbed his eyes vigorously and got very upset when he blinked them open to find that Jack and his friends were still there. "No! I'm not seeing this. I'm not! Your insanity is infectious! I'm not going to listen to any more of it."

"Nobody asked you to listen to anything," Allegra said.

"I know I didn't," Jazen said. "You just invited yourself up here and—"

"I invited *myself*?" Calhoun asked, failing miserably in his attempts to ignore his visitors from the Imagine

Nation. "This is my school! You're the ones who barged in here and turned it into a war zone!"

"You better get used to it," Jack said. "This whole planet's about to become a war zone."

"Is that a threat?" Calhoun demanded. "Is that a threat?!!"

"Relax, whoever you are," Allegra said. "You're not important enough for Jack to threaten."

Calhoun nearly fell over. "*I'm* not important enough for *him* to— He's nothing but a future toilet brush cleaner!"

"Toilet brush cleaner?" Roka repeated, his lip curling upward in disgust. Allegra scrunched up her face, clearly grossed out and confused.

Jack traded a knowing look with Jazen and allowed himself a slight chuckle. "Right. I almost forgot about that one. Turns out it might have been better for everybody if I stayed here and did that after all, huh, Mr. Calhoun? That's not the way things went though."

"Your fault, not mine," Calhoun replied. "You never did what was expected of you, Jack. Never once."

Jack shook his head. "You wouldn't like it if I did what people expect me to do these days. You were wrong about me. Everyone here was. You people don't know a thing about my potential."

"I know you're a bad apple," Calhoun said. "Rotten to the core. I thought I was rid of you, but it appears that if you want something done, you have to do it yourself. You'll pay for this. Mark my words, Jack, I won't forget what you've done here today."

Just then the wind picked up and the clouds began to darken and twist in an unnatural swirl. Lightning crashed, and a giant flying boat burst out from behind the clouds in the skies overhead. "Don't be so sure about that," Roka said, pointing up at the Secreteer's ship. Streams of dark smoke flew down from above, and the storm winds blew with all the strength and fury of a hurricane.

"I'm going home now," Jack told Calhoun. "Sorry we wrecked your generator again. If it's any consolation, I'm pretty sure this is the last time you and I will ever see each other."

Calhoun frowned. "I should be so lucky."

The smoke grew to fill every inch of the air, and Calhoun's figure was lost within the murky vapors. "We both should," Jack agreed.

Jack felt Jazen touch his shoulder as the haze closed in. "Jack, when you say the whole planet's about to become a war zone . . . do you mean what I think you mean?"

Jack turned to look at Jazen before he vanished from sight. "That wasn't just a memory that hit me back there, Jazen. It was a vision. A vision of what they're doing right now. The Rüstov are done with those burned-out Calculan planets. They're on the move, and they're coming for us. They're coming with everything they've got."

4

Homecoming

When the smoke cleared, both on the marsh and in Jack's head, he found that he was no longer standing in the swamplands of St. Barnaby's. He rubbed his eyes and looked around at the deck of the Secreteer's ship. It was flying through the air, with what was left of the *Harbinger* in tow. Jack expected to see the New York skyline and the Statue of Liberty off in the distance, but there was nothing on the horizon in any direction. He and his friends had been flying for quite some time.

Jack got on his feet feeling groggy. Up until this point,

he'd been passed out on Jazen, with Allegra leaning up against his other side. Jack's two friends were both still asleep, along with Solomon Roka. Jack was up before them, most likely because of his Rüstov connection. His bond with Khalix always made it harder for the Secreteers to wipe his memory. It was the one situation in which Jack was grateful for his alien parasite.

The Secreteers were the guardians of the Imagine Nation's secrets and were the first line of defense against people like Calhoun finding out more than they could handle, but that didn't make Jack feel any more comfortable around them. He understood why the Clandestine Order needed to do what they did, he just didn't want to have to see them do it. For one thing, he had already had a bad experience with Secreteers creeping into his head, and for another, he didn't like the feeling of being put under for any reason. He'd had more than enough of that over the last year.

Jack only felt better once he realized whose ship he was on. As far as he knew, there was only one Secreteer with a flying boat, and that Secreteer was a friend. Sure, she also happened to be the same person who had once nosed through his memories without permission, but Jack had forgiven her for that. They had bonded when they stopped the Rüstov spyware virus and exposed the Rogue Secreteer as Glave, the Magus's master spy. Jack saw a hooded figure at the wheel of the ship and ran to her.

"Hypnova!"

The figure turned and threw back her hood, revealing herself as a tall, statuesque beauty with pale skin, stark white hair, and cold, penetrating eyes.

Jack stopped short. "What the . . . ? You're not . . . Where's . . . ?"

The Secreteer gave Jack an impatient look. "Try thinking about what you want to say, and *then* saying it. It usually works better that way."

"I know you," Jack said, putting an end to his surprised stammering. "You're the head Secreteer. Oblivia. I remember you from Gravenmurk Glen. I thought this ship belonged to . . ."

"Hypnova," Oblivia said, finishing Jack's sentence. "Yes, I heard you. I'm afraid that she's no longer with us. She was expelled from our order for violating the vows of secrecy."

58

Jack's face twisted into a mask of outrage and disbelief. "You mean you didn't take her back? She helped defeat the Rüstov's spyware virus. She stopped the Rogue Secreteer!"

"Did she? I seem to remember the rogue escaping . . . with you."

Jack thought for a second. Oblivia was right, of course. Hypnova had told him the only way the Clandestine Order would take her back was if she captured or killed the Rogue Secreteer. Everyone had thought Hypnova killed Glave, the Rüstov spy who had been masquerading as a Secreteer, but he survived. Jack knew that better than anyone.

Oblivia shook her head. "You shouldn't have come back. Your presence here puts us all in grave danger."

Jack held out his hands. "What else could I do? The Imagine Nation is my home."

Oblivia raised an eyebrow. "Do you really still believe that? After everything that's happened?"

"Leave him alone, Oblivia," a voice called out before Jack could answer. He turned around to see Solomon Roka standing behind him. "It's been a while, but I'm pretty sure the Secreteers are still the Imagine Nation's secret keepers, not its gatekeepers."

Oblivia gave Roka a disgruntled "Hrrmmpph" and turned back to the wheel.

"Roka?" Jack said, looking back and forth between the space-pirate and Oblivia. "You guys know each other?"

Roka nodded. He had a hard look in his eyes. "We've met. You're not the only one going home today, kiddo."

Oblivia shook her head. "I told you before. This isn't your home anymore."

"Not your call to make," Roka said. "Not for either of us."

Oblivia gave Roka an icy stare. "Wake your friends," she said to Jack. "The island is up ahead." Jack turned back toward Jazen and Allegra, but Oblivia tapped his shoulder before he went to them. "A word of advice before we return . . . Don't expect a warm welcome. It's no secret where you've been all this time."

Jack frowned and touched the Rüstov mark around his eye. Oblivia was, of course, correct. A whole new battle was waiting for him once he got home. Winning over the people of Empire City was going to make escaping the Rüstov look easy by comparison.

"Nice," Roka said to Oblivia as he put his arm on Jack's

shoulder and ushered him toward the others. "Real nice."

As the Secreteer's ship made its final approach to Empire City, Jack stood at the front of the ship, leaning out over the railing with Jazen and Allegra, taking in the view in all its glory: the island, impossibly floating over a ring of waterfalls, that roamed all around the ocean. The massive translucent mountain behind it that framed the setting sun's rays with a rainbow glow. The Imagine Nation's diverse capital city, like six worlds pushed together, one from every genre of comic book that Jack used to read. What once was just a fantasy was now his reality. It *was* his home. No homecoming parade would be waiting for Jack when he returned, but the Imagine Nation belonged to him as much as anybody else. He was going to fight for it, and for his place in it.

The flying ship coasted gently past the statue of Legend, who was once the Imagine Nation's greatest defender. Jack stared at the towering tribute to the fallen hero in solemn silence. One day in the future, or fourteen years ago, depending on how one looked at it, Legend would die at Jack's hand. Jack had known this for years. He had always refused to believe such a horrible act was in his future. Now he couldn't be so sure. It all depended on what the Rüstov had done to him. A large crowd had assembled at Hero Square, awaiting Jack's return. Like Oblivia said, everyone knew he was coming and nobody was happy to see him. The people of Empire City watched the ship approach, pensive and quiet.

"Getting that déjà vu feeling again," Jazen told Jack. "It's just like that first time I took you here, isn't it?"

"It's worse," Jack said. "Back then they were just worried about my Rüstov infection and what it might mean. Now they think they know my future for a fact." Jack shrugged. "Can't say I blame them. I'm the one who told them all about it."

Two years ago, Jack had met Revile, a future version of himself who was supposedly the key to the Rüstov's eventual victory over the Imagine Nation. One year ago, Jack had confessed that fact to his friends and enemies alike. His honesty and candor had failed to put his detractors at ease, and his subsequent abduction by the Rüstov had no doubt added to the problem.

"Oblivia said I'm putting everyone in danger by coming back. She might be right, Jazen. Nobody wants me here."

An orange-white flash filled the sky, and Jack blinked

through blinding lights to find he'd been transported directly below the sphere in Hero Square. "I wouldn't say that," a friendly voice told Jack.

"Stendeval!" Jack said, rushing into his old teacher's arms as Jazen, Allegra, and Roka materialized beside him. A barrier of red energy particles behind them held back the crowd, for the time being at least.

"Jack," Stendeval said, holding him tight. "Thank the stars." He separated himself from Jack and knelt down to look him in the eye. Unlike everyone else, he didn't flinch at the sight of Jack's scar.

"There he is!" Blue's booming voice called out. "Welcome home, little man!" Before Jack even had a chance to turn around, he felt himself being snatched up from behind and tossed in the air like a stuffed animal.

Jack came down laughing. "Hey, Blue."

"C'mere, lemme look at ya!" Blue caught Jack and held him out in the air. His reaction to Jack's face was the exact opposite of Stendeval's. One look at Jack's eye and Blue cringed like he'd just seen a bad car accident. "Yikes."

Jazen came up alongside him. "Same old Blue . . . Worst poker face ever."

"What? No!" Blue stammered. "Hey, I'm sure it's fine," he said, trying to recover. "I mean, it's just . . . you know, it's, uh . . ." Blue swallowed uncomfortably and shook his head. "They gotcha good, huh, kid?"

Jack nodded. "They got me all right."

"Yeah, they did. That's gonna go over real big here," Blue said, his voice dripping with sarcasm. "Don't worry, though. Sounds like you're still you. That's all I care about. You are, right? Still you, I mean . . ."

Jack shrugged. "So far. It's been a rough year, Blue."

Blue set Jack down on the ground. "Just take it one day at a time, partner. You're safe now. Ol' Blue's always got your back, you know that." The blue giant put up a fist for Jack to bump.

"Thanks," Jack said. He pushed his knuckles into Blue's, but he didn't feel the least bit safe. Blue couldn't protect him from himself.

"I also bid you welcome, Jack," Chi said, coming out of nowhere and startling Jack. Falling snow made more noise than the Circleman of Karateka. "Unfortunately, not everyone in Empire City is going to share Blue's enthusiasm. You must prepare yourself."

"They'll share his enthusiasm," Virtua corrected Chi. "Just not in a positive manner." The gorgeous Circle-woman of Machina touched a holographic hand to the mark on Jack's eye. "Not to worry. I'm sure Jack expected nothing less."

"I kind of figured," Jack said, looking up at Virtua. The last time he saw her, the Mechas were rioting in Machina, and she was blinking out of existence. The Circlewoman had resigned herself to certain death if the heroes of Empire City couldn't stop her and her people from doing the Rüstov's bidding.

"I never got to properly thank you for saving Machina from the Rüstov virus." Jack's actions a year ago had been vital in stopping the Rüstov plot and saving Virtua's people.

"I haven't saved anything yet," Jack said.

Virtua's glowing holographic image changed color, turning into a cool, somber blue. "No, perhaps not. Still, my people and I remain in your debt for what you've done. I'm sorry your heroics continue to be met with such inadequate rewards."

"Don't be sorry," Jack said. "I got exactly what I had coming to me."

Jack's friends all started talking at once, but he waved off their protests.

"I mean it," Jack said. "I'm going to handle things differently this time around. I'm through lying to everyone. There's no point anymore. It's not like I can hide what the Rüstov have done to me."

"There is nothing you ever need to hide from me," Virtua told Jack. "As long as I'm in charge of Machina, you will be welcome there, and you will have a home." Virtua turned to Jazen. "And you . . ."

Jazen bowed his head in respect. "Lady Virtua."

"I'm glad to see you back in one piece as well, Commander Knight."

Jack's head turned at the mention of Jazen's new title.

"You can thank Jack for that too," Jazen told Virtua. "I wish I could take credit for busting him out, but he did more than anyone to get us back home."

Solomon Roka cleared his throat loudly.

"And Roka, too, of course," Jazen added. "He was the one who actually went in and got Jack."

"Ah, yes . . . the incomparable Solomon Roka," Stendeval said. "So good to see you again."

Roka turned to Stendeval with a confused look.

"You know *him*, too?" Jack asked Roka.

"Everyone knows who Stendeval is," Roka said. "Not sure how he knows me, though."

"Your reputation precedes you," Chi said. "Our fellow Circleman, Prime, was negotiating an alliance with the Calculan Delegation when Jack's distress signal came in. It was Stendeval who suggested that we engage your services to free him."

All eyes turned back to Stendeval. He shrugged and said, "I simply explained Jack's value in the war effort and proposed to the Calculans that it would be worth commuting your sentence if you could successfully retrieve him."

"And they agreed, just like that?" Roka eyed Stendeval suspiciously. "Doesn't sound very Calculan to me."

Stendeval tilted his head. "I can be very convincing."

"That's it, then?" Roka asked. "I'm free to go?"

"Circleman Prime is meeting with the Calculan Delegation as we speak," Stendeval assured Roka. "We'll see to it your record is cleared."

Roka rubbed his beard. "I'll believe it when I see it.

How'd you know the Calculans had me, anyway?"

Stendeval smiled again and shook a finger in admiration. "Very good. They asked me the same exact question."

Before Stendeval could finish his answer, he was interrupted by the noise of someone banging against the energy barrier. It made a loud humming sound as fists pounded away at it from the other side. People were calling out to be let through in voices that were every bit as unfriendly as they were familiar: "Stendeval! Enough of this. Drop these shields and let us pass!"

Stendeval frowned at the energy barrier. "I'm afraid this oasis of civility in a sea of angst can't last forever. I can put this off a short while longer, but—"

"No," Jack said. "Let them in, all of them. I've got news they need to hear and none of it's good."

The *Harbinger* of Doom

Stendeval waved his hands, and the red energy particles that made up the shields protecting Jack evaporated into thin air. Jazen and Blue stepped in front of Jack as an angry crowd came into view, with Smart and Hovarth at its head. The chairman and CEO of SmartCorp and the warrior king of Varagog Village walked toward the sphere with clear, angry purpose. Jack's old School of Thought classmate and former friend Skerren was there too, just behind his king. None of them were smiling. Jack didn't expect Hovarth or Smart to welcome him back, but the look on

Skerren's face hit him hard. The two boys had started out as enemies and became friends, only to have that friendship derailed by secrets and lies. Skerren had been one of Jack's closest friends in the Imagine Nation, second only to Allegra. Jack had hoped that Skerren had forgiven him for hiding his connection to Revile, but as the young swordsman fell in behind Hovarth, it was clear that he had not.

"It's about time," Smart grunted as he crossed into the area directly below the Inner Circle's sphere. "Outrageous behavior, this. It's bad enough you fought to bring the boy back here, but to disrespect your fellow Circlemen this way . . ."

"He got elected Circleman again?" Jack asked Jazen.

"Not yet," Smart said as he strode in confidently. "Don't worry, that will come soon enou—" He stopped short when he saw Jack's eye. He glared at Stendeval.

"Where is he?" Skerren asked. "Where are they hiding him?"

"Og's blood!" Hovarth called out, pointing. "His eye!"

Smart shook his head like a man who knew better than everyone else. "Stendeval, you damnable fool." He gave a slight smirk as he tapped away at his handheld holo-computer. Flying NewsBots swooped in to record Jack's image for SmartNews as another figure fought his way through the crowd.

"Let me through!" the voice called out. "Step aside! I'm a Circleman, you disrespectful proles!" Clarkston Noteworthy broke through the mass of people just as a score of SmartNews holo-screens appeared throughout the square showing a close-up of Jack's face. A collective gasp ran through the crowd at the sight of him. Frightened exclamations rang out through Hero Square.

"His eye!"

"It's the mark of the Rüstov! He's one of them now!"

"He's going to turn into Revile!"

Jack felt like he was being stoned with words, but again, he couldn't judge his critics too harshly. They weren't saying anything he wasn't worried about himself. Noteworthy inched forward toward Jack, moving with both extreme caution and intense curiosity. "I don't believe it," he said, reaching toward Jack's marked eye. "I'd heard you were coming back, which was bad news all by itself, but I never expected . . ."

Jack pushed Noteworthy's hand away, and Smart

grinned like a creepy jack-o'-lantern. "Get used to that reaction, Jack. Things have changed since you left. I'm taking this city back."

Jack sighed. "We don't have time for your games, Smart. Not now. The Rüstov are coming for us."

"Coming?" Virtua said. "They're coming now?"

"Everybody!" Jack shouted, trying to get the attention of the crowd. "Listen to me, you need to hear this! The Rüstov are on their way right now. They're ready, and they've only got one target: Empire City. We need to get ready. We need to . . ." Jack trailed off. It was no use. The crowd was too big. The people were too loud. Only the people closest to Jack on the plaza heard what he had to say. Jack threw up his hands and turned to Smart. "You have to listen for once in your life. We can't afford to mess around here. War is coming. They're finally coming back."

"I understand," Smart replied. "You can tell your Rüstov friends that this time we'll be ready for them."

Jack scrunched up his face. "Rüstov friends?"

Smart snapped his fingers, and a series of holographic circles projected out in front of his face. He cleared his throat, and the sound echoed across Hero Square. The holograms amplified his voice, and he addressed the crowd with booming authority.

"People of Empire City!" he shouted as his face flickered onto every screen in sight. "A dark day is dawning. . . . The Rüstov's secret weapon has returned to the Imagine Nation. Or should I say, it has *been* returned to us by the shortsighted, overly Zen, and potentially treasonous contingent of the Inner Circle."

"Treasonous!" Virtua spat out, literally turning red. "How dare you?"

Smart ignored Virtua and kept right on with his speech. "He comes bearing threats, promising that his Rüstov brethren are coming to save him!" Smart tapped away on his holo-computer and cued up a hastily edited broadcast of Jack's warning:

"The Rüstov are coming," Jack's voice said. "They're finally coming back!"

The audio file played over and over. Taken out of context and repeated in a loop as it was, Jack's voice sounded happy on the recording. Gleeful, even.

"That's not how I meant it and you know it!" Jack yelled at Smart, but the roar of the crowd drowned him out.

"Every second we let this boy live is time spent nurturing our future executioner!" Smart shouted. "We are all familiar with his history and how he covered up a deadly Rüstov virus that nearly destroyed our city. As for his future, he has already confessed the role he is bound to play in the enemy's relentless campaign against us! He is the cornerstone of a future where the Rüstov have already won. Baffling as it may be, the Inner Circle continues to protect him. I want to protect *you*. We can defeat the Rüstov, but not if this boy is allowed to grow up and become Revile. Jack Blank cannot be allowed to fulfill his destiny!"

The people in Hero Square were nodding, agreeing with Smart. Many began to cheer him.

"Enough!" Stendeval shouted. He voice cut across the plaza like a thunderbolt, causing everyone, including Smart, to jump up and quiet down. Stendeval levitated above the crowd and took control of Smart's holo-screens, replacing Smart's voice and visage with his own on every one. "I have heard all I care to hear about destiny, Jonas. That is quite enough, thank you."

Smart pounded away at his handheld, taking back his

holo-screens one at a time, but it was slow going. Jack could see that Smart wasn't going to stop Stendeval from having his say.

"Friends!" Stendeval called out to the crowd. "I implore you, now is not the time to give in to fear. Now is the time to stand together. If the enemy is indeed coming back, we need to be brave. Be strong! I believe in Jack Blank. I have long maintained that he is the key to our victory over the Rüstov, and I have fought to bring him back here for that purpose! Forget what you think you know about his future. Destiny is a choice we make, not a road we are forced down against our will."

Jack had never seen the reserved and mysterious Circleman of Cognito speak with such passion. He wanted desperately to lend his voice to Stendeval's and talk about getting ready to fight the Rüstov, but all of a sudden, he felt dizzy. His infection was spreading. Blue moved in to offer Jack his arm as subtly as he could, but his weakened state did not go unnoticed by Jonas Smart.

"Spare us your inspirational greeting card messages," Smart told Stendeval. "Your faith in this boy proves nothing except your naïveté. By your own actions you force

the people of this city down a road against *their* will . . .
a road to ruin! I say let them choose what they want for
their future. Let them decide whether or not they want
Jack Blank to be a part of it. Look at his eye! He's losing
the fight with his infection, just as I always said he would.
He's the Rüstov's hero, not ours. What will it take for you
to understand the threat he represents, Stendeval? His
boot heel on your neck?"

"Jonas is right," Hovarth said. "The time for your assur-
ances is past. Let the boy speak for himself. If he is truly
going to save us from the Rüstov, I want to hear it from
him. How is he going to avoid his future? How is he going
to bring anything but death and destruction down on our
heads?" All eyes turned to Jack. "Well?"

Jack steadied himself and found his voice. "I don't know."

Noteworthy joined the dissenters in interrogating Jack.
"You say the Rüstov are coming," he said, poking Jack in
the chest. "How do they plan to find us? Are they tracking
you?"

Jazen pushed Noteworthy back. "That doesn't matter."

"They're tracking him!" Noteworthy shouted. "We
have to get him out of here!"

"It doesn't matter if they're tracking Jack or not," Jazen said. "They don't need him here to find this place. They just have to believe in it, which they obviously do. Getting rid of Jack won't stop them from coming. This fight is on its way here either way. It's time to stop running . . . time to stop being afraid. We have to face them and finish it."

"And he'll help us do that, will he?" Skerren asked. "How? What are you going to do when the fighting starts, Jack? Can you use your powers to smash the Rüstov Armada?"

Jack cleared his throat and grimaced at the anger burning in Skerren's eyes. "No. I can't use my powers on any Rüstov tech. My parasite won't let me."

"There, you see?" Smart said. "His parasite, also known as Khalix, the Rüstov prince—soon to be known as Revile! He's stronger now as a result of what they've done to you, isn't he?"

"Much stronger," Jack admitted. "I have to work hard to shut Khalix up. In fact, he's trying to talk me right now."

Roka leaned over Jack's shoulder and spoke quietly in his ear. "Kid, I know I just got here, but you might want to play some of these cards a little closer to the vest."

Jack shook his head. "I'm not sugarcoating things anymore. I'm telling it like it is, good or bad. I'm not hiding from anything or anyone."

"Turned over a new leaf, have you, Jack?" Smart asked. "You may have won back your friends' trust with your candid admissions and newfound openness, but I'm not fooled. You're hiding something. . . ." Across the plaza, Oblivia's ship was docking at the flying shipyards. Smart's NewsBots were there to record its arrival as it set the *Harbinger* down on land. Jack felt them digging through the *Harbinger*'s flight recorder, searching for something . . . anything that Smart could use against him.

Smart snapped his fingers. "Your distress calls! If you can't use your powers on Rüstov technology, how did you make them?"

Jack held out his arms. He knew it wouldn't take the "world's smartest man" long to arrive at the same conclusion he had. "I'm not sure I called anyone."

"Exactly! It was a Rüstov plot to sneak you in past our defenses." Smart turned to Stendeval. "I know you have affection for Jack, but my logic is not clouded by such emotions. Whatever you may think you know, I say you do not know this boy well enough to trust him. Not anymore."

Smart's handheld beeped loudly, like an alarm sounding. The NewsBots had found something. Smart punched the keys of his pocket holo-computer and turned toward the crowd. "Jack spent a *year* in Rüstov captivity. That kind of experience changes a person—apparently, in more ways than one!" He reclaimed his holo-screens and put the data from the *Harbinger*'s broken Ghost Box on display for all to see. Jack's heart leaped into his throat when he saw the schematic of his new biology. According to the readout, there was something mechanical inside his chest. Something big. Frantic, Jack clawed at his collar and ripped his space suit open to get a look at it. The crowd gasped and Jack was just as shocked as anyone else. What he saw made him gag. There, implanted in his sternum, was a glowing red power core surrounded by Rüstov technology. It looked just like Revile's.

Jack staggered back a step and started hyperventilating. His fingers shot up instinctively toward the glowing crimson circle in his chest. He pressed down hard against it and felt around the edges, investigating the foreign object in his body. He tried to slow down his breathing and get himself under control, but he couldn't do it. This thing . . . this machine was real. It was in him. Khalix's voice crept into Jack's head, taunting him:

"*Surprise, Jack.* I was wondering when you were going to notice that."

Frightened screeches ran through the crowd. Anyone who wasn't worried about Jack's loyalties before certainly was now. Jack heard the crowd wail and the accusations fly, but it was all just noise. He couldn't focus on anything except the power core in his chest. It horrified him. What was this thing? How had he missed it? What had the Rüstov done to him?

"I've seen enough," Smart said. He keyed in another command on his handheld, and a hundred man-size battle droids that were hidden in the crowd sprang forth. Smart raised his handheld to his lips:

"Jonas Smart to all points . . . attack."

CHAPTER

6

War Machines

Smart's robot fighters charged through the crowd and opened fire. Endless rounds of ammunition flew across the square, and people ran off screaming in every direction. Jack didn't move. The revelation of the Rüstov technology implanted in his chest had him in a total state of shock. The only thing that kept him from being torn apart by laser blasts was Jazen and Blue. They covered Jack on both sides, using their bodies to shield him from the bullets. Gunshots and laser blasts careened off their backs and out into the crowd. Deadly ricochets rebounded away from Jack, following random, haphazard paths and very nearly claiming innocent lives. Luckily, Stendeval was able to generate several more force fields throughout the square. Without him, countless bystanders would have become casualties in Smart's latest attempt on Jack's life.

"Jack, I'd like you to meet SmartCorp's latest development in homeland security—the WarHawks!" Smart yelled. "Don't bother trying to stop them. Each one is fully equipped with its own power nullifier. I'm putting an end to your machinations here and now!"

Jack was barely listening. He was lost inside his own head, even as Smart's armored soldiers rushed him on all sides. The WarHawks were not lumbering tank-men that marched forward like Frankenstein's monster. They were fast, agile commandos, each one carrying the firepower of a full platoon. One of the WarHawks leaped over Stendeval's protective barriers, landed on its shoulder, and rolled toward Jack. It sprang up and dove right at him, but Chi got there first. He came in hard on the WarHawk's blind side with a fist that burned with blue flames. Once the WarHawk was down, he plunged his fist through its armored breast plate and pulled out a handful of circuits. The WarHawk stopped fighting, but it was just one of a great many.

Blue crouched over Jack as a fresh wave of bullets poured in and shredded his clothes. "No place like home, eh, partner?"

"What?" Jack asked. He looked around, beginning to take notice of the raging firefight.

"I don't want to say I told you so, but I called it!" Blue said. He ripped off a WarHawk's firearms and tossed them over to Jack. "I told ya your new look wasn't going to win you any popularity contests."

"Yeah, yeah, yeah," Jazen said. "You just hate being right, don't you, Blue?"

Jack shook his head and looked at the weapons Blue had given him. He didn't start shooting. He didn't even prime them for use. He just watched the action unfold as if he were sitting in the stands at a football game.

"Jack, snap out of it!" Allegra said, thrusting a liquid metal hand into his face. Her mercury-like skin shot up his nose, jolting him out of the daze he was in. It was just the slap in the face Jack needed. "Are you with us or what?"

Jack grabbed the bridge of his nose and pressed down

hard. He blew out a strong snort of air, and when he blinked his eyes back open, his head was clear. "Thanks, I needed that."

"Don't mention it," Allegra said, moving in to shore up the gaps in Jazen and Blue's perimeter. She morphed her body into a wide, flat shield, offering Jack more bullet-proof cover as he took aim at the WarHawks and started shooting. Together with Jazen and Blue, she formed a protective circle around Jack. He was lucky to have friends who cared enough to stand their ground and back him up like this in a fight. He was even luckier that they were all people who could take a bullet and keep on fighting. The trio stood up to a wall of WarHawk gunfire like it was nothing more than driving rain. Spent shells piled up at their feet, their energy wasted, but Jack knew they couldn't stay there forever. They were vastly outnumbered, and the WarHawks were coming in hot. "Allegra, take my place!" Jazen shouted as he ran to meet them.

Allegra stretched herself over to cover Jazen's abandoned post as he ran out and grabbed one of the War-Hawks by its neck. Jazen turned the WarHawk's guns to face the other shooters and cut the front line of Smart's soldiers to ribbons with their own bullets. A ricochet glanced off Jazen's brow, exposing the metal frame underneath his skin, but the damage was purely cosmetic. Not everyone in Hero Square would be able to say the same. The square was filled with hysterical people trying to escape before they were crushed in the stampede or cut down by random gunfire. Jack felt a mixture of guilt, shame, and frustration at the effect of his return to the Imagine Nation. He had wanted to warn everybody about the coming invasion but had only managed to make everyone more afraid. Not just a little more afraid, either. The crowd had descended into chaos. Jack touched the cold metal in his chest and felt a powerful rush of fear, not just for himself, but for the Imagine Nation as a whole. Everyone was doing exactly what the Rüstov wanted. Empire City was in no way ready for war.

"Jonas, this is madness!" Stendeval shouted as he used his powers to hold back scores of WarHawks and shield the people of Empire City. "You have to stop. You're going to get somebody killed!"

"Yes!" Smart replied, safe behind a row of WarHawk guards. "One person in particular! I'm counting on it."

"There are innocent people here, Jonas! Children!" Virtua said as bullets passed harmlessly through her holographic form. "What about them?"

Smart's face betrayed no emotion. "Desperate times call for desperate measures, Virtua. What I do, I do for the good of the Imagine Nation. Today is the day I save us all from tomorrow."

"My circuits . . . you're insane!" Virtua said, just before a stray bullet tore through Projo, her image-caster. Virtua blinked out of sight, and Projo fell to the ground with a clank.

"Virtua!" Jazen shouted.

The broken image-caster rolled across the square and came to rest at Jack's feet. "Projo," he said, picking up the feisty little orb whose job it was to carry Virtua's image to the unplugged world. Jack wasn't getting any kind of reading from him. He looked up at Jazen and the others. "He's gone."

Roka ran into the safe zone behind Blue, Jazen, and Allegra with his hands up held in a duck-and-cover position. "What is going on here?" he shouted. "Has everybody lost their minds?"

"No, just the smartest man in the world," Jazen said.

Roka looked around. "This is just a thought, but how 'bout we get out of here?"

Jack fired away at Smart's soldiers. The square was too congested to make a break for it. "We'll never get through this crowd."

"Roka, you're up," Jazen said. "We'll cover Jack. You find us a way out."

Roka leaned forward, touching both hands to his own chest. "Why me?"

"You're not bulletproof. We are. Jack needs all the bulletproof people right here in front of him." Jazen winced as another laser blast meant for Jack hit him in the back, effectively making his point. "Besides, you've got a job to finish. If Jack doesn't get out of here alive, you don't get your pardon. You're not off the hook yet, you know."

Roka gave Jazen a dirty look. "That's how it is, huh?" He nodded slowly and scanned the square for a few seconds. The plaza was a study in the madness of crowds. People were in hysterics, jamming the exits and colliding. Roka drew a blaster from his hip holster, slapped a fresh cartridge of ammo into its handle, and ran out into the frenzy without another word. Jack wondered if he planned on coming back. He laid down cover fire for Roka as he went bobbing and weaving through the mob, ducking laser blasts all around.

Roka disappeared into the crowd and was out of sight for only a few seconds when a horde of medieval warriors charged out from the teeming masses. "Incoming!" Blue shouted as an antiquated battalion of archers, knights, and other chain-mail-clad fighters rushed forward. The people of Varagog Village were joining the fight, and they weren't rushing to Jack's aid.

Chi pulled his fist out from the chest of another fallen WarHawk and turned to face the Varagog attackers. He kicked a pair of Smart's drones out of his way and went to work redirecting the laser blasts that filled the air all around him. He cut across the square, karate chopping through the laserfire and reflecting the shots over toward Hovarth's people, disarming them with frightening grace and precision. Jack ducked down below Allegra's shield-shaped body as a volley of arrows rained down on him. He switched his gun's setting to stun and picked up where he left off, firing at the angry mob from Varagog as well as the WarHawks.

Stendeval appeared beside the lord of Clan Varren. "Hovarth! What are you doing standing by? Control your people!"

"They are under control," Hovarth told Stendeval. "They're following my orders."

"Hovarth . . ." Stendeval shook his head. "This helps no one." He used his powers to try and disarm Hovarth's men before they hurt anyone, but there were so many of them. Hero Square was in a state of pure anarchy. The combined forces of the WarHawks and Varagog Villagers overran Jack and his friends. Jack ran out of ammo, and used his laser rifle to bash in the face a large, smelly man who came at him with a mace. He was busy looking for another target when Skerren flew in and sliced his gun in two.

Jack backpedaled as Skerren pressed forward, swinging away with his two unbreakable swords. One of Skerren's blades cut through his shirt and grated against the glowing power core in his chest, producing sparks that skittered out across the marble flagstones of Hero Square. Jack fell backward and landed on his side. He threw both halves of his now useless weapon up at Skerren, missing wildly with the first but nailing him in the forehead with the second.

That only made Skerren mad. He raised his sword high in the air and took a step toward Jack but fell backward instead when a pair of liquid metal hands grabbed him by the ankles and pulled his legs out from under him. Skerren scrambled to his feet to find Allegra standing in between him and Jack. "Step aside, Allegra," he warned.

"Skerren, no," she said, holding out her hand like a crossing guard. "You're not going to cut through me to get to Jack, and we both know it, so just stop."

Skerren held one sword at his side and pointed the other at Allegra. "You want to bet your life on that? In Varagog, those who side with traitors are sentenced to share their fate."

"You couldn't hurt me even if you wanted to," Allegra said. "I'm unbreakable."

Skerren scraped his swords together. "And my swords can cut through anything. Maybe it's time you and I had a rematch."

Jack didn't like where this was headed. Allegra's liquid metal body was about as strong as taffy when she was scared, but it was downright invincible when she wasn't. On the other hand, Skerren could cut through anything with his swords as long as his heart was in it. They had clashed once before and Allegra came out victorious. Jack didn't want to find out whose will was stronger at the moment.

"Skerren, we don't have time to fight each other," Jack said, trying to reason with his former friend. "The Rüstov are coming. We need to get ready, and you need my help to defeat them."

Skerren scoffed at Jack's claims. "Don't even try that with me. You're more one of them now than you are one of us . . . if you ever *were* one of us. I won't be fooled by you again."

"Skerren, he stopped the Rüstov's spyware virus," Allegra said. "You saw him do it. We did it together!"

"So *you* say," Skerren shot back. "How do I know if he left any codes hidden in those machines?" He pointed a sword at Jack. "We don't trust *any* machines in Varagog, and you're as much a machine as you are a person now. Even if we did trust you, we couldn't let you in on our plans. The son of the Magus hears every word you say." Skerren spun his swords around and held them out in attack positions. "No more!" He ran at Jack and Allegra.

Allegra morphed one arm into a shield and the other into a sword to match Skerren's, but before the two clashed, a throng of WarHawks and Varagog knights forced Jazen and Blue back into both of them. The swarm of combatants all collided with one another, and Jack went flying down a flight of marble steps, taking several Varagoggers with him in a tangled mess of bodies.

When Jack got up, he felt no great pain beyond a few new bumps and bruises. That was especially odd, because a large knife had been plunged into his chest during the fall.

Jack breathed in a huge gulp of air, nearly choking at the sight of his wound. He tugged at his already ripped shirt to find that the blade had been stabbed deep into the mechanical implant in his sternum. Black oil spurted out around the hilt of the dagger, right next to the glowing Rüstov power core in his chest. Jack shut his eyes tight and quickly pulled out the knife before he lost his nerve. The cybernetic implant, which had been damaged by the blade, instantly began to repair itself.

"It's working," Khalix said. "Jack! The Revile process . . . it's working! Stop fighting it. Join us. Join me, and these people will never be able to hurt you again."

As Jack listened to Khalix's voice in his head, he began to worry that Skerren might have had a point after all. Maybe he really was becoming more Rüstov than human. The machinery in Jack's chest was foreign and unfriendly. He had never seen its like before. He didn't understand it and it wasn't talking to him. Jack felt at the groove Skerren's sword had carved into the thick red glass that covered his power core. Unlike the damage to the core's metal casing, the cut in the glass didn't heal itself. Jack was busy wondering why as the WarHawks came galloping down the staircase to kill him. He noticed them a second too late, but just before they got to him, a glowing Chinese dragon flew over Jack's head. Its rider grabbed him by the collar.

Solomon Roka pulled Jack up and slid back on the dragon's saddle to make room for him. "Hey, Jack. How's this for a way out?"

Jack held on tight and looked over both shoulders as his former School of Thought classmates Zhi and Trea flew past him on four more of the mystical Chinese dragons that Zhi controlled. Trea had used her powers to split into three separate versions of herself and was riding three of Zhi's dragons. Lorem Ipsum, the talented and danger-ous "daughter" of Jonas Smart, flew up alongside him, riding a fifth.

"So, Jack. How's your first day back going?" Lorem asked Jack.

Jack smirked as Trea and Zhi circled back, whipping their dragons' tails into Smart's battle droids and clearing the area for the moment. "Where the heck have you guys been?" he shouted.

Zhi intentionally bumped Jack's dragon. "You're wel-come."

"Can we get out of here, please?" Roka asked. "This is the worst homecoming parade I've ever seen."

Jack shrugged. "Oblivia did warn us."

"Don't even get me started on her," Roka grunted. He pointed to a squad of airborne WarHawks riding jet packs and armed flight pods. "Let's go. Now."

"We have to get the others," Jack said. He took the reins and brought the dragon down and around, turn-ing fast enough to leave skid marks in the air. He hugged the ground, flying underneath the fast-approaching War-Hawks, and charged back up to the top of the staircase he'd just fallen down. As soon as he reached the landing, he turned hard once again, causing the dragon's tail to fly out and sideswipe a row of WarHawks and Varagog warriors. "Climb on!" he yelled to Jazen, Blue, and Allegra.

Jazen and Blue made a break for the dragon. They would have easily made it, but Hovarth came out of nowhere. He lowered his shoulder and barreled into them, knocking them both to the ground. Hovarth's men got back up and swarmed Jazen and Blue. Only Allegra got through the mob, shifting to her most liquid state to slip in between her attackers. She stretched out her arm and wrapped it around the dragon's tail. Roka pulled her in, but Jazen and Blue were lost in the grip of Hovarth's men.

"Go!" Jazen yelled to Jack. "You're the one they want, just go!" Jack hesitated, and Jazen nearly lost it. "NOW!" he shouted.

Jack nodded and kicked his heels into the dragon's sides. He became a brilliant blur as he flew away, with Zhi, Trea, and Lorem following close behind.

CHAPTER

The Getaway

Jack broke away from the pack, following the natural instinct to fly up and away as fast as he could. He drove his dragon high into the air. A hundred arrows and five times as many laser blasts chased him into the sky.

"Incoming!" Roka shouted in Jack's ear. There was no cover up above the square. Jack was completely exposed. He turned the dragon on its side to avoid getting hit, but he was only able to protect himself, Allegra, and Roka. The dragon roared as a dozen arrows lodged into its belly and its scaly armor was riddled with bullets. The mythical beast spiraled back down toward Hero Square in a nose-dive. Jack pulled up in time to soften the blow, but they still hit the ground hard and skidded into the center of the plaza. Jack and his friends were thrown off in the crash. The dragon kept going and slammed into a speed-ing HoverCar before it finally ground to a halt.

"Is everyone okay?" Jack asked, getting up and dusting himself off.

"No," Roka said. "I gave you the reins because I thought you knew how to fly. What the heck was that?"

"Sorry, I'm better with machines."

"Guys!" Allegra shouted. She was pointing at the dragon. "She's hurt bad."

"No," Jack said, running up to the wounded creature. It was his carelessness that had gotten it shot out of the sky. Jack reached out to touch the dragon's head. "I'm sorry. I didn't think . . . I . . ." The dragon looked at Jack and let out an agonized groan. It laid its giant head against the marble flagstones and dissipated into luminescent vapors.

Jack drew back his hand as Trea and Lorem circled over-head. "Hang on," Trea shouted. "We're coming down!"

Roka shook his head, waving the glittery smoke away.

"I've got a better idea. Let's play to our strengths." Roka directed Jack's attention to the HoverCar that Zhi's dragon had crashed into. "What do you think, Jack? This thing gonna run, or is it too banged up?"

Jack coughed on the hazy remains of Zhi's dragon. Roka's words had yet to register with him. "I got that dragon killed. . . . It only took a minute."

Allegra morphed into a wall to guard against the WarHawks and Varagog Villagers as they charged across the square. Arrows and laser blasts pinged off her body. There wasn't much time. Roka took Jack by the chin and turned his head back toward the car. "Jack, focus. What do you see?"

Jack blinked a few times and looked at the HoverCar. He used his powers to scan its systems. "It's a Whisper-Craft 3000. Top-of-the-line model with hover and flight modes, bulletproof exteriors, and a hybrid warp engine under the hood." Jack nodded. "She'll run."

Roka made a clicking sound with his mouth. "I even like the color. C'mon."

The trio ran to the HoverCar and found a woozy Clarkston Noteworthy sitting in the driver's seat.

"You look familiar," said Roka. "Have we met?"

Noteworthy squinted at Roka. "What?"

"Never mind. Out you go." Roka opened up the driver's-side door and pushed Noteworthy out. He ushered Jack into the driver's seat and hopped in next to him. Allegra poured herself into the backseat.

"Hit it," Roka told Jack. He gunned the engine and sped away.

Jack blazed across Hero Square, swerving wildly to avoid people, statues, fountains, and Romanesque columns. The stone archway exits at the edges of the square were all packed with people and being sealed off. With no other way out, Jack turned away from the exits and went straight for the classical, museum-like buildings that lined the perimeter of the plaza. "Hang on," he told his passengers.

"Jack, the exit's back that way," Allegra said.

"Which one?"

"All of them! Jack!"

Allegra ducked down as Jack drove right into the building's front entrance, smashing through the brass double doors and knocking them off their hinges. He took the car through the main lobby and tore down the hallway. People screamed and jumped out of the way as the HoverCar flew like a cannonball down the wide marble concourse.

"Great. We're in a building. Now what?" Roka said.

"Don't ask me," Jack said. "I'm making this up as I go."

"We better figure something out quick," Allegra said, pointing ahead. "Look!"

Jack looked up and saw a team of WarHawks crash through the wall at the end of the hall.

"What happened to Stendeval?" Roka asked.

Jack looked out the window to his right and saw Stendeval using his powers to hold back the vast majority of Smart's WarHawks and Hovarth's medieval warriors. "He's buying us time to escape."

"Escape to where?" Allegra asked. "Where are we going?"

Through the windows to his left, Jack saw the borough of Cognito. Its skyline was starting to shift. Empire City's mysterious and ever-changing borough was home to countless superhero hideouts and secret lairs. Once every day, the borough transformed itself, rearranging every building and street within its borders and moving them to new locations. Every day, a new maze of buildings, bridges, and roads was born in Cognito. As the borough started to move, Jack realized he'd finally caught a break.

"I have an idea," Jack announced, and yanked the wheel to the left, crashing through the windows and out onto the city streets. "Hang on!"

The HoverCar cleared the building and latched onto the magnetic fields in the MagLev roadways. "You're supposed to yell 'hang on' *before* you crash through a window," Roka shouted as Jack weaved through traffic like a race car driver. "This is a convertible, you know."

"Sorry," Jack replied, speeding away from Hero Square with the WarHawks hot on his tail.

Zhi, Trea, and Lorem flew up next to Jack, keeping pace with him. "Where are we going, Jack?" Zhi asked. "What's the plan?"

The WarHawks fired missiles past Jack's car and blew up huge chunks of the road. Jack swerved to avoid the massive potholes as HoverCars crashed to the left and right of him. "We have to lose them. Follow me—and stay close!"

Jack drove straight, even as the road ahead turned hard to the right. He jumped the curb and busted through the guardrail. Allegra screamed as the car sailed out into the air and fell. Luckily, Noteworthy's HoverCar came with all the options included. Jack switched out of hover mode and dropped down four wheels, just as the car hit the brick-laid streets of Cognito. He drove head-on into the moving borough as the landscape shifted all around.

Cognito was a labyrinth that was hard enough to navigate while it was standing still. The smart thing to do during its daily scrambling of the streets was to stay put and wait it out. Jack had no intention of doing the smart thing. The very road he was driving on was moving. Buildings flipped over in front of the car, blocking its path, and wide-open streets instantly became dead ends. For every road-block Jack swerved to avoid, fresh new ones rose to take its place. Trying to drive through Cognito's daily metamorphosis was a good way to get yourself killed, but with at least twenty WarHawks firing laser blasts and exploding shells at him, there was no safer place Jack could think of.

Jack drove under a bridge that was lowering itself into the ground, narrowly avoiding getting crushed in the process. He shot a quick glance over his shoulder and saw a pair of WarHawks get clipped by a spinning building. *Two down*, he thought. Jack watched Zhi fly a slalom path through a series of newly erected towers and swat a WarHawk into the last one with his dragon's tail. When Jack turned back around, a wall had shot up in front the car, less than fifty feet away. Jack pushed the pedal all the way down and drove straight at the wall.

Roka grabbed Jack's shoulder and clutched it hard. "Jack, we're running out of road here. . . ."

Jack didn't slow down and he didn't turn. Just before the car hit the wall, the building it was attached to flipped over and the road was cleared. The landscape kept changing as Jack barreled down the street, nearly hitting more buildings, and then turning to drive down a flight of stairs as it formed in front of him. The car was quiet as Jack continued to anticipate Cognito's movements and avoid certain death.

"How are you doing this?" Roka asked.

"I spent a year living here before the Rüstov grabbed me," Jack explained. "The Secreteers put a map of these streets in my head so I could get around. I'm just following my instincts and trusting the memory implant they gave me."

"Trusting the Secreteers," Roka grumbled. "Great."

Jack came up on an unfinished bridge and kept driving.

"Let's hope memory serves," Allegra said.

Jack drove off the end of the bridge and right onto the other half as it swung by on its way to connect with a completely different road. A WarHawk in Jack's rearview mirror held up a heat ray, and red beams chased him across the bridge, nearly taking out his tires. Jack jerked the wheel to the right, taking the car off the bridge and over Cognito's rooftops as they rose up to form a makeshift road beneath the car. As soon as his wheels were back on the road, Jack drove in an erratic, serpentine pattern to keep from getting hit. He couldn't give the WarHawks a straight shot at him. That was the key to getting through this. In Cognito, the WarHawks' firepower didn't matter half as much as maneuverability. The WarHawks kept pace flying after Jack, but the changing landscape was slowing them down. So were Zhi's dragons. Trea and Lorem were mainly focused on keeping Jack in sight, but Zhi had called the last two of his seven dragons into the fray. Using his mirrors, Jack saw them swirling through Cognito's moving skyline, catching Smart's mechanized soldiers in their claws and ripping them apart. They quickly cut the WarHawks' numbers in half, but the handful that remained were dangerous enough all by themselves. Jack couldn't be sure, but it looked like one of them was carrying someone on his back.

A thought struck Jack, and he shouted, pointing at an empty street corner, "Allegra, grab that lamppost and hold on tight!"

"What lamppost?"

A lamppost shot up from the ground, and Allegra stretched out a hand to grab it. She wrapped her arm around the pole several times and strained to hold on as the car swung around a hairpin turn. A WarHawk that had almost reached Jack's car started its turn too late and rammed straight into a wall. Trea, Zhi, and Lorem nearly shared the WarHawk's fate. They looped up and around to avoid the wall at the last possible second.

Checking the rearview, Jack saw the handful of remaining WarHawks turn the corner and keep coming. They were gaining on him. A flash of light twinkled in the rearview mirror and Jack cringed as a laser blast buzzed by his right ear, burning a hole in the windshield.

"This stopped being fun about five minutes ago," Allegra said.

"I'm with her," Roka agreed.

Jack couldn't argue with either one of them. It was too dangerous to stay in Cognito any longer. His friends on the dragons couldn't anticipate the borough's movements like he could, and it was only a matter of time before one of them got hurt. Jack's eyes darted around, looking around for the way out. The WarHawks torpedoed the ground in front of him, creating a massive crater in the road. Jack used a flight of stairs as a ramp and jumped it, hitting the ground with a screech. Sparks shot out from below the HoverCar as it scraped against the pavement. Jack saw the edge of Cognito up ahead. He was on a straightaway path out of the borough, but it wasn't going to be there much longer. The street was narrowing as he drove down it. The buildings on his left and right—every one of them—were sliding toward each other like the walls of a hallway closing in.

"This is it," Jack called out to his classmates. "Pull up! I'll see you on the other side!"

Zhi and the others nodded and took their dragons up above Cognito's shifting landscape. The WarHawks stayed on Jack. With Smart's soldiers right behind him and the walls closing in all around, Jack pushed the pedal all the way to the floor. At this point, speed mattered above all else. He couldn't waste even one mile per hour swerving to dodge bullets. "Allegra, cover us!" Jack shouted as the WarHawks opened fire. Allegra spread out her hands to form a large flat shield that deflected their shots but also caught the wind like a sail, costing precious seconds in the race toward Cognito's border. "Angle it down!" Jack yelled. "Angle it down!"

"Sorry!" Allegra said, morphing into a hardtop roof for the convertible and covering everyone without sacrificing the car's aerodynamic shape.

"Kid, when you said, 'I'll see you on the other side,' you meant the other side of the street out there, right?" Roka asked, pointing up ahead. "Right?"

Jack didn't say anything. He just pushed the car as fast as it could go, aiming for the shrinking gap between the last two towers at the end of the road. Stone walls scraped against the sides of the car as it passed the last two buildings, and Jack *just* made it through before they met with a heavy *thud*.

As soon as Jack and his friends burst out of Cognito, he slammed on the brakes to avoid flying out onto a busy

MagLev highway. Noteworthy's HoverCar ground to a halt just short of a speeding mass of cars. Jack switched back into hover mode and looked at the wall that had just closed behind him. A WarHawk battle drone was trapped in between the last two buildings. It was still functioning . . . still reaching out, trying to get at him. It tried to shoot him, but its wrist cannon was too damaged to do anything but misfire. Jack felt something rather unexpected as he looked into the dying machine's eyes. Before he could tell if it was just his mind playing tricks on him, the WarHawk's power source burned out, and it was gone.

"I'm gonna file that under 'too close for comfort,'" Roka said. He gave Jack a light punch on the shoulder. "Starting to be a habit with you, kid."

Jack laughed and looked up at Zhi, Trea, and Lorem, who were flying down toward him. Squinting through the sunlight, he saw only silhouettes, but he could tell that Trea had reabsorbed her multiple selves, as there were only three people coming down on the backs of dragons. Then Jack saw a fourth person sprinting across the rooftops. He knew in an instant who it was—the same person who'd been crazy enough to hitch a ride through Cognito on the back of a WarHawk.

"Is that Skerren?" Allegra asked.

Jack got the car into gear as Skerren leaped off the edge of the last roof. "Unbelievable," he muttered. Jack mashed down the accelerator pedal with his foot, and Noteworthy's HoverCar surged onto the freeway. Jack forced his way into a lane of traffic and crisscrossed up the street, cutting cars off left and right. Behind him, Skerren grabbed onto the tail of Lorem's dragon, swung his legs out, and let go. He landed on Trea's dragon, ran a few steps toward her, and jumped again. This time he landed on the hood of a moving HoverCar.

Trea made a run at Skerren, aiming her dragon straight at him. "Back off, Skerren, I mean it!"

"I can't do that, Trea," Skerren said as he drew out a sword. He ducked down and cut the strap of her saddle as she flew past him. Trea fell off her dragon and would have hit pavement if not for Lorem Ipsum. She swooped in to catch Trea, and Skerren ran forward, jumping from car to car until he was right behind Jack.

Allegra stepped out onto the trunk of the car to face Skerren. The cars changed lanes, and Skerren took an off-balance swing that Allegra easily blocked with a super-strong shield arm. "Skerren, you're being ridiculous. You know how this is going to end." Jack was impressed with how good Allegra had gotten at being indestructible, but Skerren's attack was just a feint. He spun around and sliced a paper-thin sheet of metal right out from under Allegra's feet. As Jack swerved left to avoid a car in front of him, Allegra went sliding off to the right.

"Allegra!" Jack called out. Her body slammed into a car, caving in its hood. Thanks to her liquid metal body, she was okay, even if the car she hit was not. Skerren took her place in the backseat of Noteworthy's HoverCar, and Roka put up his fists. "All right, punk, off the car. I don't want to hurt you."

"You won't," Skerren said. He planted a sword in the backseat for leverage and kicked Roka's jaw hard enough to make him see stars. The space-pirate staggered back a step. "Ow."

Zhi came racing toward Skerren as Jack turned the HoverCar around a corner. Everyone inside the car swung to the right, and Skerren leaned into the front seat to open the passenger-side door. He gave Roka a gentle nudge and called out to Zhi: "Catch!"

Zhi shot forward on his dragon as Roka fell out of the speeding car. Zhi wasn't strong enough to catch Roka, but the dragon he was riding was. Zhi pulled up, and the flying beast latched onto Roka with its talons. Roka was saved, but Jack was left alone with Skerren. The young swordsman reached for the blade he had stuck into the backseat.

"Skerren, don't," Jack said, turning around to look back at him. "C'mon, you can't do this. . . . We're friends."

Skerren pulled his sword free and shook his head. "We *were* friends."

Jack shot a quick glance at the road and saw that he was about to hit a car. He slammed the brakes and Skerren tumbled forward into the seat next to him, losing his grip on the sword. Jack swerved to avoid another collision and Skerren nearly flew out the open passenger-side door. "Skerren!" Jack shouted as he grabbed him by the collar and pulled him back in.

The two boys sat next to each other in silence for a few

seconds. Jack kept driving. "Just in case you're keeping score, I saved your life back there," Jack said.

"If you really wanted to save lives, you'd do the right thing and lay down your own. That's the only way to guarantee you won't turn into the enemy's ultimate weapon."

Jack grimaced. "You don't think there's any chance I make it? Not even a little?"

"You lied to me." Skerren flipped open Jack's collar to get a look at the glowing core in his chest. "You lied about that thing inside you. You don't get another chance." Jack could see that the friend he once had in Skerren was gone. It was as if he never existed. Skerren reached for the sword in the backseat. "Any last words?"

Jack nodded as he pushed down on the gas. "Buckle up."

Jack fired the car up a hill, and the wall surrounding Machina came into view. He was coming up on a fork in the road. A floating holographic sign laid out his options: Hightown to the left, and Machina to the right. Jack aimed for the divider in the middle.

Skerren forgot about the sword for a second and gripped the armrest. "Jack . . ."

Khalix forced his way to the front of Jack's consciousness, crying out with the same fear Skerren felt. "JACK, NO!"

Skerren tried to grab the wheel, but Jack fought him off and drove right at the wall. He knew this one wasn't going to move, but thanks to his powers, he also knew something Skerren and Khalix didn't. The safety features in Noteworthy's HoverCar were state-of-the-art. Seconds before impact, extra seat belts shot out of the cushions, connecting around Jack's and Skerren's waists and chests. That was nice, but the car's real value became clear when its front end put up three separate layers of force fields to soften the crash.

When the car hit, it still hit hard. It hurt, just like Jack knew it would, but aside from a sore head and a ringing in his ears, he was fine. And if not, he'd *be* fine with a little rest. That was all he needed. Just a second to catch his breath. He blinked his eyes, and time seemed to jump forward. Zhi, Trea, Lorem, and Roka had all caught up to him. They were talking, but Jack didn't hear a word they said. He locked eyes with Skerren and couldn't help but notice that his former friend looked a little out of it. He almost felt bad for him. After that, things got fuzzy. Jack leaned back in his seat, and the world faded to black.

Head Games

"Jack. Wake up, Jack . . ."

Khalix's voice crept into Jack's ears like a spider. He came to in total darkness. It could have been an hour after the crash or it could have been a week. Nothing would have surprised him at this point. The last time he closed his eyes, he lost a full year. Jack looked around. Why couldn't he see? Where was he? Where had everybody gone?

"You gave me quite a scare back there," the Rüstov prince told Jack. "For a moment I was afraid you'd decided to follow your friend's advice and do the 'honorable' thing.

I should have known better. That's not your style."

Jack ignored Khalix and took a second to concentrate on once again shutting the royal parasite out of his mind. *Royal pain is more like it*, Jack thought. Once he was satisfied he'd silenced Khalix, he got up on his feet. He found it odd that he didn't feel any aches and pains after hitting the wall like that. He moved about cautiously in the pitch-black void, reaching his arms out in front of him as he went.

"I suppose he's really more of a former friend, isn't he?" Khalix asked Jack. "He doesn't seem to like you very much now that you're one of us."

Jack nearly jumped out of his skin when he heard Khalix pop up again, undeterred. "I'm not one of you," he shot back. Then he walked into a wall. His face rammed into a hard steel plane, and Khalix laughed at him in the darkness.

"You don't know what you are, Jack. Not anymore."

That was when Jack realized the Rüstov prince's voice wasn't in his head. It was there in the room with him. Jack spun around, half expecting to find Khalix standing right behind him. "Where are you?"

"Where am I? Where do you think? I'm here. I'm always here."

The power core in Jack's chest lit up, flashing on and off with a faint red glow. Jack's shoulders tensed up and the hair on the back of his neck stood on end. He'd almost forgotten about the core. Just the thought of Rüstov machinery in his body gave him goose bumps all over. The fact that it had become so much a part of him that it escaped his notice absolutely filled him with dread. Jack's first instinct was to try and turn it off, but he couldn't do that. He decided instead to use the light to look for Khalix. He sounded like he was close by. How was that even possible? Jack panned around the room, using his chest like a flashlight. The walls had all the characteristics of Rüstov design. They were a disorganized assembly of various metals welded together without rhyme or reason. It was if someone had told a mason to craft a wall using broken machine parts instead of bricks. Jack inched around the room, keeping one hand on the wall, as the light blinked on and off. He saw a dim red light that held for a few seconds, then nothing . . . a dim red light, then nothing. Then the light blinked back on and Khalix was two inches away from his face.

"Boo."

"Aah!" Jack jumped back. He tripped over his feet and fell to the floor. Khalix stood over him, laughing. He was enjoying himself immensely. Jack stayed on the ground looking up as red light washed over his parasite a few seconds at a time. His blood ran cold when he realized what he was looking at—a vision of himself in the final stages of Rüstov infection. Khalix had his body . . . he had his face! The Rüstov mark around his eye was pronounced and metallic. Circuits ran all along the surface of his skin. Cybernetic growths protruded out from underneath.

"So you're the famous Jack," Khalix said with a smile. "I'm so glad we finally have the chance to meet . . . face-to-face."

Jack shook his head. "This isn't happening. You're not here."

"I'm not?"

"No. You're a hallucination. I'm woozy from the crash. Or maybe I'm out cold." Jack snapped his fingers. "That's it. This is a dream."

Khalix smiled like a boxer who knew the fight had been fixed in his favor. "Whose dream, Jack? Yours or mine? In case you haven't noticed, you're not in control here.

117

You might be able to shut me out while you're awake, but that requires concentration. When you sleep . . . that's my time." He leaned down and tapped at the glowing light in Jack's chest. "Soon, all your time is going to be mine."

Jack had nothing to say to that. He felt at the glowing power core in his chest and shuddered as he sat on the cold metal floor.

"Here, allow me," Khalix said, offering to help Jack up. Jack batted away the hand Khalix had offered and stood up on his own. The Rüstov prince looked wounded. "Jack . . . don't be like that. We're going to be together for quite some time. The least we can do is try to get along."

Jack's lip curled up. "Get along? Are you kidding?"

Khalix raised his shoulders. "I agree you've been anything but a gracious host up to this point, but I'm willing to forgive all that. It's always better when we work together."

Jack couldn't believe his ears. "*You're* willing to forgive *me*?"

Khalix offered his hand again. "We can be partners, you and I. Let's start over. You might as well. We both know how this is going to end."

Jack turned his back on Khalix, looking for a way out of the dream or, at the very least, the conversation. "You're just trying to mess with my head."

Khalix snickered. "Oh, we've already done that. You can't *imagine* the things we've done to you. Perhaps you'd like to see for yourself?"

Khalix held his hand out and a spotlight switched on across the room. Jack shielded his eyes, which were sensitive to the light after being in the dark for so long. Still, he couldn't turn away. The light seemed impossibly bright, but there was no way he could ignore what was going on beneath it. A surgical team was prepping a patient on an operating table. It all seemed eerily familiar to Jack, and he had a good idea why. When his eyes finally adjusted, his suspicions were confirmed. The patient on the table was him.

"What is this?" Jack asked.

Khalix walked toward the light with his hands clasped behind his back. "The first day of the rest of your life."

Jack steeled his nerves and followed Khalix to the operating table. He saw himself lying there, heavily sedated and stripped to the waist. Rüstov scientists dressed in clear plastic scrubs surrounded the table, checking instruments, strapping sensors to his body, and monitoring his vitals. None of them paid Jack any mind as he approached. He turned to Khalix. "Can they hear us?"

Khalix shook his head. "This is just a memory. One of mine. Not yours."

Jack watched the surgical team move about the lab, getting things ready. It was a surreal experience for Jack to stand apart from himself and watch this all play out. He felt like he was watching actors on the stage. He wanted to believe this was all just a dream, but he remembered flashes of this moment. Some of them had hit him in the swamps next to St. Barnaby's. Snippets of Khalix's memory were bleeding into his own.

At the edge of the light, a Rüstov doctor, presumably the head surgeon, was speaking with someone else Jack remembered. Glave. He was still using Obscuro the Secreteer as a host.

"I don't want to hear any more excuses," Glave told the surgeon. "There will be no more delays. The Magus has waited long enough already."

"But, sir . . . ," the doctor began.

"He's not known for his patience. Perhaps you've forgotten that?"

The doctor sighed. "No, sir. Of course not, but this is the Magus's son we're talking about. This procedure . . . it's untested. Entirely theoretical. We never even considered such a possibility before you returned to Rüst with this talk of Revile."

"I grow tired of this argument, Doctor."

"We're pushing too far. Too fast. Augmenting the infection this way could very well kill the host, and that would mean the death of the—"

"Enough," Glave interrupted, putting up a hand. "It's going to work," he assured the surgeon. Jack watched Glave tap on his forehead like he was a prop. "I know the host's mind. He has actually come face-to-face with the results of your work. He's seen the future. You've already succeeded, Doctor. There can be no other outcome."

"But what we've discovered here . . . the possibilities are endless. There are options that don't risk the prince's life. I just need more time."

A Rüstov guard marched up to Glave and snapped to

attention. "Sir. The Magus awaits your presence on the observation deck." Jack looked up, and more light faded in from above. He saw the Magus sitting in a gallery overlooking the lab.

Glave nodded to the guard. "I'll be there at once," he said, and then turned back to the surgeon. "I'm afraid the time is now, Doctor. Not to worry. If you don't believe me about the future, just remember that necessity is the mother of invention."

The surgeon frowned at Glave. "What are you talking about?"

Glave grinned. "I'm talking about the fact that if you *do* happen to harm the Magus's son, you will experience pain like never before, and it will last a very long time. I say you can't help but succeed, but you know full well that you can't afford to fail." Glave clapped the surgeon on the shoulder and laughed. "Good luck, Doctor. You have my full faith and confidence."

Glave followed the guard out of the operating room, and the surgeon muttered something unpleasant about Glave's mother once he was out of earshot. Jack was inclined to agree with the doctor.

"You don't like Glave either, I see," Khalix said. "I can understand that. Most people don't. He's not very nice, but he does get results. That's how he got where he is today. My father has rewarded him handsomely for his role in my rescue and safe return."

Jack didn't respond to Khalix. He was transfixed by the scene before him. The Rüstov surgeon barked a few orders at his staff, and the members of the surgical team took their positions around the table, making final preparations. Two holo-screen monitors popped up, showing images of Jack's body lying still on the table with action all around. The word "Recording" was flashing in red on each screen. Jack felt his stomach tighten as he watched one of the Rüstov doctors draw a black dotted line from his neck to his abdomen, laying out the points of incision. Meanwhile, two more doctors were running through a checklist of surgical tools. As each terrible new tool came into view, Jack's anxiety jumped ten levels. It didn't even matter that it was just a memory of him lying there on the table. The idea of these things being used on him was bad enough. Out of all the items on the list, the Rüstov saved the worst for last:

"Is the implant ready?" the first doctor asked.

"Ready," the other replied, holding up a crystal shard. It was a thin, red sliver of glass no larger than a blade of grass, but Jack could tell mountains of power nested within it. He knew in an instant that it was the same red crystal that powered the Rüstov core in his chest. It terrified him to see how much the object had grown while inside his body.

"There it is," Khalix marveled. "From little packages, big things come, eh, Jack?"

Jack swallowed hard. "Why are you showing me this? Trying to scare me?"

"I'm just trying to help you understand your situation. It's high time you accepted that this isn't your body anymore. It's *our* body. Your conscious mind might be able to tune me out, but I'm still there beneath the surface of every thought, tightening my grip on your subconscious. How else could I have rendered your powers useless against us? Your powers aren't enough to stop me anymore. The truth is, they never were. This is about willpower as much as anything else, and we broke your will, Jack. Don't bother trying to deny it."

Jack had no snappy comeback for Khalix. The cold logic of his reasoning was hard to dismiss.

"We had you for a year. A whole year. What you see here is just the beginning. I haven't even gotten to the Theater of War yet."

"What's that?"

Khalix smiled. "You'll see. We've done more than infect your body, Jack. We've infected your brain. Changed the way you think. Deep inside your mind, you already know how to be one of us, and when my father gets here . . . you will be."

Jack's infected eye tingled at the mere mention of the Rüstov emperor. He looked up at the Magus and worried that maybe Khalix wasn't just trying to psyche him out. Everything felt wrong. The mark on Jack's eye and the ruby-red crystal growing like a tumor in his chest made it painfully clear that Khalix was getting stronger, and then there was the matter of his father. Jack could feel the Magus's presence up in the gallery lending his son power and support on the operating table. He remembered feeling the Magus's anger back when he escaped on Roka's ship. Somehow he had known the Magus's feelings as well as he did his own. The Magus shared a powerful connection with his people, and Jack worried about how much stronger Khalix would get once his father returned. What if Khalix was right? What if he couldn't beat him anymore?

"It's like Glave said, we've already succeeded. You fought well, longer than anybody ever has, but there's no point in holding out any longer. We're too strong."

Jack did his best to sound brave. "Not strong enough to hold me. I escaped."

Khalix stifled a laugh. "That's right. I forgot."

"What's so funny?"

"Oh, I think you know. Understand this, Jack, you do nothing that we don't intend. Everything you do from this point on can only serve to weaken the Imagine Nation. You may think you're going to fight to the bitter end, but you don't know what you're going to do when that moment finally comes. I do. You're our greatest weapon and we've got you exactly where we want you. Revile is part of both our futures. It's fate. You can't escape destiny."

"I don't believe in destiny."

Khalix laughed out loud. "Oh, Jack. Really . . . you need to wake up."

Fight or Flight

Jack's eyes shot open and his whole body shook. There was somebody next to him with a hand on his arm. He tried to scurry away but his back was against a wall. There was nowhere to go.

"Jack, it's okay. It's okay!" Roka said, grabbing him and holding him steady. "It's a dream. You're dreaming."

"No, it's . . ." Jack shook his head and blinked his way out of his disoriented state. He was breathing hard. "Right. A dream. I knew that."

"It's all right, Jack," Allegra said. "You're not there

anymore. The Rüstov don't have you. You're safe. You're here with us."

Jack took a deep breath and looked around. He knew exactly two things. One, he had no idea where "here" was. Two, he wasn't safe anywhere. He rubbed his eyes and the world came back into focus. It was nighttime. He, Allegra, Trea, Zhi, Lorem, and Roka were all hiding out somewhere dark, wet, and dirty. "Where are we?"

"Lowest point in Lowtown," Roka said. "We're in one of the drainage tunnels under the foundation of the city. Used to hide out here in my younger, troublemaking days. Never really outgrew those, I guess."

"There aren't any security cameras this far down," Lorem said, looking up out of the mouth of the tunnel. "We should be okay here for a little while at least. It's a lead-lined tunnel, so even if Daddy's new toys have X-ray vision, they can't see through it. They'll make their way down here eventually, though. You can bet he's got them all out looking for you."

Jack nodded. Lorem Ipsum had been created by Jonas Smart in a lab experiment and subsequently locked up by him when she didn't do as she was told. She knew a thing or two about hiding out from her "father." Jack reached out with his powers and monitored the police scanners. "He's looking all right. Everybody's looking for us." He could tell Smart's WarHawks were still scanning the upper levels of Hightown for them. For the time being, they were off the grid. "Does anyone else know about this place?" Jack asked Roka.

"Not anymore," Roka replied. He looked sad for a moment, but he shook off his brooding expression and quickly put his guard back up. "Don't worry. No one's gonna find us down here."

"Okay," Jack said, leaning back against the inside of the tunnel. "Let me just catch my breath for a second." He closed his eyes. He was exhausted after the melee in Hero Square and the chase through Cognito, but he didn't dare rest. To relax his mind was to open the door for Khalix. His parasite had gained far too much ground on him already. Jack opened his eyes. Everyone was staring at him. They looked nervous. They were trying to hide it, but Jack could still tell.

"Jack, how are you feeling?" Allegra asked.

"Yeah, are you okay?" Lorem asked. "That was some dream."

"I'm all right. It's just . . . it's hard to explain."

"You don't have to," Roka said. "You talk in your sleep."

Jack froze. Even among friends, he felt naked not knowing exactly what he'd said. "So, you heard . . ."

"Everything," Trea said.

Jack sighed. On the one hand, he felt betrayed by his own body. On the other, at least he didn't have to tell his friends what was going on with him. They already knew. "When I sleep, he's there now. Khalix. He's stronger than he used to be. I don't know what they did to me, guys, I . . ." Jack trailed off and pressed a hand to his forehead. There was no point in denying it. He was feeling nervous too.

"Don't let him psyche you out, Jack," Zhi said. "You're stronger than Khalix. You held him off for this long, didn't you? You escaped."

Jack snorted. "Not according to Khalix. He says they let me go, and I think he might be telling the truth. It's harder for me to fight him off now. Khalix draws strength from the Magus. All the Rüstov do. It's harder for me to fight him when his father is nearby, and then there's this." Jack pulled his shirt open to let everyone get a good look at the mechanical implant in his chest. It was glowing with a red light, just like in his dream.

"Does it hurt?" Trea asked, leaning in to inspect the core.

Jack shook his head. "It doesn't feel like anything. I know what it is, though. It's Revile's regenerative core. This is where he comes from. I really am part machine now. Sure, I'm able to hold Khalix off for the time being, but when the armada gets closer . . . when the Magus gets here? Who knows?"

"What do you mean, *who knows?*" Allegra asked Jack. "You have a plan, right?"

Jack zipped his shirt back up. "A plan? Allegra, I spent the last year in a coma. I'm only here now because they want me here. What kind of a plan would I have?"

"Hey," Lorem said. "I know you're upset, but don't take it out on her. She's only trying to help."

Jack looked at Allegra. She was staring at him with her arms folded in front of her body.

Jack let out a sigh and went up to her. "I'm sorry, I didn't mean to . . ." He put a hand on her shoulder. "This isn't your fault. You were there for me when I needed it. You all were. It's just, I don't know that you should be anymore. You guys are trusting me when I can't even trust myself. Zhi, I got one of your dragons killed."

"No you didn't," Zhi said. "He just needs time to heal."

"Zhi, I watched him evaporate this morning. He's gone."

"My dragons are mystical creatures, Jack. The only way to get rid of them would be to sever their connection to this world. To kill *me*."

That made Jack feel a little better, but only a little. "So we got lucky this time. What about next time?"

"You sound like Skerren," Trea said.

"Skerren," Allegra repeated. She said the name like it left a bad taste in her mouth. "He and I had kind of a falling-out this past year. Over you."

"The way he went after you today, it's hard to believe you were ever friends," Zhi said.

"He's still mad about what went down with the spyware virus," Allegra explained. "He believes that prophecy about your future without question."

"The *prophecy*," Jack said. "I can't believe I'm saying this, but I'm starting to think he might be right."

Jack's words took the air out of the tunnel. "I can't believe you're saying that either," Allegra said, breaking the silence. "What's wrong with you?"

"Look, I know this isn't what anyone wants to hear, but how I feel is how I feel. At least I'm telling the truth." Jack looked at the faces of his friends as they digested what he had said. Judging by their expressions, they didn't have any great appreciation for the truth. This time, it was Roka who broke the silence:

"Kid, I know we just met, but if my opinion counts for anything, I don't think you mean what you're saying. Not really."

"No?"

"No. I think you're scared, and that's fine. You should be. But we've all got two main instincts that kick in when we find ourselves in situations like yours. Fight or flight. I've seen you fight when you needed to fight, and I've seen you run when you needed to run. I watched you fly from one end of the galaxy to the other at light speed for crying out loud."

"What's your point?"

Roka held up his fingers, counting off Jack's options. "Fight or flight. They're both survival instincts. You don't strike me as the kind of guy who likes to give up."

Jack nodded slowly as he turned Roka's words over in his head. He was forced to admit: "No, I'm not."

"Pretty sharp for a space-pirate," Lorem Ipsum said.

"He prefers 'adventurer,'" Allegra said.

"Or entrepreneur," Roka added. "Thank you, Allegra." He turned back to Jack. "So if you're not gonna give up, I guess the question is, what are you going to do?"

Jack ran his hands through his hair. "Whatever it is, I can't do it alone. This is going to be a hard fight, guys. The odds are against us. Way against us."

"I once met a woman who dealt with far worse," Stendeval called out from the end of the tunnel. "She was blind and deaf, but she wasn't alone. She said walking with a friend in the darkness is better than walking alone in the light."

"Stendeval!" Jack said as his old teacher stepped into the tunnel. Blue and Midknight, the veteran hero of Hightown, followed him in.

"Whatever the future holds, we'll face it together, Jack. Our job is not to predict the future, but rather to build it."

"How did you find us?" Roka asked.

"We had help from an old friend," Stendeval said, stepping aside to reveal a cloaked figure standing in the tunnel's entrance. It was a Secreteer.

"I would have found you eventually," Midknight said. "This is my borough, after all."

If Roka heard a word Midknight said, it was impossible to tell. He was leaning forward toward the Secreteer in disbelief. "It can't be . . . ," he began. "Rasa?"

The Secreteer pulled back her hood to reveal her face. Jack leaned around Roka to get a look at who it was. Hypnova shook her head sadly.

"I'm sorry, no."

Roka cursed himself under his breath. "Of course you're not her. How could you be?"

"All these years, and still you remember," the former Secreteer marveled.

"Like it was yesterday," Roka said. "Can't seem to forgive and forget, no matter what you people try to pull."

For a moment, Jack's own problems took a backseat

to an intense curiosity. He didn't know what Roka and Hypnova were talking about, but it was obvious there was no love lost between his newfound friend and the Clandestine Order. Whatever their history was, it didn't seem personal for Hypnova, but Roka clearly felt otherwise.

"You should know what happened was the matriarch's decision. I had nothing to do with it. I'm not even part of the order anymore."

Roka shrugged. "Neither is Rasa. But that doesn't matter now, does it?"

Hypnova's eyes widened. "You know what happened to her?"

"Why do you think I spent the last ten years raiding Rüstov ships?" Roka said. "This isn't my first trip home."

Hypnova frowned and looked away. Jack was about to ask Jazen if he had any idea what Hypnova and Roka were talking about when he noticed his android friend was missing.

"Hey, where's Jazen?" Jack asked.

Blue kneeled down next to Jack. "Jazen didn't make it out, partner."

"Didn't make it out?" Jack repeated. "What are you talking about? Where is he?"

Midknight stepped forward. "Smart took Jazen prisoner. He says if you don't come out of hiding and surrender, he's going to dismantle Jazen and shred his parts. You've got until tomorrow night to turn yourself in."

CHAPTER

10

A Friend in Need

As soon as Jack heard Jazen was in trouble, he immediately changed gears. He had one priority—Jazen Knight. Jack used his powers to grab hold of an advertising holoscreen that was floating around the lower levels of Hightown. He pulled it down toward the tunnel, switched off its regular rotation of commercials, and changed the channel to SmartNews. The picture rolled and Jack saw Drack Hackman, the slick SmartNews anchorman, interviewing Jonas Smart:

"I don't like this any more than you do," Smart said. "I

prefer to solve problems peacefully, with ideas that benefit the greater good. Unfortunately, when faced with such obstinate resistance and immediate danger, my hand is forced. I have to think of the people of this city. This city and beyond."

Hackman waved his hands at Smart. "Please, sir, there's no need to explain yourself. No one questions your motives. You've been the only consistent voice of reason ever since this whole Jack Blank affair began." Hackman turned toward the camera. "Here at SmartNews, we gave Jazen Knight a chance to appeal to Jack Blank and ask him to do the right thing. I'm afraid we can only show you a portion of his statement."

An window opened up on the screen with an image of Jazen inside it. He was sitting in a dark room underneath a bright light. His hands were tied behind his back and he was struggling to break free of his restraints. "When I get out of here, I'm going to shove my fist so far up your—"

The window blinked out before Jazen finished. Hackman was shaking his head with a disappointed look. "You see, this is what I'm dealing with," Smart said.

"Meanwhile, Circlewoman Virtua is no better," Hackman replied. "We have a statement from her as well."

Another window opened up on the screen, this time showing Virtua at a lectern, speaking to a group of people.

"Jonas Smart is clearly out of control. His actions on the square today are proof enough of that, but his abduction of Commander Knight is a hostile act against Machina that will not stand. I am demanding his immediate release. If Mr. Smart should choose to ignore me, he does so at his own peril and that of his borough. I will not hesitate to send troops into Hightown to take Commander Knight back."

"By force?" a reporter in the crowd asked.

Virtua's features hardened and her color turned deep crimson. "By any means necessary."

The window showing Virtua's press conference vanished from the screen. Drack Hackman threw up his hands as if he didn't know where to begin.

"Sending Mecha troops into Hightown would be an act of war," Smart warned. "I wish I could say I'm shocked by the Circlewoman's comments, but the truth is, none of this surprises me. I've had my eye on Machina ever since the riots there last year. For all we know, that entire borough is still under the control of the Rüstov."

Hackman nodded. "I suppose you're also not surprised that the Calculan Delegation has officially withdrawn its support for an alliance with the Imagine Nation now that Jack Blank has returned?"

"What?" Allegra blurted out.

Smart shrugged. "They're merely being prudent. Would you join forces with an army that let's enemy agents walk freely within their ranks? The Calculans are logical creatures. Rest assured, we'll regain their support once Jack Blank is dead. But if he isn't dead in"—Smart checked his watch—"sixteen hours and twelve minutes, Jazen Knight will be."

"Thank you for talking with us tonight, sir. It's an honor as always."

"Thank you, Drack."

"For more as this story develops, keep your holo-screen tuned to SmartNews—the only news you need to hear."

The broadcast cut to commercial, and Jack sent the screen away.

"This doesn't make sense," Zhi said. "The Calculans helped bring Jack home. Why would they quit on us now that he's back? That can't be right."

"Yes it can," Roka said. "Makes perfect sense if you know the Calculans like I do. They don't play nice with others. They play the odds. Sounds like they don't think the Imagine Nation is a good bet anymore."

"Can you blame them?" Lorem asked.

Midknight shook his head. "We'll be an even worse bet without their help. They've got a fleet of unmanned drone fighters five thousand strong. We need that firepower if we're going to stand a chance against the Rüstov."

"How can they just completely change their minds all of a sudden?" Allegra asked. "They let Roka out of prison to go after Jack. They're the reason he's here! They can't do this."

Roka shook his head. "I'm afraid they can do whatever they want."

Jack was lost in thought as his friends argued about the Calculans. Everyone was worried about suddenly losing their support, but all Jack could think about was how his best friend was in danger because of him. Again. "Why do they keep calling him Commander Knight?" he asked.

Everyone got quiet. Blue patted Jack's shoulder. "After the riots in Machina, Jazen had to resign his position as an emissary. Now he's head of Machina Security and uh . . . special assistant to the Circlewoman."

"Jack, I know you're worried about your friend, but we have to look at the big picture here," Midknight said.

"Big picture?" Jack repeated. "Are you kidding? We need to get Jazen out of there now."

Midknight put his hands up. "Jack, calm down."

"No!" Jack shouted. "Smart's gonna kill Jazen because of me. I can't just stand by and let that happen."

"We gain nothing by fighting among ourselves," Stendeval said. "Midknight is correct."

Jack couldn't believe his ears. "Stendeval!"

"And Jazen would agree," Stendeval continued. "If you confront Smart directly right now, it can only make matters worse. Our actions need to serve the greater good if we want to make a difference in the conflict ahead. Machina can't be at odds with Hightown days before a Rüstov invasion. We need to work together if we want to survive."

"How do we do that?" Jack asked. "This city can't work together. The only people who trust me are here inside this tunnel."

"Then that has to change," Trea said. "We should talk

to the Calculans. If we can change their minds about Jack, things will calm down a little. Then maybe we can pressure Smart into letting Jazen go without a fight."

"We turn the screws on Smart and shore up our defenses at the same time," Midknight said. "I like it."

"I don't," Roka said. "The Calculans don't listen to anybody. They crunch numbers and make decisions. They've *decided*."

"Based on what they *think* they know," Stendeval said. "If they're leaving because of Jack, they should at least meet him before they go. And they will."

"What makes you so sure they're going to like what they see?" Jack asked as his chest lit up with red light. "Look what the Rüstov did to me."

Stendeval put his hand on Jack's shoulder. "All they've done is give you the strength you need to defeat them. You'll never be their weapon. Never be Revile unless you decide to be."

"Stendeval, you're the one who always says we can't know the future. What makes you so sure? How do you know I can keep from becoming Revile?"

"I just know."

Jack shook his head. "You're not helping."

"The Calculan Delegation is staying with us at the Garrison," Allegra said. "I can get us all in."

"And I can fly us there," Zhi said.

Jack took a deep breath and nodded. He didn't like it, but he didn't have any better ideas. "All right. Let's go."

As Jack and his friends left the depths of Lowtown and made their way to the alien borough of Galaxis, he couldn't shake Khalix's words out of his head:

Everything thing you do can only serve to weaken the Imagine Nation.

How were they going to convince the Calculans otherwise? So many bad things were happening, all because of him. Jack didn't think he could turn that around, no matter what Stendeval said.

CHAPTER

11

The Cold and the Calculating

Allegra keyed in her personal access code at a side entrance to the Valorian Garrison. "Quick, inside!" she shouted. Jack and the others all ran safely into Prime's massive dome-shaped headquarters in the heart of Galaxis. Traveling by glowing Chinese dragon was anything but discreet, and Jack had been recognized by several people on his way over from Lowtown. He knew being spotted at the Garrison would bring his enemies to Prime's door, but there was no avoiding that. His enemies were everywhere. Allegra led the group through the building to Prime's chambers. The Valorian Guardsmen they passed along the way took little notice of Jack. They were not afraid of him or his future. Valorians knew no fear. They did, however, know considerable frustration with people who lacked their courage and convictions. Prime was no exception. Jack and the others found him locked in a heated argument with the members of the Calculan Delegation.

"Ambassador, this is madness," Prime pleaded. "To come all this way only to turn right back around . . . you can't be serious."

There were three Calculans in the room with Prime. Two of them were busy with a large holo-tech computer. Numbers and figures floated through the air all around them. Jack understood the numbers easily enough, but the rest was in a language he didn't know. Prime, the Calculan ambassador, and his fellow delegates all paused to notice Jack and the others come in.

"Stendeval?" Prime said. "Jack! What are you doing here?"

Stendeval stepped forward. "Please forgive our intrusion, Prime. I hoped we might help convince our Calculan friends to stay. If they are leaving because Jack is an unknown factor, we can at least remedy that."

Prime rubbed his chin a moment, then nodded. "Yes. Very good. Jack, come here, please."

Jack stepped forward, and two of the Calculans turned back to their work at the light computer. The tallest one stayed with Prime, studying Jack with narrow black eyes. Jack assumed that he was the leader, but the Calculans all looked the same to him. They had thin, humanoid figures and wore identical V-neck robes. They had elongated fingers and wrinkled, gray skin that made Jack think of elephant hide. They had no noses, and their foreheads extended upward a foot or more, leveling off into a flat, angled surface without hair. The Calculan leader stood across from Prime and the others with his hands clasped. He said nothing. His face was an emotionless mask.

"Ambassador Equa. May I present Jack Blank of Empire City," Prime said. "Jack, please meet the distinguished Ambassador Equa, a board member of the Calculan Planetary Conglomerate and head of this delegation."

Jack started to offer the Ambassador his hand, but Prime pushed it back down. From the look on Equa's face, Jack realized that shaking hands was not a Calculan thing to do.

"We thought it best that you two meet before you decide to take your leave," Stendeval told the ambassador.

"And now we have," Equa said. "Thank you." He looked over his shoulder at his two comrades. They ran a few quick calculations on their computer and shook their heads in reply to his unspoken question. "I'm afraid this changes nothing."

Equa turned his back on the group and moved to rejoin his colleagues. Jack screwed up his face in frustration. "Wait a minute, that's it? We haven't even talked yet." He reached out and grabbed Equa's wrist. Prime tried to pull him back, but it was too late. Equa recoiled from Jack, and the other Calculans gasped in shock. Jack quickly released the ambassador and put his hands up in apology, realizing he'd committed a serious breach of protocol. "Sorry! Sorry, I didn't mean to grab you, but . . . please, Mr. Ambassador, sir . . . at least talk to me. My friend's life is on the line."

Equa grumbled and looked at his wrist like it had a disease. One of the other Calculans brought him a glowing cloth to wipe it with. "There's nothing to discuss," he said, motioning to the holo-computer. "The numbers have told us all we need to know. Numbers do not lie."

"What numbers?" Jack asked.

"The only numbers that matter when deciding on a course of action," said the Calculan who had handed Equa the cloth. "The probabilities for positive and negative outcomes of that action."

Equa handed the cloth back to his subordinate. "We do not believe, as many people here seem to, that the future is written. However, we do happen to know it can be predicted with a fair degree of accuracy based on quantifiable knowns and unknowns. This is the probability algorithm that all our decisions are made by." The ambassador waved his hand at the third Calculan, who brought up a large projection of an incredibly complex equation filled with confusing numbers and figures. "We agreed to help free you from captivity because we were led to believe your machine-controlling powers gave us the best chance of defeating the Rüstov Armada."

Equa lifted a hand, and the algorithm processed a light show of calculations that resulted in an 86 percent probability of success.

"We did not anticipate that you would return here

unable to use your powers against the Rüstov, effectively reducing your chances of positively impacting this conflict to fourteen percent."

Jack's stomach twisted and churned as he watched the numbers rapidly tick down from 86 percent all the way to 14 percent.

"Furthermore, based on the data provided to us . . ." Equa paused to give Stendeval a reproachful look. "It appears we overestimated your ability to resist your Rüstov infection." Equa pointed across the room, where another calculation was being run. "The advanced state of your transformation indicates a high probability that you are in fact a Rüstov plant, soon to be overtaken by your parasite." According to the Calculans, the odds that Jack would succumb to Khalix's will and become Revile clocked in at a staggering 99.8 percent. "We were told that your presence here would help deliver victory, but we must now ask ourselves, *whose* victory? We are more inclined to believe that you will stand against us in the battles ahead. All of this has now been factored into the holo-computer by my associates."

Equa's examples were incorporated into the larger

equation, and the entire room lit up in a dizzying display of alien math. When the last integer finally clicked into place, the only thing that Jack understood were the words to the right of the equal sign: "Success: 50%/Failure: 50%."

"We see now that, working together with the citizens of the Imagine Nation, we have no better than a fifty percent chance of defeating the Rüstov," Equa explained. "That figure was higher prior to your arrival, but your return has had a polarizing effect on the many factions of this city. We can't go to war with you against the Rüstov. You're still at war with yourselves."

Jack didn't know what to say. The Calculans' decision-making process made his head spin, but he couldn't fault them for feeling the way they did. The fact was, he felt the same way. But Jazen needed him. He couldn't let them go without a fight. He had to make this work.

"Please, Mr. Ambassador. We need your help. I'm fighting this infection as hard as I know how. You can't just abandon us."

"I'm sorry, but this isn't about your future. It's about ours." Equa nodded, and the Calculan at the computer adjusted the variables in the equation. The probability of success increased to 53.2 percent. "By our calculations, the conglomerate's interests are better served by leaving Earth to fend for itself and letting the Rüstov take the planet. It will take them a long time to burn through all of Earth's resources."

"Forty-seven Earth years," the Calculan at the computer interjected.

"Forty-seven Earth years," Equa repeated. "And during that time, we can increase our own military might enough to improve our chances of defeating the Rüstov by ourselves. At the very least, we will be able to hold them off long enough to fall back to a new position and buy ourselves more time to make a final stand against them at some point in the future."

"You're just gonna kick the can down the road and hope for the best?" Roka asked. "That's your plan?"

The ambassador grumbled with annoyance. "Nothing is keeping you here, Mr. Roka," Equa said, ignoring the question. "You gained your freedom as a result of all this. If I were you, I would do the smart thing and leave while you still can."

"It's *Captain* Roka, thank you, and I've never done the

153

smart thing in my life. I'm not gonna start now."

Ambassador Equa turned away from Roka. "If memory serves, that's the kind of thinking that got you put in prison."

"Your bureaucratic nonsense got me put in prison, you bean-counting freak."

"That will do, Captain Roka," Prime said, holding up a hand.

"Don't worry about offending them," Roka told Prime. "They only care about their precious numbers. It doesn't matter how nicely you ask them, the only way they're going to stay is if that stupid equation up there tells them they need us."

Hypnova pulled Roka back before he said something he *really* meant. Meanwhile, Trea had split into what Jack assumed were her three hyperintelligent selves. They were all trying to make sense of the Calcluan equations. Judging by their expressions, Jack guessed they weren't having much success.

"Ambassador Equa," one of the Treas began. "I can be pretty smart when I need to be, but I can't even pretend to understand all the different variables you've factored into this decision."

"So we're not going to argue with you about that," the second Trea cut in.

"Right, we're not," the first Trea continued. "But even if we accept all the assumptions inherent in your equation . . ."

"Which we don't," the third Trea interjected.

The first Trea sighed and pulled herself together, putting an end to the interruptions. "The odds you seem to prefer are not significantly better."

"No, but they are better and that's all that matters to us."

"You're making a mistake," Stendeval told the ambassador. "No equation can measure a child's potential. Our best chance of defeating the Rüstov is right here in this room. I wonder, have you ever considered the possibility that you're wrong?"

Ambassador Equa leaned toward Stendeval. "Have *you?*"

Jack was pretty sure that Stendeval had never once doubted him, but with everything that was going on, he had enough doubts for the both of them. Almost as many as there were people in the crowd forming outside. Jack looked out the window and saw Jonas Smart leading an angry mob into Galaxis.

"Jack Blank, we know you're in there!" he called out on a loudspeaker.

Smart's voice shook the room. Everyone spun around to face the window and look outside. Jack gritted his teeth. The last time someone had yelled those words at him, he was hiding out in the library stacks at St. Barnaby's. Back then all he wanted to do was keep his head down and not get caught. Things were different now. Jack was tired of hiding. When he saw Smart, he thought of Jazen and made a fist so tight that his knuckles cracked.

Jack looked out the window with the others. It was just before dawn, but Smart had assembled an impressive crowd. He was there with Hovarth and his men, people from Hightown, and of course, an army of WarHawks. A giant holo-screen projected Smart's image into the air so that all his followers could see him, no matter how far back they stood in the crowd.

"Typical Smart," Midknight said. "He can't go anywhere without bringing a giant billboard to put his face on."

Blue slid open a glass door that led out onto a balcony. "I might have to pound that face until he lets my friend go."

No sooner had Blue opened the door than a trio of WarHawks flew up to it. A captain of the Valorian Guard appeared at Prime's side. "Sir, the Garrison has been surrounded by Smart's WarHawks."

"Surrounded!" Prime balled up his fists.

"Circleman Prime," the lead WarHawk's robotic voice announced. "I come bearing a message from Jonas Smart."

"And you may deliver my reply." Prime's hands lit up with energy, and the WarHawk went flying backward, falling out of the sky. It hit the ground hard and broke apart, its head rolling across the street to rest at the feet of Jonas Smart.

"I see we've gotten your attention, Circleman Prime," Smart said.

"Jonas Smart!" Prime bellowed. "What gives you the right to surround my home?"

"We have every right to do what is necessary to protect ourselves against the Rüstov, " Smart shot back. "We will not be threatened by your decision to safeguard the enemy's ultimate weapon!" Smart motioned to Hovarth. "As you can see, Varagog Village stands with Hightown. If you continue to harbor Jack, you will be branded an enemy of the state, just like the Mechas. This Garrison is under siege until you surrender him to us." The crowd cheered. Prime simmered.

"Get the men ready," Prime told the Valorian captain. "We're going out there."

"Prime, don't," Stendeval said. "This is not the way to convince the Calculans that we aren't at war with each other."

Prime took a deep breath. "I know of only one way to respond to threats, Stendeval."

"Don't take the bait," Stendeval told Prime. "We gain nothing by fighting each other. We need to bring people together."

"How do you propose we do that?" Roka asked. "That's not exactly Jack's fan club down there, you know."

"There are always alternatives," Stendeval said. "That's what our imaginations are for."

"I will not cower in my home while Jonas Smart parades his mechanical soldiers outside my door," Prime said.

Jack looked around at Smart's show of force. As far as Jack was concerned, the WarHawks were the least of their problems. He was about to say so when Clarkston Noteworthy fought his way out from the back of the crowd and marched up to Smart. "What do you think you're doing?" Noteworthy demanded.

"I'm simply trying to ensure the future of the Imagine Nation," Smart replied. "It's good of you to finally join us. I hope we're not keeping you from something less important."

Noteworthy scowled at Smart and Hovarth. "Hovarth, I'll thank you to conduct borough matters with me in the future." He pointed a finger in Smart's face. "*I'm* the Circleman now, Jonas. *I* speak for Hightown, not you!"

Their confrontation played out on the giant holo-screen Smart had brought with him, which was just the way he wanted it. "You can't speak for Hightown when it comes to Jack, Clarkston. You're too close to the situation. Too emotionally attached."

"Emotionally attached!" Noteworthy repeated. "Really. And why, pray tell, is that?"

"It's simple." Smart grinned. "Jack Blank is your son."

CHAPTER

Smart Bombs

Just like that, Jack's world blew up. "What?" he shouted, and clutched the balcony railing. Smart's statement nearly knocked him right out the open window.

Down on the ground, Noteworthy was even more shocked than Jack. "How dare you?" he shot back. "HOW DARE YOU! My son is dead. You know full well we lost him during the last invasion."

Smart grinned. "You'd like to believe that, I'm sure. No doubt you're wishing that was the case right now, but he's alive and well. He's right up there, and unless we do something about it, he's going to kill us all."

Smart's calm demeanor was the antithesis of Noteworthy's fiery rage, which infuriated the socialite Circleman even more.

"That's a lie! You're lying!"

"On the contrary, I have proof," Smart said, holding up a glowing sheet of SmartPaper. "It think it's time the truth be told. I have in my hand a backup copy of Jack Blank's history file, direct from the Hall of Records. The blood drop inside it that identified Jack's Rüstov infection corrupted the file when he first came here, but over time I have been able to restore the lost data in this file, byte by byte."

The crowd murmured, clearly impressed with his achievement. Jack knew it was all a lie. Smart had hidden the truth about Jack's family name back when he first arrived in Empire City. He'd done it because it made him a mystery. As long as Jack was a mystery, he was a potential threat and something to be scared of. Smart had risen to power by fighting Rüstov threats, and he held on to it for so many years by reminding people to be afraid of them.

"When I finally analyzed Jack's digitized blood drop, I was able to identify a positive match with the Noteworthy family's DNA." Smart handed the paper to Noteworthy. "See for yourself, Clarkston. It's all right there."

The crowd gasped as Noteworthy read over the paper.

Jack couldn't believe his ears. A year ago, the Rüstov agent Glave had led him on with promises of meeting his father, only to blindside him with the revelation that he had actually meant Khalix's father, the Magus. This time, Jack was getting sucker punched right from the start. Noteworthy was his father? *Noteworthy?* It couldn't be. He prayed that Smart was lying. Noteworthy took the news just as hard.

"This doesn't prove anything! A document written on SmartPaper that you *say* is genuine?" He threw the paper back at Smart. "It's a forgery."

The Calculans didn't seem to think so. They keyed up a facial-recognition program using pictures of Noteworthy and Jack and found enough points of similarity to support Smart's claims. According to their calculations, there was a 100 percent probability that Jack and Noteworthy were related. Jack was speechless. One hundred percent? They didn't even think there was a 100 percent chance he'd turn into Revile!

Jack stepped back from the window completely devastated. He already had enough trouble figuring out who he was now that the Rüstov had turned his own mind and body against him. This was the last thing he needed. To find out about his family like this, and find out that Noteworthy was his father . . . it was terrible. But if anyone was in a position to know who his parents were, it was Smart. It made sense that he didn't go public with Jack's Noteworthy lineage back when everybody considered him to be a hero. Back then it would have helped Clarkston Noteworthy to be associated with Jack. Now that Jack was public enemy number one again, Smart could use what he knew to get back at the man who took his seat on the Inner Circle.

"Don't act so surprised, Clarkston," Smart said. "Deep down you knew, I'm sure." He looked up at Jack. "My hypothesis is that he suspected you were his son shortly after you returned, but decided to remain silent. Given your condition, you don't exactly fit the Noteworthy pedigree." Smart turned back to Noteworthy. "I'm right, aren't I? You wouldn't let a Rüstov agent poison your family tree. You'd put the Noteworthy name first, even before your own son. Don't apologize. It's quite understandable."

Smart's observation ground salt into Jack's wounds. It was entirely possible that Noteworthy suspected Jack was his son and never said anything. The bump in popularity he would have gotten from being revealed as Jack's father would not have outweighed his desire to protect the Noteworthy name. It was more than possible, actually. It was likely. The socialite Circleman had once told Jack that no matter what good he did in the world, he'd always be tainted by his connection to the Rüstov. Jack hated to think that Noteworthy might be his father, but it made too much sense. Too many puzzle pieces fit neatly into place for it to be a lie.

Noteworthy's hands lit up with green electric flames. The glowing fire settled into the form of two energy glaves, which he brandished in front of Smart. "Of the two of us, I'm not the one who needs to apologize. Jack is *not* my son. Call him that again and it's going to be the last thing you ever say."

Smart put his hands up. "It's the truth. I don't know what you want me to do about it. He's your son."

Noteworthy didn't wait. He swung both glaves at Smart before he finished his sentence. Smart didn't

164

flinch. His WarHawks rushed forward to shield him. Noteworthy lunged at Smart, and Hovarth got in between them. Jack was taken aback by Noteworthy's violent reaction. In all the times he had dreamed about meeting his mother or father, the imaginary reunion had never played out anything like this.

Allegra touched Jack's shoulder. "Don't let this get to you, Jack. We don't know if it's true."

"She's right," Blue agreed. "Smart's just using you to make Noteworthy look bad."

Jack swallowed hard and looked at the image of his face, side by side with Noteworthy's. "Yep. Being related to me would do the trick."

Blue's face fell. "Jack, I didn't mean . . ."

"It's okay, Blue. I know what you meant. Unfortunately, it doesn't mean Smart is lying."

Jack's Rüstov-infected eye tingled, and he felt a shooting pain in his sinuses. He grabbed the bridge of his nose and squeezed.

"Jack, I know this is hard, but now is not the time for this discussion," Stendeval said. "It's a distraction you can't afford."

"Stendeval is right," Hypnova said. "This isn't as bad as it seems."

Jack let go of his nose and nodded with a grim realization: If history had taught him anything, the situation was probably much, much worse.

"Enough!" Hovarth said, pulling Noteworthy back and separating him from Smart. "I don't care if Jack is your son or not, Clarkston. It doesn't change what needs to be done about him." He looked up at Jack. "What say you, boy? Are you going to surrender, or are you going to keep thinking only of yourself?"

Before Jack had a chance to open his mouth, Blue answered for him. "Nobody's surrenderin' nothing! And you're going to let my partner go, Smart, or I'm gonna come down there and bust some heads!"

"Commander Knight is exactly where he belongs," Smart replied. "You're talking about the Mecha who brought us the boy destined to destroy us—something I can prove will happen if Jack lives." Smart snapped his fingers, and his image on the holo-screen was replaced by the words "Loading TimeScope Footage."

"You all know of my wondrous device, the TimeScope,"

Smart boasted. "I've used it to bring the Imagine Nation countless innovations by looking through the lens of time into tomorrow. But the future is not always filled with promise. See what it holds for Jack Blank and, by extension, all of us!"

"What now?" Jack wondered aloud as a task bar on the holo-screen slowly climbed from 0 toward 100 percent.

The Calculans came out on the balcony and took up places at the railing. "Ambassador Equa," Smart said, offering a slight bow to the Calculan diplomat. "I don't suppose you've changed your mind about leaving, have you?"

Equa rotated his head from side to side, surprising no one. Smart shrugged at the response. "I'm afraid this won't help."

Jack gripped the railing and stared at the screen as Smart's video played. He saw himself, dressed in the same clothes he was wearing now. Jack recognized the setting. It was SmartTower. He was standing in Smart's personal lab. He leaned back like he was fainting, but as he fell he was caught by an invisible force and began to float. The red crystal circle in his chest glowed bright enough to burn away his shirt, and as the flames ate away at his clothing, metal poured out of his chest. It overran his body like weeds taking over a garden in a time-lapse video. Jack shuddered as he watched himself change into Revile.

"Don't turn away, Jack," Khalix whispered, creeping into Jack's brain. "You need to see this."

Jack felt sick, but he couldn't have turned away if he tried. It was just like he'd always imagined. His worst fears were playing out before his very eyes. It was like watching the moment of his own death. The images on the screen froze, and the word "Buffering" appeared. The onscreen task bar quickly ran to 100 percent once more, and when the TimeScope footage returned, Jack was blasting a hole in the wall of SmartTower. He flew out to where the Calculans' army of drone fighters were docked. Everyone watched in horror as Jack, now fully transformed into Revile, systematically destroyed the Calculan fleet.

"That's definitely not going to help convince the Calculans to stay," Lorem said.

The Calculans looked at each other in alarm. The two junior delegates hurried back to their holo-computer and started adjusting odds. The probability of successfully fending off the Rüstov plummeted as the images of Jack destroying the fleet played on.

"Is it any wonder the Calculans won't stand with us?" Smart asked. "Their planetary host has offered sanctuary to the very person who will destroy their fleet!" The crowd around Smart roared with outrage. He fed off their energy. "Take a good look, Empire City. The closer the future is, the clearer the images in the TimeScope are. These things are going to happen unless we stop them. We want the boy, Prime. Give him to us!"

The crowd seemed nearly out of control, but Prime was not shaken. "What I will give you is ten seconds to remove yourself from my door. Starting now."

"Not without Jack!" the people shouted.

"Traitor!"

"Whose side are you on?"

The people in the crowd continued to hurl insults, and Smart grinned up at Prime. It was clear he was holding all the cards in this standoff. Jack forced himself to stop looking at the images of himself as Revile. The TimeScope footage scared him. Jack remembered what happened when he first came to the Imagine Nation. Smart had looked into his TimeScope and found visions of Revile alive in Empire City. Those visions had come true. Jack had had to fight Revile on the roof of SmartTower and again on Wrekzaw Isle. What if Smart's latest future forecast was accurate as well? It hurt to think about—literally. The shooting pains in Jack's head returned, this time stronger than before.

"We still have the power to stop this!" Smart shouted.

"He's wrong, Jack," Khalix said. "It's already too late."

Jack reached for the railing to keep himself upright. He tried to ask for help, but nothing came out. He choked on his words and grabbed at his chest. He felt like someone had just run him through with a spear. Air came back into his lungs and he cried out, falling to the floor. The pain struck faster than lightning, just like when the Magus had attacked him with his mind. Jack clawed at his forehead as he writhed on the ground in agony. His friends ran to him.

"Jack! Jack! What is it?" Blue shouted.

"It's time, Jack," Khalix answered inside Jack's head. "My father's coming."

"No!" Jack shouted back. He forced himself to sit up.

"Not yet." He put his hands on his temples and shut his eyes tight, grunting as he tried to overcome the pain on willpower alone. The pain subsided but did not vanish entirely. The dull throbbing of a migraine remained.

"Jack, talk to us," Allegra said. "What's going on?"

A squadron of Rüstov Shardwings screamed across the sky, and Allegra had her answer. "It's the Rüstov," Jack said. "They're here."

CHAPTER

13

Shock and Awe

The crowd in Galaxis scrambled into chaos, and people ran off in every direction. The Rüstov Shardwings took over the sky, shooting up Empire City and strafing the crowd. Jack struggled back to the railing as buildings exploded in flames. People fell to the ground below as the predawn sky lit up with bright white flashes. It was like the city was being hit by a lightning storm, only the rolling thunder behind each flash was the sound of a Rüstov missile hitting its target. Concrete, steel, and glass sprayed the air like buckshot as explosions tore out the sides of buildings. Jack shielded his eyes, squinting through flying debris and laser fire. Towers crashed down to the ground, and screams of terror filled the air, all within less than a minute. It was bedlam. Jack had never seen war before. He'd been in his share of superfights, but never real war. It was horrible, and all he could think was *Not now . . . we're not ready.*

Only Prime was ready. The Shardwing fighters had yet to complete their first bombing run before he ordered his men into action. A hundred Valorian Guardsmen flew out of the dome, following Prime into battle. Their shining silver forms rose up in strategic attack formations. Their hands lit up with energy as they fired plasma blasts at the Rüstov starfighters.

The red glare of exploding ships triggered another series of memories that hit Jack like a prizefighter's punch. His vision blurred and a Rüstov war movie played in his mind. He saw more explosions. More battles. Hundreds of invasions from start to finish. It was like they were being uploaded directly into his brain.

"Get down!" someone shouted as a Rüstov ship fired on the terrace, blasting half of it into tiny pieces. The real world came flooding back and Jack tried to run inside, but the ground beneath his feet gave way. He staggered a step and fell backward. He was going over the edge, but Allegra shot out an arm and grabbed him by the collar, just catching him with his heels on the broken ledge of the terrace. She reeled him back in and they ran inside the Garrison with Jack still struggling to deal with the pain in his head. The energy core in his chest was heating up and glowing bright red.

"Stay with us, Jack," Blue said, taking him by the arm. "You can do this. You fight them, hear me? Fight it!"

Jack gritted his teeth and growled out a low, guttural noise. He could feel Khalix pushing his way around his head, trying to take him over. "Why do you do this to yourself?" Khalix asked. "You're only prolonging the inevitable. Just let go. All your pain will go away if you just stop fighting."

"Remember what Roka said," Allegra told Jack. "You don't quit, right? We didn't give up on you . . . that means you don't get to give up either!"

"It doesn't matter if you give up or not," Khalix interjected. "You've just had a crash course in Rüstov history.

You know this is pointless. Deep down, you know it. My people have never lost a war."

Jack gripped Blue's hand and got up onto his feet, reasserting himself against Khalix. He pressed a hand to his temple. Pain pounded in his ears, but not hard enough to keep him down. He'd keep going. He had to. Jack looked outside and saw Hovarth fighting the Rüstov alongside his men. Smart and Noteworthy were long gone.

"Are you all right?" Stendeval asked.

Jack gave a weary nod. "Let's get out there. I want to hit something. Hard."

Blue clapped his hands. "There you go. Let's do it."

"We can't fight them on the ground," Midknight said. "We need to get to Prime's airfield before the Rüstov blow up the only ships we've got. Stendeval, can you 'port us there?"

Stendeval turned up his palms. His hands lit up but fizzled like dying lightbulbs. "Not until dawn."

"There's an underground tunnel that connects this Garrison with the launchpads," Allegra said. "Follow me."

Allegra darted out the door, and everyone ran after her. She led the way through the lower levels of the Valorian

Garrison and out into the war zone. As they came out of the underground tunnel, Jack and the others were greeted by a crashing Shardwing. One of the Valorian Guardsmen had taken out its engine and it barreled toward them like a flaming comet. Blue ran forward and threw his shoulder into the ship, diverting its path just enough to keep it from crashing into the mouth of the tunnel. Outside, the spaceport was pure anarchy. The skyline was rife with fire and people ran everywhere. The injured were limping through the street, blind and bleeding.

"We have to help these people," Jack said. Everything he was feeling about Noteworthy, Smart, Khalix, and Revile took a backseat to the battle and its imminent casualties. He stopped to tend to an injured woman who was bleeding badly. Stendeval tore off his crimson sash to make a bandage and applied pressure to her wound. He didn't have any superpowered energy left, but he did have five hundred years' worth of heroic experiences, a cool head, and plenty of lifesaving know-how. He was helping the woman to her feet when another Rüstov missile struck the building next to him. Flames spilled out into the street, and tiny bits of debris pelted Jack and the others.

"C'mon!" Roka shouted. "If we want to help these people, we've gotta stop these bombs from falling."

The wall behind them crumbled at the base and started to topple over. Blue rushed in to brace it before it crushed more wounded innocents. "Someone's gotta stop the buildings from falling too," he said. Blue motioned with his head toward the launchpads. "You guys go ahead. I can't fly one of those things anyway."

Jack nodded. There was no time to argue, and Blue was right. He and his friends were needed everywhere.

"I'm staying too," Stendeval said. "When my power returns, I'll join you in the sky."

"Good luck," Jack said.

"And to you," Stendeval replied. "Now go!"

Jack and the others ran out into the spaceport of Galaxis and went straight for a hangar filled with starfighters. They raced to the launchpads, where a row of ships stood ready and waiting. Just before they reached them, a Shardwing tore through the hangar and laid down a blanket of blinking metal fragments on top of the parked spaceships.

"Evac, now!" Midknight yelled as the Shardwing blasted

its way out through the wall on the hangar's opposite side. The ships in the hangar exploded one after the other, all in a row. The successive blasts built on top of one another, growing in heat and intensity. It was like someone had rolled a bowling ball out into a minefield. Allegra stretched into a protective shield to guard the others against the flames and flying shrapnel. Once the heat blast had passed, there was nothing but flaming wreckage left inside the hangar.

"There!" Jack yelled. He pointed across the spaceport to another set of launchpads where more starships were waiting. Jack used his powers to slide back the canopies on a group of well-armed fighters known as Mavericks. Midknight and Roka each climbed into a ship. Jack picked one for himself and started up its side. He was nearly settled into the cockpit when Allegra tapped his shoulder. He turned around and saw that Trea, her two other selves, Lorem, and Zhi were all busy mounting Zhi's dragons.

"Don't know how to fly those things," Zhi said, motioning to the ships. He patted his dragon's back. "We'll stick with these guys."

Jack nodded and looked at Allegra. "What about you?"

"If you think I'm leaving you alone right now, you're

crazy. What's going to happen if you have another one of your episodes up there?"

Jack thought about that for a second. Allegra had a point. "All right, let's go," he said, jumping down from the ship. "We'll take that one."

Jack took Allegra's hand and ran to a larger ship with the word "MedEvac" written on the side in red letters. It looked like a flying ambulance. "That's a search-and-rescue ship," Allegra said as Jack climbed into the pilot's seat.

"Trust me, this is the one for us."

Allegra shrugged. "Where do you want me?"

Jack mentally popped open a hatch near the tail of the ship and pointed to the chair inside it. He gave a nod, and several panels on the ship's exterior flipped over to reveal a multitude of armaments. "They use these things for pulling people out of war zones. Just grab the gun and keep your finger on the trigger."

"I can do that." Allegra stretched up to the gunner's battle station and poured herself into it. Jack strapped himself in as the Rüstov fighters came back around for another attack run. It had been a crushing assault so far.

The Shardwing fighters were everywhere, and they just kept coming. His classmates on the dragons flew up to meet them. Jack used his powers to turn on the engines of the Maverick fighters that Midknight and Roka were strapped into. Roka's ship made an ugly screeching noise.

"Easy, kid! I already hot-wired mine," Roka said.

"Couldn't wait, huh?" Midknight asked over the radio.

"Waiting's never been my strong suit."

"Don't wait on me, then, get going!" Jack shouted. The city wasn't ready for this fight, which meant he and his friends had to be. Jack fired up his engine, and seconds later he was up in the sky, joining Prime and the Valorian Guard as they brought the fight back to the Rüstov.

CHAPTER

14

Returning Fire

Jack and Allegra shot down a pair of Shardwings on their way up, reducing them to the metal shards they took their name from. They received some businesslike nods of appreciation from Prime and the other Valorians, who went right back to shooting plasma blasts at the Rüstov fighters and gang-tackling enemy ships to pull them apart. There were more heroes in the air fighting as well. Jack didn't recognize many of them, but it looked like they hailed from all the different boroughs. He was glad to see people dropping everything and jumping into the fight when it counted, but it didn't change the fact that Empire City had been caught sleeping. The whole situation burned Jack up inside. It wasn't supposed to be like this. He had warned everybody this was coming. They could have been ready. Jack cursed Smart and his endless power plays, kidnapping Jazen and turning the city against itself. He was probably holed up in a bunker somewhere by now. Meanwhile, the crowd of people he had led to Prime's door were all caught in the crossfire.

Jack brought the ship around to face the Rüstov and charged forward into a wall of enemy fire. Roka and Midknight followed him in. Jack bobbed and weaved through the onslaught of enemy laser blasts and around the advancing starfighters, narrowly missing head-on collisions by inches and swirling through the air. He couldn't use his powers against the Rüstov, but his own ship was another matter entirely. The aircraft Jack flew was built for med-team extractions, not aerial assaults, but with him at the helm it was like an untouchable stealth fighter. He used his powers to help the targeting system tag Shardwings the second they came within range, and Allegra blew them out of the sky. Jack's friends flew actual stealth fighters and did the same. Midknight squared off in a dogfight against three Shardwings and picked them off one by one. Shardwings chased Roka through the air from the opposite end of the sky, but he and Midknight flew at each other like they were playing chicken and veered off at the very last second. The Rüstov fighters behind them crashed into one another, exploding into a gorgeous fireball. Every time they took out a Rüstov gunship, they saved lives. As Jack flew across the city, with Allegra firing away, he could see the whole battlefield. Jack could feel how many ships were out there. He was surprised that there weren't more of them. Things had felt more chaotic on the ground.

"He's not here," Jack said over the radio. "The Magus isn't here yet."

"First good news we've had all day," Roka said. "This isn't the full invasion. Not enough ships. This is just the first wave."

"The bad news is, the first wave is winning," Midknight said.

"Of course we are," Khalix gloated inside Jack's head. "We have destiny on our side."

Jack bristled at Khalix's constant interruptions. "You talk too much." He took control of the weapons systems for a moment and sent six tiny missiles out at the same number of Shardwings. "You all do," he added as the Rüstov ships burst into flames. "I'm listening in on their radio chatter," Jack called out to his friends. "It's filled with static, but I can make out enough to run with. Roka's right. This attack is just them trying to break us. They're setting up a command post with ground troops on Wrekzaw Isle, and Glave is there! That's where we need to go."

"Wrekzaw Isle it is," Midknight said. "Let's go, people."

Midknight turned his Maverick toward Wrekzaw, the downed Rüstov vessel from the first invasion that still circled the Imagine Nation like a ghost ship. Jack and Roka rocketed after the old hero, bearing down on a legion of fighters that had created a blockade off the coast of the island. There were more Shardwing squadrons and several midsize gunships as well. It was a lot of firepower for four ships to take on, enough to make anybody think twice. "This is really just the first wave?" Allegra asked.

Jack swallowed hard as he approached the blockade. Allegra had a point. The amount of fighters in the sky definitely put the might of the Rüstov Armada in perspective. Jack didn't know what was scarier, the fact that this was just a minor force, or the major damage it had already done. Far off in the distance, Jack could see the ships forming an escort for a giant Rüstov battleship. Jack had never seen its like before, but he was about to get a very good look at it.

The air between the Imagine Nation and Wrekzaw Isle was alive with bullets and exploding shells—enough to make the airspace over the city seem peaceful by comparison. Luckily, Jack had experience dodging bullets. Just like he had with the *Harbinger*, Jack bypassed the ship's controls in favor of flying with his mind. His reaction times were amplified by a direct connection with the ship's radar system, helping him anticipate enemy movements and change course with the speed of thought. The Rüstov Armada pressed the advantage of superior numbers against Jack from every direction, but they couldn't touch him. He searched the sky for the *Apocalypse*. Nothing. He felt for the Magus with his powers. It was definite. He wasn't here. Jack breathed a sigh of relief. "Your father isn't here yet, Khalix. You lied about that." *What else were you lying about?* Jack wondered.

"I don't need to lie to you, Jack. The truth will set me free."

Another slideshow of graphic combat images poured into Jack's brain. A century's worth of battles in the Rüstov's infinite war. Why was he seeing this again? Jack fought through this onslaught quicker than the last, but mental time-outs of any duration are not an option while flying an aircraft. When Jack's head cleared, alarms were blaring and red lights were flashing in the ship's cabin. "Rüstov on our six, Jack!" Allegra shouted. "They've got missile lock!"

Jack shook his head and dove his ship down toward the ocean, trying to shake the Shardwing on his tail. The enemy ship followed right behind like it was magnetically attached. Roka swooped in and blew it out of the sky, but not before it fired three missiles at Jack.

"Rüstov warheads, coming in hot!" Allegra shouted.

"I got 'em," Roka said over the radio. "Just give me some space." Jack turned back toward the city and pushed his ship hard, trying to put as much room as he could between his tailfin and the missiles that were chasing it. As he crossed back over Galaxis, Roka swooped in to pull

186

them off his tail. He cut across Jack's jet wash, and the missiles locked onto his ship's heat signature instead.

"Roka, they're on you now!" Jack shouted.

"Got 'em right where I want 'em," Roka said. He spun around and raced back toward the blockade, zigzagging on through in the direction of a midsize gunship. Just like when he was playing chicken with Jazen, Roka pulled up at the last possible moment and swung the Rüstov warheads straight into one of their own ships. The resulting explosion took out a gunship and the two Shardwings closest to it.

"Nice moves, Roka!" Midknight said.

Roka snorted out a small laugh. "You don't last long raiding Rüstov ships if you don't have a few tricks up your sleeve."

"I wondered if Roka has any idea how hard it is to get a compliment like that out of Midknight," Allegra said.

"Doubt it," Jack replied.

Midknight and Roka kept up their aerial assault, trying to poke enough holes in the Rüstov blockade to break it down, but they were up against a lot of ships, and the odds grew worse the farther away they got from Empire

City. They were hopelessly outnumbered over Wrekzaw Isle. Jack's sprint away from the missiles had taken him as far as Hightown. He had to get back out there and help his friends. He turned his ship around and nearly crashed into a train that was running down the side of a building.

Jack went into another spiral dive and flew alongside the train as it went. "What is this thing doing?" Jack wondered as he pulled away from the track. "It's running straight into the battle zone." In his rearview, Jack saw the train level off and charge into an open-air station. He stopped the train there, and hundreds of people ran out screaming. Rüstov Shardwings flew overhead shooting at them, and Jack circled back to provide cover. He parked himself over the train and Allegra shot up at the Shardwing fighters in wide, sweeping arcs. They were saving lives on the train platform, but off the coast of the island, Jack saw Roka and Midknight both get blasted with direct hits. "No!"

He was relieved to see them both punch out before their ships crashed into the sea. The ejection seats in the Maverick fighters didn't pop parachutes. They transformed into jet packs for greater maneuverability, but Jack's friends were still surrounded. He wanted to help, but flying out to them meant leaving the people on the platform defenseless.

Just then several glowing streams of light shot past Jack's ship. They looped back around and whipped their luminous tails into the Shardwings at the station. As the Rüstov fighters went spinning away, Zhi, Trea, and Lorem pulled up alongside Jack's ship.

"Everybody okay?" Allegra asked.

Lorem beat out a small fire on her sleeve. "Close enough."

"Zhi, Roka and Midknight need help," Jack said, pointing. "They're sitting ducks out there in the open!"

Zhi nodded and gripped the reins of his dragon. He became a brilliant blur as he raced out past the edge of the island. Two empty dragons followed close behind. Jack kicked his ship back into gear and did the same. "C'mon, guys, we've got a job to do."

"You're telling us?" one of the Treas said, flying up next to Jack.

"We've been training all year for this," another Trea said, flying in on the other side. "You're the one who's been away on vacation."

Jack laughed. "Vacation! Yeah, right."

"Blah, blah, blah . . . ," the third Trea said. "Enough with the talking already. Let's go!" She dashed ahead of the group, and everyone followed her back into the fray.

As Jack flew back across Galaxis, he saw that even more heroes had joined the fight. A glowing blue streak of energy was bouncing off buildings and into Rüstov ships, disabling them. Jack recognized the energy signature of Allegra's old mentor, Ricochet. Chi's ninjas were pouring in from Karateka, and Smart's WarHawks were in the air too, fighting alongside the aliens of Galaxis. Jack saw Smart's soldiers pulling people out of harm's way, throwing their fists into Rüstov ships, and cutting Shardwings in half. Jack turned away from the city and headed back to Wrekzaw Isle. He didn't think the WarHawks were going to bother with him, not with the Rüstov attacking all around, but he didn't want to take any chances.

As Jack closed in on the blockade of Rüstov ships surrounding the island, he saw that Midknight and Roka had both ditched their jet packs in favor of Zhi's dragons. The Shardwings were running interference for the giant battleship that lumbered toward the city. Once the ship got close enough, Jack realized what it was.

"Guys, that ship!" he shouted into his radio. "It's a carrier! The whole thing's loaded with Para-Soldiers. We can't let it reach the city!"

No one heard him. Roka and Midknight weren't on radio, and even if they were, it was going to take more than Zhi's dragons to bring down a ship of that size. Jack aimed his ship at the carrier and went in on his own. The Shardwings and midsize gunships opened fire on him as he flew in to attack. Jack looped around a string of exploding shells from a Rüstov cannon and dropped down below the carrier, rolling into a controlled spin that danced directly through the ship's laser fire. Allegra emptied the plasma cannons into the carrier's belly, but the Rüstov ship sustained minimal damage. Jack's friends on the dragons batted Rüstov ships into the carrier but failed to do any more damage than he had. They were denting the ship. That was it. They weren't doing enough to stop it.

The Rüstov carrier inched closer to Empire City, and a platoon of Valorian Guardsmen shot out to meet it. They tore though the carrier's escort and hit the ship hard, but a second group of Shardwings came in to push them back.

The Shardwings were flying right into Valorians, sacrificing themselves to drive them out of the carrier's path.

Suddenly, three pods shot out of the carrier and went blasting by Jack's ship. He knew in an instant that they were filled with Para-Soldiers who were itching for new hosts. Jack chased after them and Allegra opened fire. The plasma cannons were empty, so she switched to missiles, sending the last of their ammunition out after the Rüstov transports.

"This is it," she said. "Let's hope they find their mark."

"They will," Jack said, using his powers to make sure of it. He drove a missile into the first pod and blew it out of the sky, but he was too close to the blast. The shrapnel from the explosion hit his ship before he could take out the other two. The momentary distraction was enough to make him lose control of the remaining missiles, and they sailed off in wild, erratic routes that missed the Rüstov pods entirely and struck Hero Square instead. The massive Legendary Flame Monument toppled over and cracked at the neck as it hit the ground. Jack grumbled as the last two pods raced toward the city.

"You know people are gonna think I did that on purpose."

Midknight, Lorem, and Zhi took out the second pod with their dragons and knocked it into the sea. Roka and the three Treas chased down the last one, but it was too far ahead of them.

"Jack, they're not going to make it," Allegra said, pointing ahead. The pod struck Hero Square, and Rüstov parasites without hosts started crawling out like ants from a crack in the wall.

Jack heard a sound like a cannon firing and saw that the carrier had launched another pod. "Got another one over here," he said. Without any more ammo in his guns, all he could do was watch as it reached Galaxis untouched. Seconds later, Para-Soldiers were running through the spaceport. Chi's ninjas were there fighting them, but their numbers were already severely depleted from the air raids. "Is Stendeval with us yet?" Jack asked.

"I don't know," Allegra said.

Jack looked at the horizon and started getting nervous. Sunrise was still minutes away. That meant Stendeval's power was as well, and those few short minutes made all the difference in the world. Rüstov Para-Soldiers had deployed on the ground. Parasites were taking fresh hosts and there were thousands more on board the carrier. "If that ship makes landfall, it's game over," Jack said to himself. He shook his head. "Can't happen." He took his ship back into Hightown and headed straight for the mile-high train station he'd defended earlier. "Allegra, grab a headset. I need to make sure everyone's off that train."

"What?"

"No time! Just do it!" Allegra snapped a communicator over her ear, and Jack ejected her from the ship without warning. He kept flying forward toward Galaxis, and Allegra morphed her silver body to flap out a pair of wings. She swooped down toward the train station like an eagle. On his way through Galaxis, Jack took control of every ship he could and pointed them all at the Rüstov carrier. HoverCars, cargo ships . . . anything that could fly got turned on and sent out at the blockade. It didn't matter that most of them had no weapons. For what Jack had in mind, the ships were weapons all by themselves.

"Jack, the train is clear," Allegra said on the search-and-rescue ship's internal channel. "Now what?"

"Get off," Jack said. "Get somewhere safe."

"Whoa! The train just started moving."

"I know. I'm moving it." Jack pulled up and looped back around the city, going all the way past Varagog. Once he passed the Flying Shipyards, he turned around and rocketed back across Empire City, building up speed as he went.

"Jack, what are you doing?" Allegra asked.

"Yes, Jack, what are you doing?" Khalix chimed in.

"Wouldn't you like to know?" Jack said. He was focused on so many different things at the moment, he couldn't muster up the mental discipline required to shut Khalix up at the same time.

"I see what this is," Khalix said after a moment. "It won't work. The train, those other ships, *this* ship . . . you can't keep all these balls in the air, Jack. You're not *that* good."

Jack smiled to himself. He'd been underestimated his whole life and somehow always managed to prove people wrong. He sped across the city, hoping to keep that streak alive. He darted around skyscrapers and shot beneath MagLev roadways, going faster and faster. He was flying way quicker than anyone could safely go through a busy city that was under attack from hostile invaders. It didn't matter. After his light speed run across the galaxy, this flight was like a Sunday drive.

Meanwhile, he had already launched the first part of his attack on the Rüstov carrier using every ship he could take control of. It was hard to keep everything straight in his head and make sure the ships didn't hit friendly targets, but that was helped along by the fact that he wasn't trying to fly the other ships. He was trying to crash them. Jack was throwing ships at the Rüstov as if they were stones. He fired them into the Shardwings, breaking down the defenses around the carrier and crashing them into the carrier itself. He took out enough Shardwings to clear a path to the carrier and started hitting its hull, but the ships were still tiny compared to the carrier's massive size. Jack needed to hit the carrier with something heavier. Through the gaps between the buildings he could see the bullet train racing toward Galaxis. It was almost there.

Jack kept pace with the train on its way through Galaxis. It was running up to a broken bridge, but Jack pushed the ship harder and pulled out ahead. "Deploy rescue cable," he told the ship's computer, and a cable with a large claw at the end shot out of the back of the ship. "Good thing I picked this ship, huh, Khalix?"

Khalix was silent.

Jack raced down the tracks in front of the train, trailing the cable behind him as he went. He lowered himself right in front of the engine. "This is the tricky part," he said as the iron claw at the end of the cable grasped at the train. The tips of the claw scraped against the iron hoop of the train's coupling, just shy of hooking onto it. It was hard because Jack couldn't slow down. He needed all the speed he could get. "C'mon, latch on. Latch on . . ." The train closed in on the break in the bridge. Just before it reached the severed tracks, Jack heard a loud clack as the claw grabbed hold of the train. "Yes!" he shouted as he pulled the train forward, up off the tracks, and out toward the Rüstov carrier.

Alarms immediately started sounding inside the cockpit. The words "WARNING: MAXIMUM TOW CAPACITY EXCEEDED" flashed on the screen in front of Jack. The ship started to vibrate. It was straining, but it kept going forward, riding the force of its own top speed and the train's forward momentum. "C'mon, girl . . . I need everything you've got." Jack increased the ship's power, trying to get close enough to the carrier as he crashed ships into the Rüstov fighters all around. His ship started to rattle hard. He knew he was pushing it all the way up to its limit and beyond. Red lights started blinking alongside new alarms in the cockpit, and the computer's voice spoke: "WARNING: ENGINE FAILURE IN NINE SECONDS, EIGHT SECONDS, SEVEN SECONDS . . ."

"I just need four seconds," Jack said as he pulled the train past the city's edge. "C'mon, just a little bit longer . . . Release cable!"

The ship's claw released the train, and Jack pulled up and away as the speeding locomotive went crashing into the center of the Rüstov carrier. The train nearly cleaved the carrier in two, and the resulting explosion finished the job. The added velocity Jack got from releasing the train was the only thing that kept him from being burned to a crisp in the massive conflagration. He shot up into the sky as the broken pieces of the carrier fell into the ocean. The giant ship swirled into the endless maelstrom below the Imagine Nation, dragging thousands of Para-Soldiers to a watery grave. Any remaining Shardwings that were still flying turned tail and flew back to Wrekzaw Isle, spurred on by the sudden reversal of fortune. A mighty cheer rose up from Empire City, and Jack breathed a sigh of relief. The war was far from over, but this battle was going down in the win column. They'd held off the Rüstov . . . for now.

Allegra's voice came over the radio. "Jack, that was amazing. Looks like that old instinct's coming back."

Jack could practically hear a smile in Allegra's voice. He leaned back in his seat and breathed another sigh of relief. "Fight or flight," he agreed. "Maybe Roka knew what he was talking about after all."

"You know you forgot something," Allegra said.

Jack's ears perked up. "What's wrong? What'd I miss?"

"Don't you know when you do something like that, you have to have a line ready? You have to say something cool, like, 'Time for you guys to *catch the train*.'"

Jack allowed himself a laugh as he turned his ship back around toward Empire City. "I can do better than that. How about 'You don't mess with a hero . . . in *training*.' Or maybe 'This is what I call *training hard*.'"

"All right, those are terrible. You're ruining it."

Jack laughed again as he made his way back to Galaxis. He was coming in for a landing when three WarHawks flew right into his ship, going in one side and punching out through the other. They left behind a gaping hole where the engine should have been, and the ship dropped like a stone. Before Jack even had a chance to scream, the ship was caught by more WarHawks, who threw it across Empire City. Just before Jack crashed into the ground, the cockpit filled with a white foam that dried rapidly into a soft cushiony substance and helped him survive a very bumpy landing. When the ship came to a halt, Jack punched his way through the foam and fell out onto the cobblestone streets of Varagog Village. He looked up to find an army of medieval warriors standing over him with their weapons drawn. Jack groaned with frustration and put his hands up in the air.

CHAPTER

15

Captured

The next thing Jack knew, he was tied up and hanging upside down on a rail. The crowd hoisted him up and paraded him through the streets of Varagog like a pig on a spit. None of the people there had seen him fighting the Rüstov. They only knew that an enemy attack had just come down from the sky, and so had he. It came as no surprise that they all figured he'd been fighting for the other side.

Hovarth's subjects took Jack to a vast cobblestone plaza at the center of the village. From his upside-down vantage point, he saw the massive fortress of Castle Varren come into view. Jack's captors marched toward a wooden stockade near the drawbridge of the castle. Skerren stopped them.

"Not the stockade," he said. "Modern technology may not work here in Varagog, but Jack's powers still do. Use something without any moving parts." Skerren scanned the plaza. "There."

Jack craned his neck around and saw that Skerren was pointing at a stone obelisk at the center of the square. Jack grunted as he was tied to the stone pillar with knots that were tight enough to cut off the circulation in both of his hands. "Skerren, this is ridiculous. Where am I gonna go?"

Skerren tugged on the ropes, making sure Jack was bound securely. "I'm not taking any chances with you. Not this time."

A messenger sprinted through the crowd and ran up to Skerren. "The king approaches." Skerren nodded, and the people gathered around, calling for Jack's head. Only the king's mercy could save him from the executioner's ax, but Jack knew that Hovarth's idea of mercy would be to put him down like a rabid dog. He searched the crowd for someone to help him. There was no one there. No one but Khalix.

"They're going to kill you, Jack," the Rüstov prince whispered. "Look around, there's only one way out of this—me. Do it now, before it's too late. Join with me. Become Revile!"

"Shut up, Khalix."

Skerren spun around on Jack with a look that made him wish he hadn't said that out loud. "Who are you talking to? The Rüstov? What are you telling them?"

"Nothing," Jack told Skerren. "This is crazy. All of you, there are Rüstov soldiers in the city right now. You need to be fighting them, not me!"

"You say that like there's a difference between you," Skerren said.

Jack took a deep breath and tried to keep calm. He wasn't going to get himself out of this one by losing his temper. "Look, Skerren, you don't trust me. I get that. But just because I've hidden things from you in the past, that doesn't mean I'm lying now. You can't just discount everything we've been through. I was fighting for the Imagine Nation up there. I want to help. I want to keep fighting!"

Skerren sighed and looked Jack dead in the eyes. "All this time, and you still don't get it. It doesn't matter what either of us wants. This isn't about what you've done. It's about what you are. I didn't want to kill my parents, either, but that didn't change the fact that somebody had to."

"Skerren . . ."

"This is war. We harden our hearts and we do what's necessary. We sacrifice. It's the only way the enemy inside you can ever be defeated."

Jack stared Skerren down. "Stendeval says it's what's inside me that's going to defeat the Rüstov."

Skerren snorted. "Stendeval is living in a dreamworld. Don't waste your breath trying to convince me to let you go, Jack. In Varagog, the king decides who lives and who dies, not me."

The crowd parted, and Hovarth entered the square, followed by Noteworthy and Smart. Skerren and the other people in the square all took a knee and lowered their heads. Hovarth walked toward Jack and made a slight lifting motion with his hands, telling his subjects to rise. He reached the obelisk and looked Jack up and down with weary eyes. Jack could see he was bruised and bloodied from battle. The look on his face told him Hovarth had lost people during the attack. Jack wondered how many.

"Tell me, Jack, if we had put an end to you yesterday, would it have stopped your people from raining fire down on us today?"

"They're not my people, Hovarth. I helped stop them just now, same as you."

"Did you now?" Hovarth looked around at the smoke and fire rising up off Empire City. "From down here, it doesn't look like you stopped much of anything."

"He didn't," Smart cut in. "The Rüstov have established a command center on Wrekzaw Isle, laid waste to the Galaxis spaceport, and successfully deployed Para-Soldier attack squads into the city. We've suffered massive losses." Smart turned to Noteworthy. "You must be very proud."

The crowd booed Noteworthy. He stormed up to Smart, stopping mere inches away from his face. "I told you. My son is dead."

Smart motioned to Jack. "Not yet, he isn't. You still have time to say good-bye."

"I am not this boy's father!" Noteworthy shouted, pointing at Jack.

"Blood doesn't lie, Clarkston."

"But you do!" Noteworthy shot back.

The sight of the two men arguing about him made Jack sick. He was well accustomed to people lining up against him, but this was different. Noteworthy acted like being his father was the worst thing anyone could ever have accused him of. Noteworthy's visceral reaction practically tore a hole in Jack's stomach. Jack hated to think that this man who wanted nothing to do with him might have been responsible for bringing him into the world. He didn't want Noteworthy for a father any more than Noteworthy wanted him for a son, but it still hurt to be rejected so vehemently. To be cast aside with no consideration whatsoever. Noteworthy had not said a single word to Jack since Smart broke the news. He was there in the crowd talking *about* Jack, but not once did he address him directly. He hadn't even made eye contact with him. *That's how little he thinks of me*, Jack thought. It was plain to see Noteworthy didn't care a bit about his feelings. He only cared about himself.

"It's obvious what you're trying to do here," Noteworthy

told Smart. "You want to ruin me. It won't work. In fact, I'm going to put an end to it right now." His hands lit up with green energy, and he spun like an Olympian throwing a discus. Jack's eyes widened in terror as a pair of energy glaves sped toward him. He squirmed against the obelisk, but he couldn't move an inch in either direction. There would be no dodging Noteworthy's attack. He was dead.

Then Jack felt his body warm up. The heat built quickly until a bright flash of red light erupted out of his chest. Jack's stomach heaved as the wide beam of energy poured out of the power core in his Rüstov implant. It knocked everyone back a few steps and drowned out Noteworthy's glaves, vaporizing them. When the light died down, Jack saw that the core had burned away part of his shirt. Other than that he was completely unscathed. He felt like he was going to vomit.

"I can't hold them off forever," Khalix told Jack. "I need more firepower. We're going to have to work together if we want to survive this."

The entire crowd stared at Jack in silence, blown away by what had just happened. The Rüstov inside him had risen up to defend itself with a weapon that should have been useless in their corner of the city.

"That's impossible," Noteworthy said, getting up off the ground. "How did you do that? Machines don't work here."

Khalix scoffed. "As if I'm just some *machine*. I'm the son of the Magus. I'm alive. Of course I'm going to protect myself. Tell them, Jack."

Jack wasn't listening. He was busy trying to figure out which was worse: the way Khalix had just taken control of his body and used him like a human cannon, or the fact that his own father had just tried to kill him.

"Og's blood, his chest!" Hovarth said.

Jack looked down and found out that the worst development was still ongoing. His cybernetic implant was getting bigger. Jack gasped as circuits spread out across his torso like fungus growing up a tree. The crowd shrank back in fear. His condition was deteriorating before their very eyes.

"Just let it happen," Khalix said to Jack. "These people have turned their backs on you. You're not one of them anymore. Your own father doesn't even want you. Mine does. Stop fighting me. Give in to the transformation. Do it now, while they're distracted. Do it before it's too late!"

Jack couldn't speak. He couldn't even breathe. *Is this it?* Jack wondered. Was he turning into Revile now? The crowd of villagers trembled at what was happening to him. Their fear was contagious. Jack's body was changing faster than ever before, and he could feel himself slowly slipping away. It really wasn't just his body anymore. Khalix had proven that point. Jack was a shared resource now, and he was losing control. He scanned the crowd for friendly faces once again. Nothing. He was all alone, tied to a rock, and surrounded by people who wanted to kill him. His only options were to join with Khalix and escape, or stay and die. Really, he was dead either way. The only question was how many other people had to suffer as a result of his decision.

"How do we kill him?" Hovarth asked Smart. "Can we still kill him?"

"Of course we can," Smart replied. "Clarkston just isn't trying hard enough. As I said, he's emotionally attached to Jack. He can't help himself." Smart looked at Skerren. "We need someone who will swing the sword with all his heart."

Hovarth looked at his sword-wielding protégé. "I

believe you're right, Jonas. Skerren. You know what needs to be done." Hovarth didn't say the order out loud. He didn't have to. Skerren knew what he meant, just as well as Jack did. Skerren walked up the steps to the pillar Jack was tied to and drew out a sword. Before he struck, he leaned in close to get a good look at Jack's mechanical implant.

"You're turning," Skerren said. "You know you are. This is the only way for you to fight the Rüstov now. Revile is the key to their victory. If you want to kill a snake, you have to cut off its head. Unfortunately, that's you."

"It's a good death, lad," Hovarth called out. "A noble sacrifice. Legend gave his life to save us from the monster inside you. You can finish what he started. You can still be a hero."

"A *dead* hero," Khalix told Jack.

"He's not a hero at all," Smart said. "Legend sacrificed himself willingly. Jack has clung to life and pushed us to the brink of destruction. You should go to your grave knowing that you will be remembered as a selfish coward, Jack. I'll see to that."

"You hear that?" Khalix said. "No one here is going

to honor your sacrifice. Don't throw your life away. Save yourself. Save us, and together we'll make these people pay!"

Jack hung his head. His despair was growing even faster than his infection. He didn't know what to do. Who was right? Who was wrong? He honestly couldn't say. He didn't know if he was a hero, a villain, a Rüstov, a Noteworthy, or a weapon. He only knew that no matter what anyone said about him, he didn't want to make the people of Empire City pay like Khalix was suggesting. He wanted to save them. Even people like Noteworthy and the Varagog Villagers, who were clamoring for Skerren to cut him in half, deserved better than the Rüstov. The way Jack saw it, everyone who wanted him dead was broken. At their core, they were all victims, just like he was. They had all had their families ripped apart by the Rüstov. Jack wanted to save them from any more pain, but he couldn't even save himself. He wasn't going to give in to Khalix. He knew that much. The only other option was to die like Legend. To make the noble sacrifice. Jack didn't want to die, but he didn't know how else to stop the Rüstov from winning. All his doubts and fears about the future had come flooding back. During the Rüstov air strike, he didn't have time to think; he had just acted. During the battle he had gotten lost in the moment, but the moment had passed. Now it was just him and Skerren.

Skerren pressed the tip of a sword against the red crystal in Jack's chest. It rested neatly in the groove he had cut into it earlier, back in Hero Square.

"I'm sorry, Jack. We all have to make sacrifices."

"Yeah," Jack said. "Some of us more than others."

Khalix was pleading with Jack to give in to the infection and let him take over. Jack tuned him out.

Skerren closed his eyes and got ready to plunge in the sword. "I'll make it quick."

He wasn't quick enough.

Before Skerren could run Jack through, the sun came up. The first light of a new day shot across the horizon, and the world went white with blinding brilliance; Skerren froze in place. It wasn't the new dawn that filled the square with light. It was Stendeval, and he wasn't alone. Allegra, Blue, Roka, Midknight, Zhi, and Lorem Ipsum were all with him. They materialized in the air above the obelisk and dropped down all around Jack. Allegra and the others took up positions at the base of the stone pillar, guarding Jack against the crowd. Stendeval raised a hand, and red energy particles pushed the residents of Varagog back with considerable force.

Jack shuddered and let out a deep breath of air when he realized what was happening. He continued to breathe heavily for a few seconds as his friends rushed to his side. He couldn't form a sentence. He was saved . . . for the moment, at least.

"What treachery is this?" Hovarth asked, his body locked in an awkward stance. "I can't move."

Stendeval swooped in next to Hovarth. "And you won't. Not until after we're gone. If I can't talk any sense into you, I'm afraid we'll have to do things the hard way." Hovarth's men brandished their weapons, ready to charge. Stendeval shook a finger at Hovarth. "Don't give them an order they'll live to regret following. I can do much more than this, as you well know. However much energy I waste fighting your people instead of the Rüstov is entirely up to you."

Hovarth's eye twitched with anger. "Hold," he told his men. Hovarth's army reluctantly lowered their weapons.

"Allegra," Stendeval said. "Get Jack down from there if you would."

"Right," Allegra said, stretching herself around to the back of the pillar. "Let's get these off you."

"Stop!" Smart shouted. "Stop right there, or I'll have Commander Knight shredded immediately. All it takes is one phone call."

"Allegra, wait," Jack blurted out. "He still has Jazen."

Allegra froze in place, but Midknight reached in and cut Jack free himself. "Nice try, Smart, but that's a phone call you can't make in Varagog. No tech works here."

Smart scowled and put his phone away. Jack was relieved that Jazen was still safe, but just like with him, it was only for now. How long could he realistically hope that safety would last?

"You're putting us all at risk by letting him live," Noteworthy said.

"How can you do this?" Smart asked. "We've seen his future! Why are you still supporting him?"

"Both sides in this war need Jack's power to win," Stendeval said. "Through him, we have a chance to turn the Rüstov's greatest weapon against them."

"Or we can simply take that weapon out of their hands," Smart replied. "Stop acting like a child, Stendeval. If you're not ready to make the hard decisions, then let the adults take charge. We're out of time! We can't save Jack any more than we could save any other infected person. We have to think of ourselves!"

"What if Jack could save everyone?" Allegra asked.

Jack looked at Allegra. "What? Allegra, I can't—"

"What if Jack's powers could take control of the Rüstov?" Allegra continued. "He just needs a chance. He could wipe out their fleet. He could bring the infected back."

"If he could do that, he would have saved himself already," Hovarth said. "He's powerless against them. Look at him, he's beaten and he knows it! Why can't you see that?"

All eyes turned to Jack. He knew what his friends wanted to hear. They were all waiting for him to tell Hovarth he was wrong, but he couldn't bring himself to say so. He didn't know what to say until he stepped down from the obelisk and saw something flying through the air. Jack looked up and his stomach dropped. Rüstov

Para-Soldiers lined the walls of the buildings all around.

"Look out!" Jack shouted as one of the falling objects landed right behind Stendeval and exploded. The blast sent them both flying through the air. Stendeval's head slammed hard against the stone pillar that Jack had just been tied to. He fell down unconscious as more bombs were thrown down by the Rüstov. The cobblestone plaza erupted with fiery explosions as geysers of flame and rock shot up all around. Rüstov Para-Soldiers descended on the square, repelling down the sides of the buildings and pouring in through the alleyways.

Suddenly free to move, Hovarth swung at Jack with his battle-ax. "Jack, run!" Blue shouted, jumping out in front of him. He locked onto Hovarth and tried to push him back. Jack went to run, but there was nowhere to go. More Para-Soldiers came in from every direction, throwing bombs and swinging weapons. They were all wearing fresh hosts with little to no technological decay on their bodies. Just like Jack, they were all still more human than they were machine, but unlike him, their parasites were in total control. The sight of innocent people being used as puppets by the Rüstov gave Jack the chills. They still looked like the people they once were, but Jack knew they were lost. They were Rüstov soldiers now. That was his future. That was how everyone saw him. The more his infection grew, the easier it was for him to understand why.

The Rüstov blitz was as perfectly executed as it was overwhelming. The people of Varagog ran for their lives, and those who stayed to fight were either killed or taken by the Rüstov. Jack couldn't help but feel responsible for the body count, but the most crushing blow had yet to be delivered. When it came down, Allegra was standing in the same place she always stood, right in between Jack and any danger. She was struggling with Skerren, who no doubt deeply regretted those extra few seconds he had taken before stabbing Jack through his power core.

Allegra pushed Skerren back and stepped toward him. She was focused on the threat directly in front of her. The threat to Jack. She didn't see Hovarth mortally wound a Rüstov Para-Soldier two steps behind her. The Rüstov abandoned its host and went for Allegra. Jack saw the whole thing. He felt like he was watching it in slow motion and he still wasn't fast enough to stop the bug from crawling up Allegra's leg and into the small of her back. She gagged and clawed at her back, trying to pull out the parasite. It was too late.

"Allegra!" Jack screamed. She locked eyes with him and froze in place. He watched with tears streaming down his face as the infection took root in her heart. A Rüstov mark appeared around Allegra's eye, and circuits swam through her liquid metal skin. Skerren backed away from her as she transformed in front of him.

"You!" he shouted at Jack. "This is your fault! They came here for you!"

At that moment there was no hole on Earth deep enough for Jack to crawl into. There was no place low enough to hide. Jack's heart shattered as what was once Allegra reached for him with the knifelike fingers of an enemy. Roka grabbed Jack and ran in the other direction, but there was nowhere for them to go. The Rüstov had taken the square. Jack cursed his stupidity. Their attack shouldn't have come as a surprise to him. He'd known the Rüstov were in the city. He should've known they'd be headed after him.

"You knew they were coming," Jack said under his breath. "Didn't you, Khalix?"

Khalix's arrogant snicker bounced around Jack's head. "Let's just say I wasn't entirely honest when I said there was only one way out of this." A Rüstov ship flying high enough to avoid Varagog's effect on modern technology passed overhead and dropped down a series of cables. The Para-Soldiers on the ground, Allegra included, rigged the cables together with steel nets and herded Jack and his friends inside. The ground troops waved up at the ship, and the net rose into the air carrying Jack, Stendeval, Blue, Roka, and scores of Varagog Villagers. Once the net cleared Varagog airspace, it lit up with electricity, stunning Jack and his friends into submission.

They were now officially prisoners of war.

CHAPTER
16
The Darkest Hour

The next several minutes were a blur to Jack. The net continued to shock him and his friends at random intervals, keeping them off balance, disoriented, and powerless. Jack figured the electric current was intended more for his friends than it was for him. He couldn't have done anything to sabotage the Rüstov technology holding them, with or without the electroshocks. Jack could feel Khalix's power amping up as they pulled away from the city. The Rüstov prince was elated, and the pain in Jack's head was growing.

The Rüstov ship flew over Wrekzaw Isle and dropped

the net. Jack and his friends hit the hard, uneven terrain with a painful *thud*. They had landed in a small clearing, surrounded by Para-Soldiers on all sides. Before anyone could muster the strength to stand, they were accosted by the Rüstov and forced into holding pens. Jack was being grabbed at and pushed from every direction by Rüstov hands. He didn't put up much of a fight as they herded him along. He couldn't take his eyes off Allegra or, rather, what had *been* Allegra. She was busy processing the prisoners alongside her fellow Rüstov. By the time Jack realized what was going on, it was too late to do anything about it. He, Stendeval, and Roka had been separated from the others and loaded onto a small ship. An iron door shut behind them, screeching as its metal frame scraped into place. They weren't tied up, but Stendeval was still unconscious, and Jack and Roka were in no condition to fight. Jack heard the engines ignite, and the ship shot into the sky.

The force of the ship's sudden liftoff knocked Jack and Roka to the floor. They were in complete darkness, save for a small porthole window on the door. Jack struggled to his feet and looked out as the ship sailed up through the clouds. He could see that the bulk of the Rüstov

Armada had gathered around Wrekzaw Isle and the Imagine Nation, completing the enemy's blockade. It was a scary sight, especially since the wall of ships was made up entirely of Shardwings and midsize fighters. Jack didn't see a single dreadnought among them, which meant the Rüstov's real firepower was still being held in reserve. Jack, Stendeval, and Roka were taken up to the very edge of the atmosphere, where the Rüstov dreadnoughts and super-dreadnoughts were all lying in wait.

The higher they climbed into the sky, the more the pain in Jack's head intensified. Jack put his back to the door and slid down into a seated position, rubbing his temples. He opened his eyes and saw Roka holding on to Stendeval's unconscious body. "Is he all right?" Jack asked.

Roka shook his head. "He has a concussion. Don't know how bad."

Jack leaned over and took Stendeval's hand. With his other hand he dabbed away some of the blood on Stendeval's brow using the cuff of his sleeve. Jack's friend and mentor had taken a bad blow to the head. He had just lost Allegra. He didn't even want to think about losing Stendeval, too.

"You don't look so great yourself, kid." Roka put his hand on Jack's forehead and grimaced. "You're burning up."

Jack winced as a jolt of pain ran through his eye. The machinery in his chest was moving too. It was like someone had just switched it on. Roka banged on the wall. "Hey! Where are you taking us?"

"That should be obvious," Khalix gloated. Jack's head throbbed with every syllable.

A set of doors slid open to reveal a Rüstov officer flanked by two imperial guards and the Rüstov Allegra. The only thing stronger than the anguish Jack felt about Allegra's condition was the anger he felt toward the Rüstov officer beside her.

"Glave." Jack scowled, recognizing him immediately. He was still using Obscuro's body as a host, although the Rüstov virus had done it considerable damage over the past year.

Glave puffed up his chest. "It's General Glave now. The Magus thought the title to be a fitting reward for my service. How are you feeling? Ready to see your father again?"

Jack swallowed hard. Just the thought of the Magus sent another shooting pain through his head. "The Magus isn't my father," he said.

"That's true," Glave replied. "*Your* father wants nothing to do with you. You're an embarrassment to him. A political liability." He waved a finger at Jack. "Not to worry. That doesn't matter anymore, as you well know. In a short while, there won't be any difference between you and Khalix. Soon you'll have a new father, and he's very happy with you both. You've done well, boys."

"It's true, Jack," Khalix said. "The invasion is nearly ready to begin. The Rüstov will take the Imagine Nation and roll over the Earth without any resistance, all thanks to us."

"There is no us. Stop saying that," Jack said. He tried to use his powers to probe Allegra's infection but couldn't make contact with her Rüstov components. "Allegra, talk to me. I know you're still in there. You have to—*b-ahh!*" Jack screamed as the core in his chest lit up. Circuits continued to slowly worm their way out of it.

"How sad," Glave said. "Lost your girlfriend, did you? It appears the two of you have something in common, Captain Roka."

Jack saw a fury in Roka's eyes he'd never seen before. "You son of a—"

Roka lunged at Glave, but the guards sprang forth with

their staves charged at full strength and shocked him back.

"Such grim determination," Glave said. "I'm curious, do you think Rasa put up this much of a fight?"

Roka propped himself up on the ground. Smoke was rising up off his clothes. "Don't talk about her. You're not good enough to even say her name, you piece of rust-covered filth."

"But I feel like I know her so well." Glave smiled. "She was a Secreteer, wasn't she?" Roka's face gave it away. Glave snickered with sinister glee. "Just like my host," he said, looking at his withering hands. "I'm going to miss this body when it's gone. Normally, I wouldn't go before the Magus in such a deplorable state of decay, but the strategic value of this body has been immeasurable. And the memories? Simply delicious."

Roka flew at Glave once more. Once more he went down, but he didn't go easily. He fought hard against repeated prodding until he finally collapsed. Glave shook his head at the space-pirate's resolve. "Amazing. Some of you simply don't understand the futility of fighting us. Most of you learn it so well. Let's see . . ." He closed his eyes and took a deep breath, seeming to search his memories for the one that would cause Roka the most pain. "The Clandestine Order forbade you and this Rasa from being together. They tried to make you forget her, but they just couldn't get through that thick skull of yours, could they?" Glave smiled. "I suppose it didn't matter in the end. She's gone now. Became one of us, did she? That's perfect. Thank you for illustrating my point."

Stendeval grunted. He was coming around. "What point is that?" he asked.

"That nothing you do matters," Glave said. "You can't fight the future." He snorted out a laugh at Roka. "Don't despair. If nothing else, you can share her fate." Glave crouched down next to Jack. "You all will. Check his progress," he told the Rüstov Allegra. Glave handed her a small metal device no bigger than a stick of gum. She uncapped the device, exposing a sharp needle, and pricked Jack's arm, drawing a drop of blood. Jack hardly felt the needle, but the dead look he saw in Allegra's eyes was more painful than anything he had ever experienced. In her, he saw the face of a friend, only with a total absence of everything that she was. She was lost. The Rüstov Allegra handed the device back to Glave, who smiled when he saw the readout on its display. "Very good," he said, holding the device out for everyone to see. It read, "Infection Level: 37%."

Stendeval sat up against the wall. "You haven't won anything yet. He still has a long way to go."

"Ah, Stendeval. Ever the optimist." Glave nodded to the guards, and they pressed lightning-tipped staves into Stendeval's chest, shocking him back into silence. Roka jumped up to defend him and got the same treatment.

"Let me ask you. When you cut down a tree, does the ax need to go all the way through the trunk to bring it down, or does it simply topple over under its own weight once you cut away more than half of the base? We *have* won," Glave said as his prisoners nursed their wounds. "It is quite literally a matter of time." He motioned to Jack. "Look. Revile is being born before our very eyes." Jack felt at his face. Thin lines of circuitry were rising up beneath his skin. He could feel them growing across his chest and out from his eye. "The future is coming. It's practically here, and quite frankly, you deserve every second of it. You had years to prepare your defenses, but you chose to fight one another instead of us." Glave knelt down next to Jack and patted the back of his head. "You were a big part of that in recent years. You're the key to victory in so many ways."

"You hear that, Jack?" Khalix asked. "You're a hero. It's just like you always wanted."

Jack would have liked to fire off a fearless comeback at Khalix, but nothing came to mind. His heart just wasn't in it. The ship shook as a tractor beam locked onto it and brought it in to dock with what Jack knew had to be the *Apocalypse*. The Magus was getting closer. Jack could feel his influence—the power he lent to Khalix by his very presence. Rüstov components were growing inside of Jack. He was fighting the transformation into Revile, but he could tell he was losing the battle. The ship lurched forward and ground to a halt. The door behind Jack opened up with another metallic shriek. Fresh-faced guards wearing new hosts appeared at the door. Glave waved them in. "Take them to the emperor."

Jack fell into a dazed and delirious state as the guards dragged him through the ship. The pain in his head grew increasingly worse until he couldn't see straight. He felt like he was watching a movie, but with everything out of focus and the audio timing slightly off. Lights glared with bright starbursts, streaking across his line of sight. Voices echoed in his ears, coming through magnified and distorted. Visions of the Rüstov ship hit Jack in unnatural staccato bursts, like a film that kept breaking and jumping to new scenes without any clear transitions.

The guards reached their destination and deposited Jack on the floor. His senses settled down a bit once he finally stopped moving, but he still felt wrong. Everything was wrong. Turning his head too fast brought on a throbbing pain behind his eyes and pulled bright, glowing trails out from all the lights in the room. Jack got up into a crouching position and looked around. Tiny specks of light danced about his head like glowing embers from a fire. As they faded in and out, Jack realized they weren't really there at all. He was seeing stars but still recognized where he was. He was back in the Magus's throne room. His memory of this place was fresh and clear, as if he'd just been there yesterday. Did he really remember this, or was it more of Khalix's memories mixing with his own? Jack tried to get up and nearly fell over. His heartbeat pounded in his ears, and the walls seemed to pulsate in time with each thump. This close to the Magus, the Rüstov infection inside him was spreading faster and faster. Meanwhile, his own strength was dying.

Seated on the large iron throne on the far side of the room was the Magus. The Rüstov emperor's perfect, unblemished host was in peak physical condition, just like it was the last time Jack stood at his feet. And just like the last time, the imperial guards knocked Jack to his knees, forcing him to bow before the Magus. The guards pushed Stendeval and Roka down as well. Glave stepped forward to make his report:

"Sire," he said, bowing his head. "I bring you news from the front."

The Magus motioned with his hands. "Speak."

Glave lifted his chin and faced the Magus. "Your glorious armada surrounds the island below. Your forces have crippled Empire City's defenses, and your troops are taking new hosts on the ground, even as we speak. We have reclaimed your former flagship, known here as Wrekzaw Isle, and established your command center there. Your loyal subjects stand ready to fight and die in your name.

We await your order to deliver the Imagine Nation's death-blow."

Glave bowed his head once more and stepped back, awaiting his master's response. The Magus applauded Glave, slowly clapping his hands together three or four times, but no more than that. "Very good," he said. "Very good, indeed." The Magus stood up and flexed the iron spikes that fanned out of his back like wings. "I see the vessel of our enemy's destruction has been reclaimed as well." He walked up to Jack and rested a heavy hand on his shoulder. "It's almost time, my son."

Jack was down on all fours, trying to hold the line against the virus that was relentlessly attacking his body. He didn't have the strength to offer up a defiant retort, and even if he had, he remembered all too well how the Magus made him pay for his back talk last time.

"Who do we have here?" the Magus asked, looking over his other two prisoners.

Glave had the guards prop up Stendeval, who was conscious but badly injured. "My lord, I present to you Stendeval, a most powerful hero. One of the leaders of the Imagine Nation."

"Yes, the great Stendeval," the Magus repeated, clearly pleased. "Glave tells me it was you who hid my son from me all these years. You're going to pay for that." He took Stendeval by the chin and looked him over. "I've heard much of your abilities. I'm going to enjoy using them against you. What do you think of that?"

Stendeval jerked his chin away from the Magus's grip. "I think that in five hundred years on this Earth, I've never met anyone with a more overdeveloped opinion of his own self-worth than you. And I've met Jonas Smart."

The Magus scowled at Stendeval. He balled up his fist, ready to strike him.

"You did ask my opinion," Stendeval said.

The Magus stared at Stendeval. His expression relaxed and he dropped his hand to his side. "If you were anyone else, you would pay dearly for such impudence."

Stendeval raised an eyebrow. "But?"

The Magus took Stendeval by the chin and examined his wounds. "You're already injured. It does me little good to cause you any further damage. Cutting off your nose would only serve to spite my face."

The Magus turned his eyes to the next prisoner in line.

Glave cleared his throat and introduced him. "I believe you will recognize our next prisoner's name as well. May I present Solomon Roka."

"Ah," the Magus said with a grin as he looked Roka over. "An amusing prize, if nothing else. You've been a thorn in our side for many years, haven't you, space-pirate? Raiding my transports . . . disrespecting my authority . . ."

"For the record, I prefer adventurer or entrepreneur. Space-pirate is so . . . Ow!" The guard behind Roka jabbed him in the back with his electro-staff, and then once more for good measure. Roka cried out and fell to the ground. "What was that? I thought it did you little good to cause us any further damage."

"My standards aren't as high as the emperor's," Glave said. "Hit him again."

The Rüstov guards jolted Roka with electricity, and the Magus walked over to an observation window beside his throne. "A grand day is at hand," he announced as he looked out on his armada. "This is the day we shed the defeat and dishonor we've been saddled with ever since the last invasion. For fourteen long years, we licked our wounds in that pathetic Calculan star cluster, but now it's time. Time for revenge. It's time to finish what we started."

"I'm ready . . . Father," Jack said.

The Magus turned in surprise. It was Jack speaking, only it wasn't Jack. It was Khalix, speaking through him. The voice was strained and weak, but it was more powerful than it had ever been before.

"Your son grows strong, sire," Glave said.

Jack was horrified. Khalix had just taken control of his body and used him like a puppet. Jack was suffering intense physical pain from being this close to the Magus, but the mental anguish caused by his body surrendering to the Magus's influence was greater by far. "He's *not* strong," Stendeval said of Khalix. He gave Jack a reassuring look. "Standing on his father's shoulders won't make your son tall." Stendeval looked right at the Magus. "Jack can beat Khalix. And we can beat you."

Jack was sure the Magus was going to hit Stendeval this time, but the Rüstov emperor just laughed at him instead. "If that's true, why is there fear in his eyes?"

Jack said nothing. The Magus saw right through him. Jack needed to win the battle of wills with Khalix to be able to use his powers against the Rüstov, but right now, standing next to the Magus, that seemed downright impossible.

"You only think you can win because you have no understanding of war," the Magus told Stendeval. "My people spend their lives in a state of infinite war. No mercy. No peace. Just a never-ending game of strategy, planning, spycraft, battle, and conquest. Jack has seen it with his own eyes. He knows there's no hope." The Magus gave Jack a light tap on his cheek. "You remember what you learned in the Theater of War, don't you?"

Jack winced as another memory hit him. He was strapped into a chair with his eyes taped open. Rüstov war movies played all around him on a dozen different holo-screens and Jack was unable to look away. Grisly images of death and destruction assaulted him in high-definition 3-D with audio that made him feel like he was living through each battle.

Jack felt the Magus pat his shoulder, and he was jolted out of his flashback and into the real world. "You've seen everything we're capable of. Deep down, you know you can't win. It's only a matter of time before my son turns off your heart and Revile is born."

"You're wrong, Magus," Stendeval said. "The heart of a hero never stops. We will fight you until our dying breaths."

"Who is this *we*?" Glave asked. "I hope you're not still holding out hope that the Calculans will join your cause. They can't desert you right now because of our blockade, but they will soon, I assure you. Ambassador Equa will make every attempt to escape once the invasion begins."

"Of course he will," the Magus replied. "The Calculans understand that this battle has but one possible outcome. All of this is part of a grand design." The Rüstov emperor nodded toward Jack. "Do you honestly believe that he *escaped*? That he was able to send out distress signals telling you where to find him?" The Magus stepped up to Roka. "Do you *really* believe you were able to steal my only son out from under my nose?" The Magus shook his head. "I wanted Jack here, sowing discord and confusion. My son's host is more than just the perfect vessel for Revile. He is a seed of destruction planted in your hearts and minds. I always intended to complete his transformation here with all of you watching. This is how we break the Imagine Nation's spirit. The true battle begins long before the first shot is fired. It starts up here." The Magus tapped his temple. "Once people start thinking about what to do when they lose, they have lost. We always believe we will win, which is why we always do."

"Why me?" Jack croaked, fighting through the pain. "Why did you have to make me the one to do your dirty work?"

"You think you're special?" Glave asked. "That you as a person somehow matter? What is happening here is much bigger than you."

The Magus nodded. "When we invaded Earth fourteen years ago and Revile appeared, we didn't know what he was. Who he was. We had yet to even imagine developing the technology to create him. It wasn't until Glave discovered the truth about Revile in your memories . . ." The Magus swelled with pride and patted Jack's shoulder. "My son . . . not only alive but destined to become something greater than I ever imagined. We know what the future holds. That's why we're here. You have already lost. The individual cannot stand against what is meant to be. You cannot stand against fate."

Stendeval surprised Jack by laughing. "This isn't fate.

It's chance. You came into Jack's life by accident. You may be partly responsible for making him what he is, but you're not ready for what he's going to become. And it isn't just Jack you've underestimated . . . you've misjudged the strength of all my people. We're not going to make it easy for you. If you want to win this war, you're going to have to come down to our level. You're going to have to get your hands dirty."

The Magus leaned into Stendeval's face with a look of death. "That sounds like an invitation. Consider it accepted." The Magus raised up his arms and dropped to the floor in a heap. The guards thrust Stendeval forward at him.

"Stendeval!" Jack shouted. He knew what was coming next. The Magus's hostless form crawled out from beneath his robes and snapped its claws. The rusty metal scorpion shot up Stendeval's leg, climbed onto his back, and latched on. Just like the last time Jack saw this happen, there was nothing he could do to stop it. He could barely move. He was still in agony, still fighting off Khalix's assault on his system.

"Your turn," Glave said to Roka, and followed his emperor's example.

Roka turned to Jack. He knew what was coming. "Fight them, Jack. Don't ever stop, you hear me?"

Glave relinquished his hold on Obscuro's body and traded up to Solomon Roka's.

"No!" Jack shouted as Glave pounced. It was absolute torture. His friends were dying right in front of him and he couldn't do anything but watch.

Roka was turned almost instantly, but as the Magus dug his way into Stendeval's back, he was met with considerable resistance. Stendeval lit up with superpowered energies, fighting back against the Magus's infection with everything he had. Red energy particles swirled around him, and he rose up into the air with his arms spread out. It took Jack a second to realize what was happening, but it soon became clear that the more the Magus labored to overcome Stendeval's will, the less physical pain he felt. Jack heard a voice in his head, and for the first time in a long time, it wasn't Khalix. It was Stendeval.

"I can't keep this up forever," Stendeval said to him. "I'll buy you as much time as I can, but you have to run. There's no time to argue."

"Run where? I can't leave you here like this."

"There's no time to argue!" Stendeval said again, shouting inside Jack's head. "Your job is not to save me. You're here to save the Imagine Nation. You can't do that on board this ship. We need you, Jack. You have to make the difference in this war."

"Stendeval, no! I can't do this alone. The Magus was right. I can't stop what's happening to me. I don't know what I'm going to become. I don't even know what I am right now."

"I *do*. You are what you are when you don't have time to stop and think about it. When you simply act. That's you, Jack, and you're not alone! There are people down there who believe in you. Forget the future and believe in yourself! The only future that matters is the one you decide on. The one you create. *You* decide your future, Jack. You decide—"

Stendeval winced in pain and broke off his connection with Jack. Speaking telepathically required superpowered energy, and Stendeval clearly needed every ounce he had to fight the Magus. A dark line was forming around his eye. He was losing the battle. Jack had gotten used to Khalix speaking up at times like this, but with Stendeval currently demanding the Magus's complete attention, the Rüstov prince was silent. Jack's head cleared. Khalix was drawing zero strength from his father, and that meant Jack could use his powers again—even on the Magus's ship.

"Go, Jack! Go now!" Stendeval yelled out loud.

Jack got up onto his feet and backed away from Stendeval. He didn't think. He just acted, going for the first exit he saw. Jack reached out with his powers and opened the window behind the Magus's throne. The sudden change in air pressure created a powerful vacuum, pulling everything toward the window. Everyone grabbed hold of whatever they could to try and keep from getting sucked out. Everyone except Jack, who ran for the open window. Leaving his friends behind, he went flying out into the sky, running for his life and falling to his death at the exact same time.

CHAPTER

17

The Eve of Destruction

For the second time in as many days, Jack found himself plummeting through the sky without a parachute. The wind roared in his ears, and air whipped into his face as he fell. With the Magus otherwise engaged trying to take over Stendeval's body, Jack had his powers all the way back. He had to act fast because there was no telling how long that was going to last.

Jack commandeered a Shardwing from the Rüstov blockade surrounding the Imagine Nation and pulled it up toward him. Jack squinted, trying to make out the ship as it approached from below. He had reached terminal velocity and he couldn't just bring the ship up underneath him. He had to time things just right, or hitting the Shardwing would have been no better than hitting the ground. He made the ship fly up past him and then loop back around into a nosedive. Jack flattened out, spreading his arms and legs to control his descent as the ship came up behind him. He waited until the Shardwing had caught up and matched his speed before reaching out. The irregular shape of the ship's exterior came in handy as Jack found two good handles to grab hold of. He climbed on board the Shardwing's back and slowed it down, ready to ride the ship home.

The Shardwing pilot banged on the canopy from the inside, but Jack shut him up in the cockpit and cut off his radio. Jack still had to go through the Rüstov blockade, but it was set up to keep ships from getting out, not from getting in. Also, he was riding a Rüstov ship. Jack blew out one of the Shardwing's twin engines and steered the damaged ship toward Empire City, leaving a trail of black smoke in its wake. Jack got through the blockade looking like a malfunctioning ship that was crashing to the Earth. He flew past the city limits and brought the Shardwing down in the Outlands. He didn't land so much as slow down, fly over an open field, and jump. Once he was finally back on the ground, Jack sent the ship high into the sky and then forced it to dive down and crash. It was the super-powered equivalent of slamming a door. A massive fireball shot out from the point of impact. Jack watched the ship burn, momentarily hypnotized by the dancing flames. Just like the Rüstov, the fire consumed everything.

Jack thought about what his enemies had taken from him. It was too much. Allegra, Stendeval, and Roka were all infected. Blue had been captured by the Rüstov, and Jazen was Jonas Smart's prisoner. They would both soon be dead, if they weren't already. Everyone close to Jack was gone. Skerren hated him and wanted him dead. So did his own father. Jack looked at the hunk of machinery in the center of his chest. He wanted to rip it out with his bare hands. His lungs felt tight and he couldn't draw a full breath. Jack knew he didn't have much time left. He had lost so much more than a year of his life. The Rüstov had taken every-thing that made today matter, all his tomorrows as well.

"Your friend Stendeval has fallen," Khalix said, piping

up for the first time since he had shocked Jack by speaking through him. "He fought hard, but in the end he succumbed to my father's will. You all do, eventually. I just thought you'd like to know."

Jack coughed a painful cough. With Stendeval gone, Khalix was getting his power boost from the Magus again. His short vacation from the Rüstov prince was over.

Jack ignored Khalix and turned toward Empire City. He had a long walk ahead of him, made even longer by thoughts of Stendeval and Allegra. Their blood was on his hands. The same was true of Roka, who could have just left and saved himself if he'd wanted to. None of them had ever doubted Jack. The memory of each person was like a hundred-pound weight on Jack's back. He started walking and stumbled immediately. He was getting weaker by the minute, but it wasn't guilt that was sapping his strength. It was Khalix.

"Are you really still trying to keep going? Why do you do this to yourself?" Jack didn't waste energy responding to Khalix's taunts. It took all his concentration just to keep putting one foot in front of the other. "What could you possibly hope to accomplish at this point? Do you really think you're going to save the Imagine Nation like that fool Stendeval said? He's gone, Jack. He's my father's host now, nothing more. What do you think you're going to do, get your powers back? Crush our ships? Expel us from your bodies? Please."

"Nothing's impossible," Jack grunted.

"It is for you. The only way for you to get rid of me is death, and you're too scared . . . too selfish to fall on your sword. You're mine, Jack, now and forever. I can let *you* go, but you can't push me out. You don't understand our connection well enough for that. You will when your transformation is complete, but by then it's going to be too late. You've fought well, but enough is enough. Just give up and find yourself a quiet place to die. I'll handle the rest."

Jack winced as a sharp pain stabbed through his chest. He breathed out slowly and thought about everything Khalix was saying. Jack understood where Khalix was coming from. He understood the Rüstov prince's point of view better and better with every step he took. But Jack didn't lie down and die. He hiked for hours until he reached the city and the one place in it that he knew he'd always have a home.

Jack used his powers to open up the walls of Machina

from the outside. Once he was in the city, it was just a short walk to Virtua's data center. Jack was on his last legs. He could barely stand by the time he reached the door. Virtua's guards brought him in and took him straight to her war room. It was a hotbed of activity. Inside, Jack saw several images of Virtua projected around the room as she marshaled her troops. Midknight, Lorem Ipsum, and Trea were on hand, strategizing with one of her projections. At first Jack thought Virtua was getting her forces ready to face the Rüstov. Then he saw her talking to Jonas Smart on the room's main holo-screen.

"This is your last warning," Virtua told Smart as her soldiers reported in from checkpoints along the Hightown-Machina border. "Release Commander Knight or my men are coming in there to get him."

Smart squinted at Virtua in disbelief. "You must be malfunctioning. The fact that you would even suggest invading Hightown while our city is surrounded by the Rüstov . . ." Smart shook his head. "You're clearly still corrupted by that Rüstov spyware virus. Do your worst, collaborator. My war machines are prepared to fight you and your Rüstov masters."

Jack felt Smart terminate the connection. Virtua cursed Smart as his screen blinked out. Jack couldn't believe Virtua was really going to march on Hightown in the middle of a war with the Rüstov. Apparently, Chi, Prime, and Noteworthy couldn't, either. Jack felt them dialing back in from their respective war rooms, where they had been monitoring her call with Smart. Jack used his powers to answer the calls and put them on-screen.

"Virtua, please. You can't do this," Chi pleaded. "We can't waste time fighting each other. Not now."

"We can't spare the men," Prime agreed. "We're already outnumbered as it is."

"Don't tell me," Virtua said. "Tell the Circleman of Hightown to make Smart let Jazen go." Noteworthy just tugged at his collar and stammered.

"You know Noteworthy can't control Smart," Midknight told Virtua. "Be reasonable. We have to think of the—" Midknight stopped short when he noticed Jack standing in the entryway. "Jack?"

Lorem Ipsum and Trea dropped what they were doing and ran to him the moment they saw him. "How did you get here?" Lorem asked.

"Thank goodness you're all right," Trea said.

Jack slid into a chair to keep from falling over. "Let's not get carried away. Sounds to me like we're all pretty far from all right."

Virtua's image shot out of a projector that was concealed in the data center floor by Jack's feet. Her guards informed her that Jack had come alone. "Where are the others? Are you the only one who got out? Where's Stendeval?"

"We could sure use him right now," Lorem mumbled to Trea.

Jack took a deep breath. He couldn't have agreed more, but Stendeval was gone. He looked up at everyone and shook his head. Virtua's image turned a pale white. "That can't be. Are they all . . . ?"

"I don't know," Jack said. "Blue, Zhi, and the others . . . they all got put into holding pens. Stendeval, Roka, and I were separated from the pack. They took us up to see the Magus. I only got away because I . . . Stendeval, he . . ."

Jack was still struggling to find the words when terrified outbursts filled the data center. Along with everyone else, Jack looked up to see what all the commotion was.

"What's going on?" Midknight asked.

"Look out your window," Prime called out over the holo-screen. "You need to see this."

Outside, several giant holo-screens were blinking on, projected out from the sea of Rüstov ships that filled the air. The Magus was getting ready to broadcast a message to Empire City. Everyone but Jack gasped when they realized he was using Stendeval's body as his host. Jack's eye burned as the Magus looked out from the screens. It was as if the Magus was looking right at him. Glaring lights flared up before Jack's eyes. He saw spots, like he'd spent too much time staring at the sun.

"People of Empire City," the Magus announced. "I am the Magus, supreme ruler of the Rüstov Empire. I am your new lord and master. Let it be known that I hereby declare the Imagine Nation, this planet, and everyone on it to be the rightful property of the Rüstov. You belong to us. From this moment on, your world will be known as Rüst. Your city is now the capital of the Rüstov throneworld. This is an honor. Those of you living here will serve as hosts to the upper echelon of Rüstov society, provided you do not waste your lives in foolish and pointless efforts to resist our rule. I believe you recognize my host, Stendeval the Wise. He was not wise enough to accept the inevitable. For all our sakes, I hope you will choose a different path. Stendeval's loss is proof that even your strongest heroes cannot withstand our might. Embrace your future as my willing subjects, for it is unavoidable. We have released the boy you know as Jack Blank into your city. To me, he is Khalix . . . my son. He will soon become Revile, the engine of your destruction, but only if you choose that fate. We have no desire to destroy this city or its citizens. You are valuable resources. There is no need for us to be at war with one another, but if you force our hands, you will die by them. I await your formal surrender. You have until dawn."

The screens blinked out of the sky, and a hush fell over the room. It lasted only a few seconds before everyone started talking at once. The twin currents of fear and alarm overtook the data center and drowned out everything else. Jack remained quiet. He sat in his chair thinking about how Stendeval looked with the Magus's iron horn grafted onto his head. It was the kind of sight that could make a person abandon all hope. Jack knew the Rüstov well enough now to know that was exactly what they were going for.

"The Magus using Stendeval's body . . . ," Midknight said. "This is going to scare people to death."

"He's right," Khalix told Jack. "They're all scared, and not just because of my father. They're scared of you. Scared of *us*."

Jack cast his eyes around the data center. He didn't need to scan the Mechas there with his powers to recognize the truth of Khalix's words.

"We still have a chance," Noteworthy said via holoscreen. "We have Jack."

Everyone spun around to look at Noteworthy. Jack's eyebrows shot up in surprise. Was it possible that Noteworthy was starting to believe in him? Was his father finally coming around?

"We can turn him over to Smart!" Noteworthy explained. Jack slumped in his seat. "Jonas will see to it that Jack doesn't live to become Revile. He'll release Commander Knight and we can call a truce between Hightown and Machina. We can fight the Rüstov together! The only thing keeping us apart is sitting in that chair."

"You mean your son?" Midknight asked.

Noteworthy pounded his desk. "He's not my son! Stop saying that!"

The adults in the data center argued, and Jack put his head in his hands. "We're doing exactly what they want us to do," he said to himself. "This is the way it always goes."

"What do you mean?" Trea asked Jack.

Jack looked up. He hadn't realized he was talking loud enough for anyone to hear. "The infinite war. I know the Rüstov's history. They crammed it into my brain. They break their enemies apart before they invade, that's their playbook. They infiltrate their targets, psyche out their enemies, and get them to fight each other. The details change, but the story's the same. It always ends the same way."

"Then we have to break the cycle," Trea said. "We can't just do the same things everyone else has done and expect to fare any better. If you know their history, think. What's different about this invasion? Anything we can use?"

Jack ran through all the battles the Rüstov had shown him. Every war the Rüstov had ever fought. All the reasons they gave him for giving up. In all that carnage, there was only one thing that made this invasion different from any other. "There is one thing that's different. Me." Jack looked up at the holo-screens where the Circlemen were fighting about what was to be done with him, and something clicked. They didn't stand a chance against the Rüstov if things went on like this. He was the wedge driving everyone apart. Something had to be done. "I hate to say it, Trea, but Noteworthy's right. I just wish he felt the tiniest bit bad about it." Jack touched Lorem's elbow. "Hey. How'd you get over having a father that didn't want you?"

Lorem turned toward Jack with a look that was one part pity and one part amusement. "What makes you think I got over it?" She shook her head. "I didn't get over anything, Jack, but I do know this. Family . . . real family is about more than blood. A lot more."

Jack leaned back in his chair. He found comfort in Lorem's words. He thought about the closest thing he had to a big brother—Jazen Knight. He wasn't human. He didn't even *have* blood. That didn't mean he wasn't family. Stendeval had told him something similar when he first came to the Imagine Nation. He had a family, and right now, they needed him. He had to save Jazen. He had to make Stendeval's sacrifice matter. He had to do something for Allegra, Roka, Blue, Zhi, and all the innocent people the Rüstov had taken.

Jack stood up. His body was worn-out and on the verge failing him, but he wouldn't let himself quit. "Lorem, give me your hand. I've got an idea."

Jack grabbed Lorem Ipsum's hands and spoke for two full minutes, saying nothing but absolute gibberish. Virtua, Midknight, Trea, and the other Circlemen all stopped and stared as Jack blathered on in a language only Lorem Ipsum could understand. When Jack finished talking, she touched his hand again, unscrambling his words.

"Got all that?" Jack asked. Lorem nodded tentatively.

"Got all what?" Khalix demanded. "What did you just tell her?"

Jack shook his head. "Sorry, Khalix. Private conversation. Didn't anyone ever tell you it's rude to eavesdrop?"

Midknight brought his hands together. "Very clever."

"I don't understand. What's clever?" Noteworthy asked. "What did he do?"

"Jack just cut the Rüstov out of the loop," Midknight explained. "The Rüstov prince can't listen in on his plans if it can't understand what he's saying. The question is, what was said?"

Lorem swallowed hard. "This is risky, Jack. I don't think I like it."

Jack snorted out a small laugh. "I *know* I don't like it. But this is war. Everything is risky." He put up his hand, heading off any further discussion. "Let's not say too much just yet. You can talk more about it after I'm gone."

"What do you mean, after you're gone?" Noteworthy asked. "Where do you think you're going?"

"I'm going exactly where you told me to, *Dad*." Noteworthy turned three different shades of red and started yelling at the top of his lungs until Jack got fed up and disconnected his holo-screen. "Virtua, call Smart back and tell him to get ready to send Jazen home. I'm turning myself in."

CHAPTER

18

Getting Smart

Night fell as Jack arrived at SmartTower, carried there by flying Mechas. Khalix chirped in Jack's ear the whole way. Jack could tell he was nervous as they approached the top of the building and Smart's lab. The glass from the lab's great round window split into eight curved triangles and spiraled open like an aperture door. The Mechas brought Jack and Trea inside and set them down.

"I don't know what you think you're doing, Jack, but whatever it is, I promise you it won't work."

"Said the broken record," Jack told Khalix. "Don't

worry. You'll find out what I'm up to soon enough." Jack was enjoying the opportunity to taunt Khalix for a change. He had to take pleasure in the little things, because they were all he had left. Everything else hurt. Jack's muscles ached, his head was throbbing, and his fever had climbed to a hundred and four degrees. Smart and his WarHawks were waiting in the lab when Jack got there. He locked eyes with Smart as he entered and as a result missed a small set of steps leading down toward his workstation. He stumbled and fell, hitting the ground hard. Trea helped Jack up. He was breathing heavily. His chest was glowing. Jack absolutely hated that he had made such a terrible entrance. For his part, Smart barely seemed to notice. He pointed behind him at a holo-screen that had just blinked out.

"That was Circlewoman Virtua. I didn't believe her at first. She said you agreed to come here?" Smart looked Jack up and down, frowning at the state he was in. "More likely, you were too weak to do anything about it. Don't tell me you've finally accepted your fate. . . . You're truly ready to think of the greater good and end this?"

"That's exactly what I'm here to do," Jack said, dusting

himself off. He felt flushed. He wiped his brow and found that he was dripping with sweat. "Where's Jazen?"

Smart nodded to his guards, and a row of WarHawks stepped aside to make room for the prisoner Jazen Knight. Armed escorts marched him in with his hands bound in electro-cuffs. Jack breathed a sigh of relief when he saw that Jazen was still in one piece.

Jack ran to his friend. "Are you okay?"

"Jack?" Jazen looked back and forth between Jack and the WarHawks as they deactivated his manacles. "What are you doing here?"

"He made a deal," Smart said. "He wants to do the right thing."

"What?" The WarHawks went to place Jazen's cuffs on Jack's wrists. Jazen pushed them back. "Get away from him!"

"Jazen, it's okay!" Jack said. "Don't worry, I'll be fine."

Jazen glared at Jack as he offered his wrists to the War-Hawks. "You don't look fine to me."

Jack shrugged. "I'm not really. But I will be. Now, so will you." He looked around at the lab's antiseptic white walls, organized workstations, and glaring bright lights.

"The last time you and I were in here together, you ran a pair of Left-Behinds out the window to save me. It's my turn now."

Jazen shook his head. "If you think I'm going to let you go through with this . . ."

"I'm doing it, Jazen. They took everything. I've got nothing left to lose except you, and that's not gonna happen."

Jazen's nostrils flared, but he kept his cool. "I can't leave you alone here, Jack. No way. Unless . . ." He leaned in close to Jack and whispered. "Tell me you have some kind of a plan here."

Jack tilted his head to the side. "I have an idea. We'll see how far I get with it. Don't worry, Trea's here to help."

Trea shook her head. "I don't even know why I'm here."

"We don't have time to get into every last detail," Jack told Jazen. "You have places to be. You need to get up to Mount Nevertop with Lorem Ipsum, and you need to take Roka's ship."

"Roka's ship?" Jazen repeated. "What are you talking about? Roka's ship is wrecked. It can't fly anywh—"

Jazen stopped talking midsentence and locked eyes with Jack. The two friends stared at each other in silence for a few moments while everyone else looked on with confused faces.

Smart rolled his eyes and let out a heavy sigh. "I've clearly tolerated this heartfelt good-bye of yours far too long. Enough, both of you. Circlewoman Virtua and I have come to an accord. Commander Knight, you are free to go. I suggest you take your leave before I rethink our agreement. As for you, Jack, you may consider yourself my prisoner. At least for the next thirty seconds."

"Listen to him, Jazen," Jack said. "Go."

Jack and Jazen shook hands.

"Good luck," Jazen said as the Mecha guards got ready to take him home.

"To all of us," Jack replied.

The Mechas flew out the window carrying Jazen in their arms. As soon as they were gone, twenty WarHawks trained their weapons on Jack.

"Jack, what are you doing?" Khalix asked. "You're not really staying here. You can't!"

Jack remained calm, even as a score of red laser-sight

dots danced over his forehead and chest. "I just want to say one thing, if that's all right."

Smart motioned for Jack to go ahead. "Get on with it."

Jack put up his hands. "Don't shoot."

Smart snorted out a laugh. "I don't know why, but I was expecting something more." He turned to the War-Hawks. "Fire."

Khalix screamed as Smart gave the order. Trea covered her ears and turned away.

Nothing happened.

Smart's eyes narrowed and he furrowed his brow. "Fire," he said again. Still, nothing happened. The War-Hawks stood frozen in place. Smart pounded the keys on his pocket holo-computer. "What's going on here? Fire, I said!"

Jack calmly deactivated his electro-cuffs and rubbed his wrists as the metal components of his shackles hit the floor with a clank. "Sorry, Smart. Your WarHawks work for me now. Or did you forget that I control machines?" He walked up to Smart's robotic commandos and looked them over. "This is nice hardware. Really impressive design work, I mean that."

Smart's mouth fell open as Jack walked freely around his lab, decidedly not riddled with bullets. He was at a loss. "I don't understand. My nullifiers . . ."

"Yeah, about those. They don't work on me anymore." Jack snapped his fingers and Smart's holo-computer blinked out of his hand. Smart stared at his empty palm in disbelief. "Looking for this?" Jack asked, holding Smart's holo-computer in his right hand.

"When you sent these guys after me back in Hero Square, I was so shocked by all this Rüstov tech inside me, I couldn't even think straight. I had an inkling that my powers still worked around them once I made it out of Cognito, but the WarHawk chasing me died out before I could be sure. It wasn't until you surrounded us at the Valorian Garrison that I knew for certain." Jack raised his shoulders. "I don't know if my thoughtprint is different because of what the Rüstov did to me, or if I've just grown a lot in the last few years, but either way, your software needs an upgrade."

Jack winked at Smart, and it wasn't anger he saw staring back in his nemesis's eyes. It was fear. "But if your powers work . . . you tricked me! You told that Mecha

Knight something before he left. You told him with your mind!"

"Don't worry about Jazen," Jack said. "He has his job to do. You have yours. You want to hear what it is?"

"*My job?*" Smart scoffed. "You must be out of your mind. I'm not going to be part of anything you two are up to." Smart rifled through the drawers of the nearest lab station, trying to find a weapon to use against Jack.

"Nothing you have in here can hurt me, Smart. You might as well listen. I have a proposal that I think might interest you."

"*Nothing* you have to say interests me."

There was a loud stomping noise as all twenty War-Hawks in the lab turned and aimed their guns at Smart. "Hear me out," Jack said. "While I'm still asking nicely."

Smart frowned at a useless gun he had just taken out of a desk drawer and tossed it on the ground. It didn't take the world's smartest man to realize he was completely at Jack's mercy.

"That was pretty cool," Trea told Jack.

Jack smiled. "I know, right? We can't do it this way,

though. We have to work together. That's why you're here, Trea. I need your brain."

Trea's eyes bugged out.

"Not literally," Jack said. "We're gonna be lab partners again. Smart, too, if he'll agree to it. We're going to do some work on the Rüstov virus. The one inside me." Jack tapped his chest and launched into a series of painful coughs.

Smart studied Jack with suspicious eyes. "What's your angle?"

"No angle," Jack said. "I want a truce."

Smart scowled. "This from the boy aiming twenty guns at my head."

Jack made the WarHawks lower their weapons. "I had to get your attention somehow. I told you. I want us to fight the Rüstov, not each other."

"You are the Rüstov," Smart said. "Your leader doesn't want a truce. He wants our surrender."

"He's not my leader."

"He will be," Khalix told Jack. "Soon. Very soon . . ."

Jack winced as Khalix spoke inside his head. It was a

reaction that did not go unnoticed by Smart. "He's talking to you again, isn't he? The Rüstov prince? You're about to surrender yourself. There's only one way to end the threat you pose."

"You're not using your imagination. I don't have to become Revile. Not the way you think."

"You can't stop it. You said yourself they changed the way *you* think."

"Maybe, but they couldn't change who I am. I know that now. And I know how to beat them. The Rüstov don't even realize it, but they showed me how. They gave me everything I need."

Smart remained unconvinced. "What are you talking about?"

Jack tapped his temple. "They put every page of the Rüstov history book in here. Nothing but war, that's all they know. They were trying to show me how hopeless this all is. They thought it would break me, but they don't know me. I don't quit. All they did was take me to school. Planning, strategy, battle, conquest. I'm supposed to be their ultimate weapon. That's fine. As far as I'm concerned, they just showed me how to use it against them."

"But they control what you can and can't use your powers on. From the looks of things, they're about to control more than that."

"That's where you come in," Jack told Smart. "I need you to build a new nullifier. One that's tuned in to *Khalix's* thoughtprint." Jack heard Khalix gasp and allowed himself a slight smile. It felt good to strike a little fear into the Rüstov prince's heart. Smart opened his mouth to talk but shut it without saying anything. Jack had the old man's attention. "Once Khalix is blocked out of my mind, I'll be able to use my powers on whatever I want. It won't matter how much juice the Magus pumps into him. My power will take over and shut him down, just like it's been doing ever since I was a baby. It'll just be me again. Then I can take the Rüstov apart piece by piece."

Smart rubbed his chin, deep in thought.

"It won't work," Khalix said. "He won't do it. You don't have the time."

"Khalix is scared," Jack said. "Right now, he's scared. I can feel it. Tell me this isn't at least worth a shot."

Smart was still skeptical. "If I fail, you'll turn into Revile and kill us all." He keyed up the TimeScope footage of Jack destroying the Calculan fleet after turning into Revile. "Perhaps you've forgotten about this?"

Jack shook his head, studying the images intently. "I haven't forgotten. Quite the opposite, actually."

"Think of what people will say about you if you can stop Jack's infection," Trea told Smart. "You'll be a hero. You might even get elected Circleman again. Don't tell me you don't want that."

"She's right," Jack said. "I know you, Smart. For you, the only thing worse than losing this war would be us winning it without you. Work with us. We can do it here in your lab. You can take any precautions you want. I won't fight you."

Smart stared at Jack for five endless seconds, then slowly nodded. "If we do this, we do it my way. My lab, my research, my rules. Whatever you might know about machines, you don't know mine. You don't know the intricacies of my process for identifying a thoughtprint or creating a nullifier to block it out. I won't have you questioning me. We don't have time for your usual brand of insolence."

Jack offered Smart his hand. "Don't look now, but I think you and I just agreed to work together."

Smart looked at Jack's hand like it had been dipped in raw sewage. He turned up his nose and walked away, motioning for Jack and Trea to follow. "Let's get started. Dawn is just a few hours away."

The Fate of Jack Blank

Despite his initial misgivings, Smart dove into the work with vigor. He busted out all the old favorites, zapping Jack with electroshocks, firing him around a centrifuge, frying him with heat blasts, and flash-freezing him in liquid carbonite.

"Are we almost done with this part?" Jack asked after Smart thawed him out for the third time.

"I'm not doing this for fun," Smart said. "I can't isolate your parasite's thoughtprint without mapping your brain wave activity."

Jack rolled his eyes. "And that requires tracking its thought pattern as it responds to negative stimuli. I know. I remember the drill. I'm just saying, you should have enough by now."

"Jack's right," Trea said. She had split into three supersmart versions of herself, all of whom were sitting at holo-computers, crunching numbers as the data poured in. "Check my work," the first one said, handing a sheet of SmartPaper to the other two.

The second Trea nodded in agreement. "Looks good."

"We're ready," the third Trea agreed. "We've got a statistically significant sample set. Time for phase two."

Smart grumbled. "Get on the operating table. We're wasting time."

Jack shook his head and limped over to the operating table. His strength was fading fast, so he had the WarHawks help him across the lab and lift him onto the table. He knew that using Smart's soldiers as his personal assistants grated on Smart, and he didn't want to distract the old man from his work, but he just couldn't resist.

"Take your shirt off," Smart said to Jack. "I want to

get a look at that infection." Jack pulled off his shirt, and all three Treas gasped. Smart's eyes narrowed. "Just as I suspected."

Jack looked down and saw that his entire chest was covered in wires and machinery. Khalix had been busy. Jack tried to sit up, but a sharp pain in his lungs forced him back down. "I wish I could say I'm surprised to see this, but . . ." He lifted a hand and let it fall on the table. Smart stuck sensor after sensor onto Jack's neck and forehead. He plugged a wire into the apparatus that was once Jack's chest and ran a diagnostic scan.

"Infection level: forty-seven percent," Smart announced, reading the figure off his handheld holo-computer. The handheld beeped and Smart looked again. "Forty-seven point one."

"Hear that?" Khalix asked Jack. "You're running out of time. With every inch of ground you lose, I grow stronger. Can you feel it? I know you can."

Jack's vision started to blur. He shut his eyes tight, but that was no help. He felt like he had swatches of sandpaper taped beneath his eyelids. Smart kept working, plugging more wires into him and checking the connections. He moved to a new desk and called up a holo-magnifier. Sparks started flying as he leaned over the table and fired up his tools. Jack assumed he was burning circuits into a chip. He cracked his eyes open to get a look. It wasn't easy keeping track of what Smart was up to. That's why Jack wanted Trea there, to keep him honest. Ordinarily, Jack was enough of a computer whiz to stay on top of what Smart was doing without any trouble, but in his feverish state, he was glad he had Trea there to catch anything he missed. Meanwhile, Khalix kept trying to speed up his transformation before Smart's work was done.

"The first thing I'm going to do once you turn is fly out that window and blow up the Calculan fleet," Khalix told Jack. "If only to show you that the future is exactly what we always said it was."

Smart looked up from his workstation. The Rüstov prince's words scrolled across one of Smart's holo-screens with a slight delay, no doubt due to one of the many cables that were plugged into Jack's chest at the moment.

"Please, keep talking, Khalix," Smart said, turning

back to his work. "It makes it that much easier for me to isolate your consciousness inside Jack's head. It makes it easier to block you out."

"Nothing's going to block me," Khalix replied. "Do whatever you want. It will amount to nothing."

Smart issued an amused chortle but nothing more.

"Jack's powers aren't enough to stop me," Khalix insisted. "The battle between us is about willpower. His is fading. He grows weaker with every passing second."

"That's where you're wrong," Jack told Khalix. "My body might be broken, but my will isn't. I can take you. I know I can."

"I *will* become Revile. My father will see to that."

The three Trea's checked a readout on one of the screens and whispered among themselves, quickly coming to an agreement. They motioned to Jack, telling him to keep Khalix talking. Jack nodded.

"Leaning on Daddy again. Huh, Khalix?" he struggled to say.

Khalix laughed. "By all means, mock me if it makes you feel better. Your pleasure will be short-lived. The simple fact is I am never without my father. No Rüstov is."

Jack shrugged. "Must be nice. Never having to do anything for yourself, I mean."

"I don't expect you to understand the bond we share. How could you? Your own father wants nothing to do with you."

"Hitting below the belt there, Khalix," Jack said. "You may not see it, but we're not all that different when it comes to family."

"What are you talking about?"

"You're not like all the other Rüstov. You *were* without your father . . . for most of your life, in fact. It was the same back there in the throne room, too. You were totally without him, even though he was standing right next to us. He was so busy with Stendeval, he forgot all about you. And you vanished."

"And your point is?"

"You couldn't stand up to me without his help. Your father thinks you're gonna be some invincible super-soldier once you finally put me away. What's he going to think when we finish up here and shut you down instead? What's he going to say when there is no Revile, and he's stuck with just you?"

Jack could practically feel Khalix's blood boiling. "That's not how this ends," the Rüstov prince said. "You know how this ends. You've met Revile. You've seen the future."

"One possible future. Your overconfidence is going to be the death of you, Khalix. It makes you lazy. You keep saying the same old thing over and over. Me, I've got all kinds of new ideas. And tomorrow's not going to be anything like what you remember. Not if I can help it."

"You can't help it. You can't. It doesn't matter where my strength comes from, or my confidence, for that matter. All that matters is that I'm getting stronger and you're fading away. You're going to eat those words, Jack. I'm going to set your world on fire and make you watch it burn."

"Ahem," Smart said, holding up a shiny silver microchip. "That will do."

"Finished?" Jack asked.

"Let's see." Trea snatched the chip away from him. He tried to grab it back, but she handed it off to the second Trea. She gave it to the third Trea, who then handed it back to the first. She plugged it into a holo-tablet computer and projected a schematic of the chip into the air. Its rotating image hovered above the operating table. Jack and the three Treas studied it intently.

"Careful with that," Smart said, reaching for the chip. "It's extremely delicate!"

"I just want to get a look first," Trea said.

"We don't have time for this," Smart said. "Look." He held up his handheld. It read: "Infection Level: 48.9%." "Once the infection covers more than half his body, it's going to be too late."

Jack coughed a couple of times. He tasted blood. "It's all right. I see what he did. It's fine. Let's get this done before it's too late."

"Forty-nine point two and climbing," Smart said.

"Bring it over here. Quickly," Jack told Trea. "We only need one of you for this part." Trea pulled herself together and brought the chip over to Jack. He could feel Khalix pushing as hard as he could, racing like an Olympic sprinter trying to beat him across the finish line. "Right here," Jack said, tapping the glowing light in his chest. "The infection is buried in my heart. That's where you have to load the chip."

Trea straightened her back. "In your heart? How do I—?"

Jack groaned in pain as he "opened up" the machinery in his chest. He arched his back up off the operating table and pushed Revile's power core up out of his body. His chest split open as the core rose up. "Here. There should be an open data port on the flip side."

"Forty-nine point six," Smart said, still reading the numbers off his handheld.

Trea swallowed hard and reached into Jack's chest with the chip. She fished around with her hand, looking for the data port, but couldn't get at it. "I can't reach it," she said. "The angle's no good."

"You have to," Jack said. "Keep trying."

As Trea struggled to press the chip into place, Jack's mind wandered a moment, thinking about someone who would have had no trouble reaching his heart. Allegra. Her liquid metal fingers would have found the mark easily. He couldn't let the Rüstov have her. He wouldn't. This had to work.

"I think I've got it," Trea said.

"I'm not going anywhere, Jack," said Khalix. "I'm still going to be the last one standing when this is all over."

"We'll find out soon enough," Jack replied.

"Hurry, Trea," Smart pressed.

Trea found the data port and pushed the chip into the back of Jack's heart. She retracted her hand, and for a moment, the lab and everyone in it were completely still. A clock on the wall counted the seconds in silence. Jack held his breath. His body convulsed. He shook like he was having a seizure, thrashing about violently. Trea tried to hold him down, but Smart pulled her back. Jack flailed about for another ten seconds, then suddenly, every muscle in his body tensed up. He relaxed a second later, dropping his back flat against the table. He took a few deep breaths. Waiting. Listening. Nobody said a word. It was as if someone had just turned the volume on the room all the way down.

Jack sealed himself back up and got off the table. He nearly fell over when he put his feet on the ground. "Whoa." He shot his arms out and caught his balance like a surfer riding on a wave.

"Jack, are you all right?" Trea asked. She looked at Smart. "What's the infection level at now?"

"Forty-nine point eight," Smart replied. "And holding."

". . . it worked?" Trea said.

"We don't know that yet," Smart replied. "I'm running a full diagnostic scan."

"Talk to us, Jack," Trea said. "What are you feeling? Is Khalix blocked out? Can you use your powers against the Rüstov now?"

Jack felt around the machinery in his chest as a ray of blue light from Smart's scanner washed over him. "This . . . this is unbelievable."

Suddenly, alarms started going off all over Smart's lab. Trea jumped. "What is it? What's going on?"

Jack doubled over and grabbed his chest. The pain was incredible.

"It's not working, that's what's going on!" Smart said. "Look." He called up a holo-screen projection of the nullifier chip inside Jack's power core. It was flashing with red light. "Khalix is still drawing enough power from the Magus to strain the device. The nullifier is burning out."

Trea backed away from Jack, her eyes darting left and right. "What do we do?"

Smart shook his head slowly. "There's nothing we can do."

Jack staggered back to the operating table and fell onto it. The infection level readout on Smart's holo-screen ticked up one point to 49.9. Jack's body shook as it hit 50 percent and kept going. The numbers rolled up toward 100 percent at a rapid pace. Jack's infection attacked his system completely unopposed, and Rüstov technology poured out of his chest.

CHAPTER

20

Revile Resurrected

The Rüstov infection worked fast. Nanites flooded Jack's brain. His bones vibrated as they transformed into metal, and he felt his veins turn cold as they morphed into lengths of wire and cable. His organs shook inside his body as they turned into machine parts. His blood flow slowed down as his bodily fluids thickened and became a sticky black oil. Jack's Rüstov infection was unlike any other. It didn't simply stop growing once the parasite had taken over his body. It kept going until every inch of him had been replaced with Rüstov technology. Metal grew out of

Jack's chest and covered his body like a ramshackle suit of armor. He could hear Trea screaming as his muscles gave way to iron and rubber tubing.

"I told you. I warned you!" Smart shouted. "Now we're all doomed!"

A rusty iron mask grew over Jack's face, and the last traces of his identity vanished. For all intents and purposes, Jack Blank was gone. He stood before Smart and Trea as Revile.

"Jack?" Trea asked, her eyes streaked with silver tears. "Are you in there? Please tell me that's still you in there."

The iron giant gave no reply. He simply charged forward, crashed through the window, and launched himself out into the sky. Broken shards of glass fell down like rain as he soared high above the towers of Empire City.

He went straight for the airfield in Galaxis where the Calculan fleet was parked. Five thousand unmanned attack ships sat below them, all lined up in neat little rows. He swooped over the first row of ships, firing away with his plasma cannons and lighting them up. Explosions ran down the line, building in force like a giant wave crashing into the shore. He made another pass, and a crescendo of fire ripped through the airfield in the opposite direction. Thunderous booms shook the city as the remote-controlled fighters went up in flames. Minutes later, the Calculan fleet was destroyed, and its destroyer flew away into a night sky that was filled with smoke and fire. He had left some of the Calculan ships intact, but the bulk of their fleet had been decimated in a terrifying display of firepower. It was just as the footage from Jonas Smart's TimeScope had predicted.

The Rüstov supersoldier left Empire City behind and flew to Wrekzaw Isle as dawn approached. Its once deserted surface now bustled with activity. Legions of Para-Soldiers raised their fists in the air and cheered him on as he passed over their heads. He touched down at the edge of a pit of fire. He'd been there before. In a way, he'd never left. The pit was Revile's grave, a slow-burning cauldron of flames that never went out. Up until the most recent Rüstov attack, a pair of Valorian Guards had been placed here at all times, just in case the time-traveling supersoldier was still alive in there somewhere. The guards were now host bodies for Rüstov troops, a fate many in the Imagine Nation would soon share.

He reached out to the downed mothership that made up the foundation of Wrekzaw Isle and powered down its Infinite Warp Core engine. The flames went out, and deep within the pit, there was darkness. Moments later, a flicker of light flashed in the pitch-black hollow. A circular red crystal drifted up from below with globs of molten metal trailing behind it. The fragments hovered in the air above the pit and began to cool, drawing themselves together around the crystal core. They were forming the shape of something, bit by bit. Machine components from the junkyard landscape of Wrekzaw Isle were attracted to the molten mass of metal and got pulled in from all sides. A figure began to take shape. The end result was a mirror image of the Rüstov supersoldier standing at the edge of the pit. The Revile of tomorrow had come face-to-face with the Revile of today. The Imagine Nation's troubles had just been multiplied by two.

A resounding cheer rose up from the Rüstov forces that had gathered around Revile's grave. The noise echoed across the barren plains of Wrekzaw Isle as thousands of Para-Soldiers stomped their feet and fired their weapons into the air. The raucous celebration was enough to chill the heart of even the bravest hero. Sure enough, the reaction of the Rüstov rank and file was the polar opposite of that of the prisoners in the holding pens. Blue, Zhi, and the rest of the prisoners taken in the Varagog raid huddled together in fear as the second Revile emerged from the fiery pit.

The second Revile appeared disoriented, but he was coming around. He flew a few feet away from the crater that had been his prison for the last two years, moving in an erratic, clumsy path. He took a moment to steady himself and get his bearings straight. He looked at his hands, flexing his fingers and reaching his arms out in front of him. He felt at his chest, examining his newly regenerated and very intimidating form. After being trapped for so long in the warp core engine, melting and reforming over and over in an endless loop, he was suddenly whole once more. Turning his head slowly, he scanned the surrounding area, familiarizing himself with his dreadful surroundings. The dull orange-brown hue of rusted shrapnel burned with a hideous glow beneath glaring fluorescent lights. An army of Para-Soldiers stood below him, applauding his arrival. A sea of Shardwing fighters hovered above him, filling up the sky and blocking out the stars. Judging from his reaction, it was what he saw across from him that bothered him most—a hulking mechanical soldier that might as well have been his clone. He straightened up with a jolt.

"No . . . NO!"

He instantly regained his coordination and rushed down toward his doppelgänger. He clutched him by the shoulders and looked him up and down with frantic, jerky motions.

"I'm too late," he said, letting go and pulling his hands back. "They did it. I failed." He balled up his fists and drifted away from his twin, shaking with anger. "I *told* you this would happen. I warned you!" He turned away and grabbed at his head in tortured anguish. "We've lost. All is lost . . . again."

He had come from a future where the Rüstov had not only won the war but used him to do it. He'd come back in time to prevent that future from ever happening and himself from ever existing. Seeing what Jack had become made it painfully clear that his time-traveling suicide run had not changed a thing. His mad dash through time was all for naught. As he mourned the loss of his only purpose in life, Glave arrived at the pit, marveling at the unexpected development.

"Two of you?" Glave asked. A second later, he snapped his fingers. "Of course, the one from . . ." Glave trailed off, putting it all together. "He was still in there!" The Rüstov general clapped his hands together. "Sire, you are a genius! Congratulations, Lord Khalix. Your father's faith in you has been rewarded. Your destiny is about to be fulfi—"

Glave was interrupted by a hand at his throat. He gagged and looked with shocked eyes at the newer giant supersoldier who had just grabbed his neck and locked it in a viselike grip. "Khalix, what are you doing?" he sputtered out, gasping for air. Glave thought his master's son was underneath all those layers of armor, but when the supersoldier took off his mask, there was a human face hiding behind it.

"You keep calling me Khalix. The name is *Jack*."

Glave's eyes bugged out. "Impossible!"

Jack shook his head and flashed a devil's grin. "Sorry. No such thing. I keep saying that, but I feel like nobody listens." He lifted Glave off the ground. "Roka, I know you're still in there, so I want to apologize for this in advance. I'm going to put things right, I promise."

Glave clawed at Jack's fingers, trying to pry them from his throat. "Khalix! Wake up! Stop him!"

Jack shook his head. "Khalix isn't home right now. Have fun telling the Magus that his son didn't make the cut." He turned and threw Glave as hard as he could. The Rüstov general went sailing through the air like a home run ball flying out of the park. He landed well out of sight, beyond the scrap-metal hills in the distance, and the Para-Soldiers suddenly lost every ounce of their swagger. They looked at each other in confusion, searching for answers none of them had. The old Revile, too, looked completely bewildered. He approached Jack with extreme caution, as if he were a mirage that might blow away in the ocean breeze.

"I don't understand. What is this?" he asked.

"It's simple. I'm just like you."

"Just like me . . . ?"

"I'm still in control," Jack explained. "I beat them. I just did it sooner than you did."

Despite Jack's explanation, Revile continued to share

the Para-Soldiers' confusion. He looked around, assessing their numbers. "I thought this was an occupying army."

Jack shook his head. "It's an invasion force. They attack at dawn. It's not too late. You and I can stop them."

Revile pondered Jack's words carefully. He looked across the sea and saw that Empire City was still largely intact. "Earth has not yet fallen?"

"Not yet it hasn't." Jack offered Revile his hand. "What do you say? Partners?"

Revile placed his hand on Jack's chest and listened. "You didn't beat your infection. The parasite inside you is fighting to live, even as we speak."

Jack frowned. "You can hear him?"

Revile drew back his hand. "It's not him I feel. You and I are connected. I can feel his effect on you. He'll win out eventually. That will be the end of you." He motioned to the still-intact city across the water. "The end of everything."

"How can you say that? You beat Khalix. What makes you think I can't do the same?"

"Because *we're* the same. I didn't beat Khalix when I was your age. I tried. I failed. It took years before I finally built up the anger and resentment—the willpower—necessary to take back my life."

"*I'm not you.* I'm me. Just me! And I've got plenty of anger and resentment, all right? I don't just want to beat Khalix; I want the Magus, too. I want to beat all of them."

Revile shook his head. "That's impossible."

"Time travel is impossible. This conversation is impossible, but here we are. It's not too late to change tomorrow. It's not too late for the Rüstov's victims, either. We can save them. We can get back the people we lost."

"The people we lost?" Revile looked like he was laughing beneath his mask. "You're dreaming. You'd have to know—"

"I'd have to know how the Rüstov hook into our bodies. How they bond with us. Why don't you know that? Haven't you ever tried to figure it out?"

"Of course I've tried." Revile tapped the power core in his chest. "Whatever part of Khalix that's still alive in here keeps that information hidden from me. The bond is unbreakable. You won't have any more success with it than I did. How could you? Like I said, we're the same."

Jack shook his head. "My life's been different from

yours. Different because of you. You changed things whether you realize it or not. I'm not giving up on this, even if you have."

Revile straightened up. "I never gave up. I tore a hole in time itself to—"

"To kill yourself," Jack said. "All that power the Rüstov gave you, and that's the best plan you could come up with. To kill yourself. Is that really the limit of your creativity? You can stop their ships, same as me. I regenerate, same as you. Let's fight back! They want a war, we'll give them one!" Jack saw Glave high up on a junkyard ridge. He heard the Rüstov general inside his head, trying in vain to speak with Khalix. He waved a hand at Glave and the Para-Soldiers, all of whom kept a very safe distance. "Look at them. They're afraid of us. They know what we're capable of. They know they can't fight us both. We can end this war today. We can end it forever."

Revile looked back at Empire City. "But the future . . . I remember it happening."

"Enough with the future already! If we worry about today, the future will take care of itself." Jack offered his hand to Revile once more. "Please. Fight with me."

Revile just stared at Jack's hand. "I'm no hero."

"That's up to you. A hero is just another name for a person who wants to make a difference. We can do that. We're the key to all of this. Forget about the future. Our time is now."

Revile hesitated a moment, then reached out and took Jack's hand. Jack gripped it hard and shook. With Revile on their side, the Imagine Nation had a better chance than ever before. The Rüstov's future was coming back to haunt them.

CHAPTER

Invasion

Jack and Revile's first order of business before returning to Empire City was freeing the prisoners in the holding pens. The deadly duo quickly scattered any Rüstov guards foolish enough to stand their ground, and ripped up the electrified fences confining Blue, Zhi, and the Varagog Villagers. Revile flew up and orbited the pens, sweeping their perimeter with more gunfire and holding the Rüstov back.

Blue looked up at Revile as the gates fell. "Jack? Is that you?"

"Over here, partner," Jack said, coming up behind

Blue. Blue turned with a jump. His hands were bound behind his back, held there by white-hot electric bolts emanating from a collar around his neck. Jack ripped off the metal collar like it was made of tissue paper. "How do I look?" he asked Blue.

Blue looked back and forth between Jack and Revile. It was easy to tell the difference between the two of them now. Revile was still wearing his iron mask. Blue rubbed his neck and grimaced. "You look *terrible*."

Jack laughed. "Thanks," he said, ripping an identical restraining collar off Zhi. "You guys ready to get out of here?"

"More than ready," Zhi said. "I've got our ride." He pressed a fist into his palm and bowed his head. Lightning crashed and seven serpentine dragons shot out of the ground like a geyser spouting wild, mystical beasts. They roared with feral rage and lashed out at the Rüstov Para-Soldiers with razor-sharp claws. The dragons circled the pens, adding a physical barrier to the barrage of bullets that Revile was laying down. Seconds later, the dragons were all flying back to Empire City, carrying the Rüstov's former prisoners on their backs. Jack carried Blue, whose five-hundred-pound frame felt light as a tuft of cloud in Jack's new ironbound arms.

As they flew across the sea, the tip of Mount Nevertop lit up with a blue glow, and a laser shot out from its peak. The ray of light expanded into a wide beam and rotated around the mountain like a lighthouse beacon. It blinked out after a single revolution, but not before it passed over every ship in the Rüstov blockade.

"Looks like Jazen and Lorem came through," Jack said.

"What was that?" Blue asked.

Jack smiled. "That was Jonas Smart's twisted brain coming in handy again. I never imagined he could be so useful."

Jack and Blue arrived at Hero Square ahead of Revile, Zhi, and the dragons. A massive crowd had assembled on the square, with all the leaders of Empire City present. In Jack's absence, the city had finally united against their common enemy. Virtua led the Mecha forces, Jonas Smart had his WarHawks, and Hovarth commanded an army of warriors from Varagog. Chi and his ZenClan ninjas stood side by side with the ShadowClan shogun and a horde of Ronin assassins. Prime, the Valorian Guard, and a legion of heroes and villains were all there as well. Jack recognized Midknight, Ricochet, Speedrazor, Arsenal, Backstab, and many more. Even Hypnova, Oblivia, and the Secreteers had come. They all stood ready to fight, and the reception they gave Jack reflected that.

A kaleidoscope of ammunition lit up the predawn sky. Jack turned around just in time to shield Blue from harm as the WarHawks, Valorians, and countless others opened fire. A hundred tiny explosions went off all over Jack's body. He felt like he was being pelted with scalding-hot acid rain. The blasts sent him crashing into the square. He hit hard, tearing up the marble flagstones. Blue rolled into the crowd, knocking people down like dominoes. When the bullets stopped flying, Jack stood up and dusted himself off. His body was already repairing itself. "We good?" he asked as his arms, legs, and chest sealed back up with a new armor shell. "Everybody got that out of their system?"

The crowd was about to start shooting again when Revile touched down beside Jack. At first, there was no sound at all, then frightened exclamations broke the silence.

"It's worse than I feared," Smart said as all the color

drained from his face. "This is the end. The end!" Smart's words seemed to serve as permission for the crowd to panic. Blocks of people started screaming and trying to escape.

"There are two of them!"

"Smart was right!"

"Run!"

"Hold your ground!" Skerren shouted. His call was echoed by Hovarth, and for the moment, order was restored. The lord of Varagog turned to his army. "Turn your hearts into fire, men. . . . They're going to attack."

"No they're not," Zhi said, flying into the square and setting the rescued villagers down. They dismounted the dragons and pushed their way through the crowd, rushing back to the walls of Varagog and into the arms of their loved ones.

"What is this?" Skerren asked, looking around in confusion as he saw his countrymen safely returned. "They're bringing people back?"

"Careful," Smart said. "They might be infected."

"No," Midknight said to Smart. He motioned to the Rüstov ships that filled up every inch of the sky. "They've got us completely surrounded. They don't need to sneak in sleeper agents anymore. It's too late in the game for that."

"It's not too late for us," Jack said. "Not as long as the Imagine Nation will stand together and fight."

Midknight's eyes narrowed. "Is that really you talking, Jack?"

Jack held up his scrap-metal arms. "All evidence to the contrary." He took a step toward the crowd. The majority of people bristled with fear. "It's all right. I took all the power they had to give me and I'm ready to use it against them. I survived the Rüstov transformation by nullifying my parasite's signals. Your device worked," he said, raising his chin up at Smart.

"It worked?" Smart repeated, clearly skeptical. He scanned Jack's body with his handheld holo-computer. Jack let him do it.

Trea worked her way through the crowd and went right up to Jack. She stopped a foot away from him and gave his armor a few curious pokes, trying to peel back its layers and look underneath. "I don't understand. If it worked, why did you turn into this?"

"I know it sounds crazy, but that was my choice. I had to do it."

Trea scrunched up her face. "You did this to yourself . . . on purpose?"

Jack gave an apologetic shrug. "I'm sorry if I scared you."

Prime came forward. "You did more than that. Jack, you destroyed the Calculan fleet."

"No, I only blew up half," Jack said. "I was very careful about that. I know it doesn't look like it, but I know what I'm doing. I'm fine, Prime. I'm still in control."

"Not based on these readings," Smart said, holding up his blinking pocket holo-computer. "Your body is rejecting the nullifier I placed inside you. You have an hour at best before it fails. What then?"

"There is no *what then*," Jack replied. "I'm fully infected. When this thing burns out Khalix takes over. My only chance is to get rid of him, get rid of the Magus, or both. We've got sixty minutes to end this war. That's going to have to be enough. This isn't the battle the Rüstov planned on. I'm on your side in this fight." He motioned to Revile. "And so is he."

Noteworthy pushed his way to the front of the crowd. "You expect us to believe that? Look at yourself. You're not even human anymore!"

"There he is," Blue said. "Father of the year."

Noteworthy reddened. "I am *not* his father!"

"I don't care," Jack cut in. "It doesn't matter. Only one thing matters right now. The Rüstov. Jonas Smart was right when he said it's the end. It's *their* end." Jack took a step back and looked at everyone assembled in Hero Square. He was heartened by the completeness of the turnout. "Look at us, all of us here together. *This* is an army. We can end this war today." The crowd looked doubtful. "It's true! Not only did the Rüstov underestimate the Imagine Nation's unity and resolve, but they were stupid enough to give us their ultimate weapon." Jack tapped his own chest and then pointed at Revile. "You're looking at them. They gave us two."

"Can the ultimate weapons use their powers against the Rüstov?" Prime asked.

"We can and will," Jack said.

"Can you force the parasites out of their victim's bodies?" Chi asked. The people in the crowd looked to Jack with hopeful eyes.

"No," Revile said before Jack could reply. "That we cannot do."

"Not yet," Jack added. "I'm trying." He threw Revile a stern look as the sun peeked over the horizon. Dawn had come, and the Magus, using Stendeval's body, appeared on a fresh set of giant holo-screens. As the Rüstov emperor prepared to reissue his ultimatum to the Imagine Nation, the crowd shuddered once again at the reminder of Stendeval's loss.

"People of Empire City," the Magus's voice boomed. "Your time is at an end. My generosity, however, is boundless. I give you this one last chance to spare yourselves unnecessary bloodshed and devastation. Surrender and swear allegiance to the Rüstov. Kneel before me as a sign of your undying fealty, and I will spare your lives."

Jack spun around at the Magus's image. "Is that supposed to be a joke?" he asked, flying up into the air and using his powers to broadcast his response on every screen in Empire City. His face loomed large on the sides of buildings and floating NewsNet screens. "We're not interested in any life with you in it, *Maggot*." The crowd let out a collective gasp. "I've got a counteroffer for you. Pack up your ships, leave now, and don't come back. Ever. You do that and maybe, just maybe, I won't destroy every last one of you. This offer expires in thirty seconds."

The entire city was shocked into silence by the brazen manner in which Jack had addressed the Rüstov emperor. The Magus's eyebrows rose up in surprise, but he did not explode with rage like Jack expected. He showed restraint. "I hope you enjoyed making that little speech," he told Jack, his voice calm and even. "It's going to be the last one you ever deliver. All of you, pay attention. See what happens to those who dare to challenge me." The Magus reached out his hand toward Jack. Jack braced himself, but nothing happened. As long as the nullifier held out, the Magus couldn't hurt him.

Jack snorted out a laugh and held up his arms. "I'm waiting."

The Magus looked back and forth between Jack and Revile. Jack could tell the Rüstov emperor had no idea what was happening, and that was how he wanted to keep it. "Confused?" he taunted the Magus. "It's simple, really. I had it out with Khalix and he lost. Last time we met, you tortured me by helping him attack the uninfected areas of my body. Now that I'm a hundred percent infected, you can't hurt me anymore. You've got nothing left to threaten me with."

The Magus put a clenched fist to his lips, then relaxed his grip, trying to hide his frustration. It was no use. He was practically shaking, he was so angry. "What have you done to my son?"

Jack shook his head. "I told you, he didn't make it. You're dealing with me from now on."

The Magus froze. He gritted his teeth and took several deep breaths, like a bull getting ready to charge. The realization was setting in that his son was gone. At least, that's what Jack wanted him to think. The truth was, Smart's nullifier was getting weaker by the minute. Jack just hoped the Magus wouldn't find out about that until it was too late. Jack figured his best bet was to keep the Magus angry and off balance.

"Time's up," Jack told the Magus. "I need an answer. You going to do the smart thing and run away, or what?" Jack knew the Rüstov emperor wasn't going anywhere. He was just pushing the Magus's buttons.

"I'll give you my answer," the Magus told Jack. "I'll

deliver it to you personally. I swear on my son's heart, I'm going to make you pay."

"It's my heart now," Jack said. "Bring it." He waved at his neck, making a "cut off" motion, and the Magus's holo-screen blinked out. Jack flew back down to Hero Square. The crowd stood in awe of him as he landed.

Noteworthy broke the silence. "Are you insane talking to him like that? Look what you've done!" He pointed up at the sky. The Rüstov Shardwings had begun to move.

"I'm not afraid of them," Jack said, dismissing Noteworthy as the Rüstov fighters descended. "I'm not afraid of what they made me anymore either. I know what I am, and I know what they are—bullies. Overconfident, egotistical bullies. I've been dealing with people like that all my life. You know how you deal with a bully? It's simple. You stand up."

"But you lied to him," Smart said. "Khalix isn't gone. When that nullifier burns out . . ."

"I told you. We're going to have to end this before that happens." Waves of Shardwing fighters fell on the Imagine Nation. It was a huge number of ships, but the heroes all held their ground and prepared to fight. Prime and his men moved forward to join Jack at the front of the crowd. Smart's WarHawks flew to the frontline and armed their weapons. Jack held a hand out behind him, using his powers to freeze them in place. "Stand down," he said.

"The devil we will!" Smart shot back. "Release my WarHawks this instant or I'll—"

"What? What are you going to do?" Jack asked Smart. "You can't hurt me anymore. You can't kill me, so you're just going to have to trust me. Save your bullets. These ships are taken care of."

Jack flew out past the edge of the island to meet the Shardwings. The Rüstov ships passed through him. A mixture of bewilderment and euphoric relief filled Hero Square as the Rüstov fighters streaked across the city like ghosts, unable to attack anything.

"I don't understand," Smart said as Jack flew back and landed next to him. "How is this possible?"

"We made it happen," Virtua said, appearing next to Smart. "In a way, you helped. We couldn't have done it without your SmarterNet."

Smart spun on Virtua. "What?"

Virtua smiled. "One of my tech teams made a few

alterations using the broken Ghost Box from Solomon Roka's ship. It took some doing, but we were able to rebuild the damaged systems in time and modify the SmarterNet to broadcast a phase signal at the Rüstov." She waved up at the harmless Shardwings. "These ships are useless now."

Smart was speechless. As the Rüstov ghost ships continued their futile attempts to attack the city, a wave of confidence swept through the crowd.

"It was Jack's idea," Lorem Ipsum called out, flying in on an AirSkimmer. Jazen Knight was driving. "At the risk of stating the obvious, it was a good one."

"Is that it, then?" Hovarth asked. "The armada isn't a threat anymore?"

"No, that's not it," Prime said. "We just evened the odds. The Rüstov's cannon fodder is gone, but the real firepower is waiting beyond those clouds." He turned to Jack. "Why, Jack? Why did you destroy even half of the Calculan fleet? What possible good can come from that?"

Chi tapped Prime's shoulder. "Perhaps we should direct that question to the other half." Prime turned around and saw that the remaining Calculan ships had all moved into a defensive position around the city. As the drones armed their weapons, the members of the Calculan Delegation joined the crowd in Hero Square. Ambassador Equa walked up to Prime and whispered in his ear.

Midknight held out a hand toward the alien diplomats. "I don't want to speak for Ambassador Equa, but I have a hunch that right now he's telling Prime that the variables in his decision matrix have changed."

"Changed?" Noteworthy said. "Changed how?"

"By taking out just over half of his remote-controlled battleships, I swung the odds to the point where the Calculans can't go it alone anymore. Now their best option is to fight with us." Once Jack had finished explaining his actions, Prime nodded to the crowd, confirming everything he had just said.

"That's brilliant," Blue said. "How did you come up with that one?"

Jack shrugged. *That's what a ticket to the Theater of War will get you,* he thought. It was an idea he never would have come up with if the Rüstov hadn't paraded an endless loop of military campaigns before his eyes. They thought they could brainwash and break him. All they had done was turn him into a master strategist. A veteran of a hundred wars he never actually fought in.

"What's next?" Jazen asked Jack. "Any other crazy plans up your sleeve that we need to know about?"

Jack shook his head. "The rest of this is as simple as it gets." He looked at Skerren. "If you want to kill a snake, you have to cut off the head. That's not me. That's the Magus."

Skerren stepped cautiously toward Jack. "The Magus is Stendeval."

Jack nodded. "I didn't say it was going to be easy."

"What about you?" Skerren asked. "What about when your hour is up? What then?"

"Stendeval said I'd only become Revile if I chose to be. This is as far as that goes. Look here." Jack pointed out the mark Skerren had carved into his power core. "You did that. Standing right over there, you took a slice out of me. Nothing else has even scuffed this thing. If my time runs out before I can halt this infection or anyone else's . . . if I'm about to turn into Revile for real? You'll see to it that I don't." Jack offered Skerren his hand. "Are you with me?"

Skerren paused to look at Jack's iron fingers.

"I don't like this," Jazen told Jack.

"I don't like it either," Skerren said. "But I promise you, I won't hesitate." He took Jack's hand in his. "I'm with you."

A new wave of Rüstov ships broke through the clouds and dove toward Empire City. There were fighter planes and troop transports bringing in leagues of Para-Soldiers. The massive dreadnoughts were off in the distance, and it was plain to see that they were not phased. "This is it," Jack said. "Time to end this war once and for all."

CHAPTER

The Children's
Crusade

The fight was like nothing Jack had ever been involved in before. His greatest and most death-defying adventures had never approached anything even close to this scale—an entire city at war with an invading alien force. The Rüstov fighters, both on the ground and in the air, were too numerous to count. Not an inch of ground offered shelter from the storm.

Jack immediately went into attack mode. He flew around the square, using his powers to wreck Rüstov ships and disable enemy soldiers as they came in. Revile did the same, blasting Shardwings and troop transports in every direction. The air was alive with gunfire, and the ground was filled with Para-Soldiers. The Rüstov attacked with overwhelming force, but the people of Empire City fought back at every turn. Smart's WarHawks and the people of Varagog charged into battle together with Virtua and the androids of Machina. Unmanned Calculan drones streaked through the sky alongside brave Valorians, and heroes fought side by side with their archenemies. The time for politics and infighting was over. The time for sitting on the sidelines and weighing the options was over. It was time for action.

As Jack continued his assault on the Rüstov Armada, he scanned the enemy fleet for the Magus's ship, the *Apocalypse*. "He's not here."

"What?" Revile asked.

"The Magus isn't here. We're gonna have to go to him." Jack looked around. "Zhi, where are you?"

"Way ahead of you," Zhi called out. He swooped down to Jack's level, riding one of his dragons. It was the same dragon Jack thought he had gotten killed two days earlier. The creature gave an angry snort in his direction. Zhi stroked the dragon's mane. "Easy, girl, we're all friends here." He directed Jack's attention to the other six dragons and their riders: Jazen, Skerren, Lorem Ipsum, and Trea's three selves.

"Let's take this fight to that metal monster's door," Jack said.

"I'm coming with you," Revile said.

Jack shook off his future self. "No way. The city needs you here." He motioned to the sky as Prime and the Valorians blasted away at Rüstov Shardwings. Down on the ground, Mechas, ninjas, WarHawks, heroes, and villains were all fighting for their home and their lives. "They're outnumbered. They need your firepower." He pointed up at Mount Nevertop. "Protect the SmarterNet and keep that ghost signal broadcasting. Protect the *people*. They need you more than we do."

Revile raised his left hand and blew a Rüstov Shardwing out of the sky. "You can't go up against the Magus with children. You need an army to take on that ship."

"Actually, a small force like this has the best chance of slipping through the blockade," one of the Treas said.

"And, hello? We're not just children," Lorem added.

"Thank you," a second Trea said. "We're in the School of Thought. We're better than an army." She held out her hand, and the third Trea slapped it.

Revile just shook his head and leaned in close to Jack. "You really think you can beat him? That you can break the bond between parasite and host?"

"It's not impossible," Jack said. "That's just what they want us to think. That's job one with them. Inspire fear. Think about it. All this time, they've been trying to make us give up. They've done everything they can to make sure we don't put up a fight. They want us to make it easy for them. Stendeval told the Magus he wasn't ready for us. I think he was right. That's why he waited until dawn to invade. He was waiting for Stendeval to power up again. He wanted every advantage he could get, but the real advantage is us. Me and you, fighting together. Stay here. Save lives. It's time for you to be a hero again, Revile."

Revile thought a bit more, then finally nodded and reached out to the Rüstov ships in the air around him. Metal fragments flew off their exteriors and attached themselves to his body, bulking up his armor's strength and size. Heavy artillery ripped off Shardwing hulls, drawn to him as if pulled by an electromagnet. Revile's armor came alive, integrating the additional weaponry into his systems. New plasma cannons, rocket launchers, flame-throwers, and guns heaped themselves onto his shoulders and arms. He became a walking armory. When he was finished upgrading, he rested a hand on Jack's shoulder. "I was wrong about you. We're not the same. I don't remember ever being this strong."

Jack went to touch Revile's hand, but Revile broke away and flew off without another word. Jack watched his doppelgänger go. He hoped they would both still be alive when this was all over.

Jazen tapped his wrist. "The clock is ticking, Jack. Let's go."

Jack nodded. "Follow me."

Jack led the way toward the *Apocalypse*. An string of explosions heated up the cool morning air as he ran interference for his friends on the dragons. The enemy invaders had brought out the heavy artillery to face Jack, and he was hit again and again by shots fired from large-caliber weapons. The Rüstov bombarded Jack with missile launchers and fusion cannons. The attacks came from both the city below and the skies above. Some bombs blew up right next to Jack, sending him hurtling through the clouds. Others scored direct hits and tore off whole pieces of his body. That was all fine by him. As long as he continued to draw the Rüstov's fire, his friends were able to advance untouched. It took only a few moments for Jack to recover from each hit, regain his bearings, and dive back into the fight. Try as they might, the Rüstov succeeded only in briefly disorienting Jack. He lost his focus on the battle each time he regenerated, which was an annoying side effect of his new healing abilities, but it was way better than the alternative.

Jack shook off the Rüstov's latest assault and turned to find a trio of Shardwings closing in on his friends. He reached out his right hand and made a fist. As he tightened his grip, the ship in the middle crumpled up like a piece of scrap paper and dropped out of formation. Black smoke streaked across the sky as it fell crashing into the ocean. Jack swung his arm out in a dismissive wave, forcing the Shardwing on the left to ram into the one on the right. Stendeval had always said the Rüstov would rue the day they infected him. Jack's powers were a silver bullet aimed at the heart of the Rüstov Armada, and thanks to the Revile process, he was now all but invulnerable while he used them.

As Jack's friends cleared Empire City's airspace and left the Imagine Nation behind, Jack held back. He had spotted Prime attacking an armored transport filled with Para-Soldiers. The Circleman of Galaxis had at least six Valorian Guardsmen with him as he tried to stop the ship from reaching Empire City. It took Jack only a single glance to find out everything he needed to know about the Rüstov vessel. He held out his hand like a traffic cop and halted the ship in place. Taking control of the transport's forward thrusters, Jack forced it to turn upward, exposing its weakest point. Prime's men all keyed on the ship's thinly armored underbelly and fired. White-hot energies poured out of their hands, and another Rüstov ship burned a hole in the sky. No handshakes or fist pumps followed the explosion. The ship was just one target in a field of thousands. Prime gave a cordial nod in Jack's direction and moved on. Five seconds later, he and his men had knocked five more Shardwings out of the sky. The falling ships shot Jack's body to pieces on their way down, but it didn't matter. Jack drew on them for spare parts as they fell and put himself back together at their expense. He turned back toward the clouds above and kept going up. There were still more Rüstov ships between Jack and the Magus, but he wasn't worried. They couldn't touch him. Everything they had was his for the taking. At least until Smart's nullifier burned out.

"I wonder how the Rüstov like getting a taste of their own medicine," Zhi said as the enemy ships that Jack had used to rebuild himself spiraled down into the sea.

Jazen trained a plasma cannon on a Shardwing fighter just over Zhi's left shoulder and fired. "I'm guessing not very much."

"Turnabout is fair play," said Skerren, slicing wings off a few Rüstov gunships of his own. "The trouble is, Jack's only one person."

"Actually, he's two," one of the Treas said. "Revile's still down there, remember?"

Skerren grunted. "Even the two of them can't take out the whole Rüstov fleet at once. There's too many ships."

Jack pointed ahead as the *Apocalypse* came into view. "As far as I'm concerned, there's only one ship that matters."

Jack tried to sound confident, but Skerren's point was well taken. Even with half the Rüstov fleet rendered useless, they seemed to have an endless amount of ships. The armada was far too vast for him to bring down in an hour, even with Revile's help. That wasn't how the Imagine Nation was going to win. For that, Jack needed to figure out how the Rüstov bonded with their host bodies. The war, and his own survival, depended on it. Jack used his powers to search out the roots of infection inside both himself and the Para-Soldiers attacking him. If Smart's nullifier ran out before he unlocked the secrets of his Rüstov connection, it was over. Everything was over.

The *Apocalypse*'s escort of Shardwings fired on Jack and his friends as they approached. A volley of missiles closed in on Jack, and he morphed his arms into fusion cannons. Steam rose from the barrels as he fired on the missiles and the ships that had unleashed them. With every target that burst into flames, Jack felt a pang of guilt for the host body that died with each parasite. The more he investigated his bond with Khalix, the more he felt the presence of people who were still alive inside each Rüstov invader. Jack didn't want to kill the enemy's host bodies.

They were innocent victims. He wanted to save them along with everybody else. His own constant blowing up and regeneration caused Jack no physical pain, but the battle itself was starting to take a mental toll.

Skerren seemed to pick up on Jack's feelings of remorse as they reached the Magus's ship. "Harden your heart," he told Jack. "There'll be time to mourn the dead later. This is war. Like it or not, we kill our enemies to survive. It's the only way."

Jack scrunched up his lips like he had a bad taste in his mouth. "I know." He was about to blast a new door into the *Apocalypse*'s side, but Skerren grabbed him by the shoulder and made sure he had his full attention.

"It only gets worse from this point on, Jack. You better be ready for this. Tell me now if you're not."

Jack looked at Skerren. "I don't have a choice. I have to be. If there's any chance I can get Stendeval back, I have to do it. If there's any way to save Allegra . . ." Jack shook his head. "She backed me up from the beginning. She never once thought about herself. It was always me. She was always right there protecting *me*. I can't leave her like that."

Skerren nodded. "You better be ready for what's necessary in case you can't save her. In case you can't save yourself. I don't want to hear about what choices you have or don't have. I want an answer. What are you prepared to do?"

Jack took a breath. Everything he'd learned since he came to the Imagine Nation flashed before his eyes in an instant. He used to think a hero was a man in a cape who fought bad guys in a comic book and always won. Now he knew better. A hero was someone who tried to make a difference, even when everyone else thought all hope was lost. Being a hero meant putting the needs of others before your own. Being a hero meant sacrifice.

What am I prepared to do?

Jack raised a fist toward the hull of the Rüstov emperor's flagship. "Whatever it takes."

CHAPTER

23

The Hero's Journey

The second Jack blasted his way into the *Apocalypse*, enemy laserfire blasted back out. Once again, he took point. Jack charged ahead and raced down a corridor, crashing into Rüstov Para-Soldiers as he went. He left a trail of broken bodies in his wake and cut a path for his friends to follow. The Magus was on board. Jack could feel his presence. He motioned to his friends. "Come on."

The ship's hallways were dark, with only a sporadic placement of bare bulbs to light the way. Jack led the others into a massive hangar bay filled with starfighters and other

Rüstov aircraft. Bright fluorescent lights switched on as they entered. When Jack's eyes adjusted, he saw a legion of Para-Soldiers lining the walls. There were hundreds of them inside the hangar, but one stood out from all the others.

"Is that Roka?" Jazen asked, pointing up at a figure on a balcony.

Jack pushed Jazen's arm down. "Not right now, it's not."

Glave waved a hand and turned to exit the room. "Kill them."

"Go! Find cover!" Jack yelled as he flew up into the air, shooting at the Rüstov before they had a chance to follow Glave's orders. The rotating barrels of his plasma cannons spun like wheels as he unloaded on the Para-Soldiers and drew their fire. Jack jammed as many Rüstov weapons as he could while his friends took shelter behind a group of Shardwings.

"They've got us surrounded!" Zhi shouted.

Skerren scraped his swords together. "That's their problem." He shot out at the Rüstov like a boulder fired from a Varagog catapult. Skerren's arms whirled like windmills as he sliced away at the horde of Para-Soldiers. Jazen, Zhi,

Lorem, and Trea watched in wonder as he attacked without fear or hesitation.

Jazen pulled a pair of blasters out from his shoulder holsters. "Kid's got a point. These punks surrounded the wrong people." He reached over the top of the Shardwing and fired on a ship that was parked across the room. His shots pierced the ship's fuel tank, and the resulting explosion took out at least ten Para-Soldiers. He targeted more ships as Zhi, Lorem, and Trea ran out into the fray and took on the Rüstov directly. Jack watched them go as the Rüstov knocked him out of the sky. Their bullets had absolutely shredded his body.

Pieces of Jack scattered across the hangar as he fell. He just grunted and put himself back together. As his arms and legs rebuilt themselves, a Para-Soldier moved in to finish him off. Jack hit it with a faceful of lasers before it got close enough to do any damage. As soon as Jack was back in one piece, he sprang to his feet and charged into a Rüstov platoon. They went down like bowling pins. Another squad of Para-Soldiers shot him in the back, but he took it in stride and spun around to tag them with a laser blast of his own. This one he fired out of the power core in his chest. A thick beam of red energy poured out of Jack like a jet stream of water gushing forth from an open fire hydrant. The blast burned clean through the squad of Rüstov troops, taking them all out with a single shot.

Jack ripped machine parts off the nearest Shardwing and shoved them into his body wherever he was damaged. He didn't wait until he was healed to find a new target. He didn't have time. A swarm of Para-Soldiers had piled on Jazen and was trying to tear him apart. Jack quickly pulled two of them off and tossed them into the air. Skerren cut them in half before they landed. Jazen threw off his other attackers and emptied his blasters into them. Before Jazen could even blink, a fresh unit of Para-Soldiers rushed him from behind, hitting him like a freight train. Jack ran after him, but a new group of Para-Soldiers blocked his path. He took aim at them with his plasma guns, but they all jumped out of the way as their comrades rolled in with a large cannon. A plume of smoke shot out of the barrel as the Rüstov fired on Jack. He tried to use his powers on the missile they had shot at him, but nothing happened. It wasn't until it hit him in the chest that he realized it was a cannonball.

Jack went flying back into the wall. He hit it hard and

belly flopped down onto the ground, landing right next to a wounded Para-Soldier. It was creeping up on Lorem Ipsum, no doubt looking to trade up to a new host. Jack grabbed it by the shoulder and hijacked the techno-organic armaments that covered its host body, using them to repair his own. The stripped-down Para-Soldier fell in front of Lorem like a toothless tiger. She nodded at Jack and gave him a little salute. Jack returned the gesture and went right back to shooting Para-Soldiers. Lorem did the same, going back to flipping around and fighting Rüstov invaders hand to hand. Her "gibberish touch" powers weren't much help in this battle, but she was still as agile and deadly as any hero Jack had ever seen. Zhi, who had learned karate at the feet of his mentor, Chi, was just as dangerous. His fists broke Rüstov bones like they were wooden boards in a dojo, and his roundhouse kicks sent Para-Soldiers flying through the air. Trea's three selves worked together with coordinated attack moves that the Rüstov couldn't counter, and Jazen kept going no matter what the Rüstov threw at him. Jack and his friends were more than a match for the Magus's foot soldiers, but they were still outnumbered twenty to one.

"This is taking too long," Jack said to himself. At this rate,

Smart's nullifier would burn out long before he reached the Magus, and he still didn't know how to separate a Rüstov parasite from its host body. He had to speed things up.

Jack used his powers to arm all the weapons at his disposal—every gun and missile on every aircraft in the hangar. He set his sights on the field of Rüstov soldiers fighting his friends and unleashed an unbroken string of rapid-fire shots. His connection with each ship's precision targeting system ensured he hit only the Rüstov. The Para-Soldiers all dropped to the ground and the room got very still. Zhi, Jazen, Lorem, and Trea looked around with unexpected relief. Skerren was all business. He pulled a sword from a Para-Soldier's chest and nodded to an open door on the far side of the hangar. Jack nodded back and ran through it.

The next group of Rüstov soldiers Jack and his friends encountered put up less of a fight. They were Rüstov nobles and clearly weren't expecting an assault while on board the *Apocalypse*. Jack and the others hit them hard and fast. They went down easily, but the battle was hard to stomach. The nobles had all taken fresh hosts. They didn't look like robot-zombies; they looked like people.

Their appearance made dealing with them so much more difficult, but Jack told himself he had no choice. *Until I have another way to fight them, this is it,* he thought. When it was over, Jack knelt down by the fallen nobles to try and learn something from their bodies. He had very little experience dealing with the Rüstov's upper class. He hoped they could tell him something that the withered Left-Behinds he was used to dealing with could not.

Using his powers, Jack reached out to the few mechanical parts he could find in the dying host bodies all around him. There wasn't much for him to work with. So far, the virus had only bonded with each host's nervous system enough for the parasite's consciousness to take over.

"What's the verdict?" Jazen asked. He didn't have to get any more specific than that. Jack knew what he was asking. Was he going to be able to unhook the parasites from their hosts? Was he going to be able to save Stendeval, Allegra, Roka . . . everybody?

Jack shook his head. "Jury's still out."

"Jury's still out?" Skerren repeated.

Jack reached out to every dying Rüstov infection in the room. He could see pieces of the puzzle, but he couldn't put it all together yet. "I'm working on it. I just can't figure out where the Rüstov ends and the person begins. The connection's too complex for me to unravel in my head. I can't see it."

"I don't understand," Trea said. "The nullifier's still blocking Khalix. You're using your powers on Rüstov technology now. Shouldn't you be able to see it?"

Jack touched his power core. "I can't even see it inside myself. I thought I'd be able to, once I let this happen to me, but . . ."

"What's stopping you?" Skerren asked.

Jack frowned. "Khalix is. Whatever influence he has that isn't being blocked by the nullifier is hiding this from me. It's just like with Revile."

"Not *just* like Revile, right, Jack?" Jazen asked.

Jack didn't answer.

"Jack?" Jazen said again.

Zhi tapped Jack's shoulder. "C'mon, Jack. Say something."

Jack stood up. "The clock is ticking. Let's move."

As Jack and his friends pressed on, they heard the sound of rockets launching and explosions going off outside the ship. "I wonder how it's going out there," Trea said.

Jack didn't have to wonder. That was the other reason he wanted Revile to stay behind. His future self was mostly machine, just like him. Jack reached out with his powers and looked through Revile's eyes to see how the war was going down on the ground. At the moment, Revile was in Karateka.

Jack saw Chi and his arch nemesis, the ShadowClan shogun, fighting back to back against a throng of Para-Soldiers. The master of the ZenClan ninjas and the lord of the Ronin assassins were working together. Jack could not envision any other scenario in which this could have taken place. Glowing blue lights emanated from Chi's fists as he hacked away at the Rüstov with his bare hands and threw fireballs into them. Dark black energy flowed from the wicked shogun's hands as he did the same. He swung out a flattened palm, and black light trailed from his fingertips. Revile joined the Ronin assassins and ZenClan ninjas as they overtook the Para-Soldiers, and Jack broke contact. He turned his attention back to the task at hand. He turned his attention inward. As he and his friends fought their way through the ship, he kept trying to solve the riddle of his connection with Khalix. So far, he had come up with nothing. It was hard to concentrate amid all the chaos and fire.

Jack smashed open a set of iron doors and found another small army of Para-Soldier shock troops waiting behind it. He fired two shots from his fusion cannons at them and followed that up with a six-pack of missiles, each one no bigger than a Magic Marker. Bright orange streaks of fire screamed across the sky as the minirockets took out the Rüstov's front line. Jack winced as they exploded. More lives lost . . . but what choice did he have?

Jack resolved to deal with his conscience later. Right now he had to save whatever lives he could, starting with his friends'. They didn't have time to fight through another Para-Soldier battalion. He ignited a pair of pilot lights on the insides of his wrists and pumped aerosol fuel out through tiny holes in the palms of his hands. Giant tentacles of fire leaped from Jack's arms and lashed out at the grimy Rüstov foot soldiers. He waved his hands back and forth, creating a wall of flames that they couldn't get through. Each lowly Para-Soldier's dilapidated machine parts were covered in grease and flammable liquids. They didn't dare approach Jack's fiery blockade. They could shoot through it, but they were shooting blind.

"Skerren, cut through that wall!" Jack shouted, pointing. "We're getting out of here now."

Skerren did as he was told and carved a giant circle into the wall on his left. Zhi threw a jump kick at it, and together they made an instant door. A giant piece of the wall went flying into the engine room on the other side. Everybody ran through the opening. Jack went last, still using his flamethrowers to hold back the Rüstov soldiers behind them. There were more Para-Soldiers up ahead, but the odds were much better in the engine room.

"Which way, Jack?" Jazen asked as he threw a hard right cross at an advancing Para-Soldier, dropping it where it stood. The former emissary picked the Para-Soldier up and swung it around like a throwing hammer. When he let go, the lulled Para-Soldier went sailing into the towering column of white-hot energy that powered the ship's Infinite Warp Core. Jack watched it go. The column rose up three hundred feet into the air. He felt for the Magus.

"Up there," Jack said.

"Not a problem," Zhi said as he threw an elbow into a Para-Soldier's jaw, snapping its neck back. "We've got room for my dragons in here."

Zhi was about to call in his seven flying serpents, but Jack stopped him. He used his powers to grab hold of a team of Rüstov sentries that were flying around the engine room on jet packs. "How about I give you a ride for once, Zhi?"

A minute later, all of Jack's friends were strapping jet packs onto their backs, even Skerren. "I don't like this," Skerren said as Trea helped him get his pack on. "I don't like using machines."

"You want your shot at the Magus, don't you?" Lorem asked. She reached over and hit the button to fire his rockets. "Make an exception."

Skerren went soaring up into the sky. Jack flew after him and used his powers to straighten out his flight path. Once Skerren got the hang of flying, Jack let him take the reins and go off on his own. Jazen, Lorem, Zhi, and Trea took off after them, and they all flew up alongside the gleaming pillar of energy in the center of the engine room.

Jack led the way, firing round after round from his fusion cannons up at the ceiling. The Magus's throne room was waiting on the next floor.

As Jack closed in on his target, he could feel Khalix fighting against Smart's nullifier. The Rüstov prince's power was rising within him. He didn't have much time left. *I can do this,* Jack told himself. *Stendeval was right. We can beat them. I know we can. . . .*

Jack checked in once more on the battle in Empire City. Revile was flying from borough to borough, helping out wherever he was needed. Down on the ground, Jack saw a legion of armed androids from Machina advancing on the Rüstov and pushing them back. They were moving up the streets in platoons, laying down cover fire for each other and taking back block after block. Glowing projections of Virtua were blinking in and out all over the battlefield, directing them as they fought.

Up in the air, Prime and his men were fighting alongside the Calculan drones and Smart's WarHawks. Ricochet was there too, bouncing around the sky like a racquetball made out of thermite. Powerful bursts of energy exploded on every ship she hit. Down in Hero Square, Speedrazor rushed through the crowd, cutting Rüstov Para-Soldiers to ribbons. He had reunited with a few other former Peacemakers. Battlecry, Flex, Harrier, and Surge fought with him. Villains like Backstab, Pain, Arsenal, and Fugazi were there, too. Everyone was fighting the Rüstov, even the Secreteers. Jack saw bursts of black smoke firing up out of the ground, behind monuments, and up in the air. With every cloud of smoke that appeared, a hooded Secreteer sprang out and struck a Para-Soldier, then vanished before the mists even started to fade. The Mysterrii were right there with them, flipping all around the square and stabbing at the Rüstov with little knives.

Jack's spirits were lifted by the courage of the people down below. He had to come through for them. He had to finish this. All the while he fought the Rüstov, he studied his own techno-organic makeup. He was almost there. Jack blasted through the roof of the engine room and into the grand hallway outside the Magus's throne room. The way inside was blocked by a regiment of armored guards . . . and a friend.

"Allegra?" Jack said. He knew she wasn't in control of her body, but she still looked exactly like herself. Seeing Allegra guarding the Magus's door stopped Jack's heart cold. While he was distracted, the imperial guard filled the air with cluster bombs. They blanketed the hall with explosions before Jack could lift a finger to stop them.

Shrapnel stabbed Jack like a million tiny daggers. He couldn't be permanently harmed by such an attack, but his friends were another story. He heard them scream as the bombs went off throughout the hall. When the dust settled, Jack scanned his friends for vital signs. Jazen's and Skerren's injuries were minor, but Lorem Ipsum, Trea, and Zhi were seriously wounded. He could hear the footsteps of the imperial guards coming down the hall to kill them. Jack put himself back together and got up angrily. He had seen too many good people hurt by the Rüstov for one day. This was where it stopped.

"Stay down," Jack told Jazen and Skerren. He shot out a hand, and the imperial guards running toward him froze in place. He made a fist, and their knees folded over in the wrong direction. Jack locked a plasma cannon on the next row of guards and fired. They tried to fire back, but he wouldn't let them. He rose up into the air, holding his hands out in front of him. They glowed with lines of energy that ran out in circuit-like patterns. More Rüstov guards ran into the hall shooting at Jack, then suddenly stopped and shot each other instead. Their bombs blew up while still in their hands. Their weapons misfired. Jack moved slowly toward the throne room entrance, taking the Magus's guards apart piece by piece as he went.

The Rüstov Allegra ran inside and locked the door behind her, leaving her men to face Jack alone. They didn't stand a chance. Jack was learning more and more about how the Rüstov worked. The harder he fought, the more things he discovered. The more he discovered, the more weaknesses he found to exploit. There were so many things he could do to them. Knowledge was power, and the battlefield had turned into Jack's classroom. He reached the throne room door. A few inches of iron was all that separated him from the Magus. Jack knew the Rüstov emperor didn't fear him. To the Magus, he was nothing more than a puppet for his son to control. The Magus had worked hard to make Jack accept that fate. He thought he could break him. The Magus tried to teach him the Rüstov way of life. He didn't realize Jack had been studying how to be a hero ever since he opened his first comic book.

His final test was about to begin.

CHAPTER

The Sacrifice

Jack used his powers to open up the throne room doors. They quietly slid apart to reveal the Magus sitting in his throne on the far side of the room. Glave was on one side of him and the infected Allegra on the other. Other than that, the room was empty. The Magus appeared relaxed. He and his minions were quiet and still, waiting for Jack as if on display. Jack could see what they were doing. It was more psychological warfare. The Rüstov were hiding behind the faces of his friends and loved ones, taking full advantage of his feelings for them. It was standard operating procedure for the Rüstov; Jack knew it all too well. That didn't make it any less effective. Jack steeled his nerves and walked inside, leaving Skerren and Jazen in the hall to tend to their wounded friends.

It was calm inside the throne room. Outside the ship, Jack could hear the muffled sounds of bullets and laser blasts firing without pause. In the air over the city, Valorian Guardsmen, Calculan drones, and WarHawk troopers blew up ship after Rüstov ship. Down on the ground, heroes and villains were pushing the Rüstov back, but this battle, here in this room . . . this was the key. This was where the war would truly be won or lost.

"You've got determination. I'll grant you that," said the Magus. "This has gone on far longer than I expected."

Jack swallowed hard, trying his best to keep up a brave front. "I warned you what would happen if you didn't pack up and leave. I'll give you one last chance to get out of here before we finish you." Jack hoped he sounded more confident than he felt. He could only hope Smart's nullifier would hide Khalix's presence from the Magus long enough for Jack to do what he came to do. In an ideal world, he wouldn't have forced a confrontation with the Magus until he was absolutely sure how to play his trump card and break Stendeval free of his control. He didn't have the luxury of going the ideal route. Nothing about Jack's situation had ever remotely resembled ideal. He could feel Khalix inside his mind, fighting to make his voice heard. The nullifier was holding out, but this close to his father, the Rüstov prince was at his strongest.

The Magus got up and flexed the winglike spikes on his back. "Still haven't learned to hold your tongue, I see." He shook his finger at Jack like he was a child that needed to be punished. "Kill his friends."

Glave and the Rüstov Allegra stepped down and left their emperor's side. Jack raised his weapons toward them, but that was just his reflexes kicking in. He couldn't fire on Roka and Allegra. It didn't matter how many Rüstov he'd taken down up to that point. These two were using his friends as their hosts. They walked past Jack unmolested. Out in the hall, Skerren and Jazen stood up and got ready to fight.

"Which one do you want?" Skerren asked Jazen.

Jazen shook his head. "Neither, not that it matters. I'll take Roka."

Skerren spun his swords and settled into a fighting stance as the infected Allegra closed in on him. "Jack, you have to let me know if you're in trouble. You know what I mean. If you're running out of time, I'm trusting you to say so."

Jack put up a hand. "I know, Skerren. Don't say anything else. Just hold out as long as you can, all right?"

"Right," Skerren said, ducking down as a razor-sharp liquid metal arm shot past his ear. "Easier said than done. Holding out means holding back while she tries to kill me."

"Just do your best, both of you," Jack said. "It's always been enough before."

"True," Jazen said as Glave went at him holding a pair of ion blades that glowed with deadly radiation. "Trouble is, Allegra's and Roka's best have always been pretty good too." Jack kept trying to figure out how to extricate his infected friends from their parasites, but it was hard to concentrate with the Magus right there. The fact that he was using Stendeval's body made it even worse.

The Magus got up off his throne. "You've been a worthy adversary, boy, but you've taken things as far as they can go. This only ends one way." The Magus walked up to

Jack and stopped less than two inches from his face. Seeing the look of an enemy in Stendeval's eyes was positively gut-wrenching for Jack. Talking to him on the holo-screen was bad enough, but being face-to-face with him was infinitely worse.

"Do you really think you've accomplished something here?" the Magus asked in a voice still partly Stendeval's. He motioned to the window and the battle raging outside. "That's nothing. Less than nothing. The losses out there don't concern me. The only thing that concerns me is my son." The Magus waved a hand, and Stendeval's trademark red energy particles spiraled out of his fingers. A chill ran down Jack's spine. The Magus wielding Stendeval's power was a nightmare made real. He could do almost anything now. The Rüstov emperor rubbed his fingers together and smiled. "This host body is truly something. So much potential."

The Magus pointed at Jack, and jagged, deep-crimson versions of Stendeval's superpowered energies shot down from the sky like lightning. The bolts blew a hole in the roof of the throne room and struck Jack down. He felt pain like he'd never felt before. Electric fireballs lodged in his body, bouncing around inside of him like trapped animals trying to claw their way out. Jack screamed as the red lightning burst from his chest and shot out in twelve different directions. The second it was gone, another bolt dropped out of the sky and hit him again. His body was burning and his teeth crackled with bloodred electricity. Jack was on the verge of passing out when the Magus halted his attack.

"Now. I'm going to give you one last chance to let me speak to my son."

Jack propped himself up on all fours and spit on the ground. His saliva tasted like motor oil in his mouth. He wiped his lip and gave the Magus a defiant stare. "I told you. Khalix is gone. He's not coming back." It was a blatant lie. Khalix was pounding on the door of his subconscious at that very moment, but the Magus didn't need to know that.

The Magus's eyes narrowed into thin slits. Jack could tell he was seething, but he didn't act on his anger just yet. Instead, he put his hand on the back of Jack's head and spoke softly. "Khalix. I know you're in there. If you can hear me, say something."

The Magus's hands glowed with red energy, and once

again, Jack spoke in Khalix's voice. "Father . . . is that you?"

The Magus's eyes widened, eager for more. "I'm here, Khalix. Talk to me."

Jack's eyes were shut tight. "Father, I need . . ." Jack trailed off, straining to keep the words in. "I need you to—"

"Yes? Tell me!"

Jack stood up. "I need you to get this through your thick skull . . . Khalix doesn't live here anymore." The muscles in his face relaxed into a cocky grin. "You blew it, Magus. Khalix is over. He's done."

The Magus pulled back his hand and straightened up with a jolt. Jack heard him let out a low, guttural growl as he took a step back. He didn't like being made a fool of, and he liked the idea of losing his son to Jack even less. The Magus reached out his hand again. Jack could feel him scanning his systems. He held his breath as the Rüstov emperor looked for traces of Khalix inside him.

"There's nothing there," the Magus said after what felt like an eternity to Jack but was really just a few seconds. "It's just static." He was devastated. Jack exhaled, safe in the knowledge that Khalix's voice was still being drowned out by the nullifier. His relief would be short-lived. The Magus's face filled up with enough rage to form an expression that Jack was certain Stendeval had never made once in all his years.

This is gonna hurt . . . , Jack thought.

The Rüstov emperor cried out with every ounce of wrath and fury in his body, and crimson spears of pure energy impaled Jack's arms, legs, torso, and neck. Jack staggered about in agony as they wrenched him apart like levers. His body attempted to heal itself, but the spears lit up again, crackling with the full measure of the Magus's wrath. The pain was incredible, but Jack had to endure it. The only way to hide Khalix from the Magus was to distract him with rage. To keep him angry and unfocused. Being drawn in by Jack's deception had unleashed new levels of anger within the Rüstov emperor. "Insolent meatbag," the Magus grunted as he picked Jack up. "I'll kill you for this. Kill you!"

The Magus threw Jack across the room. He crashed into a steel girder hard enough to leave an impression of his body on its face and fell on the floor. Jack got up, beginning to question the wisdom of his plan. He tried to keep thinking about unraveling his bond with Khalix, but he couldn't focus. The energy spears lodged in his body had dissipated, but the Magus had more where they came from. He materialized above Jack using Stendeval's teleportation technique and raised a fist that was crackling with power. The Magus punched Jack so hard he drove him halfway through the floor. He lowered himself down and hit Jack again. Jack went flying out of the room as if pulled by an invisible cable. He crashed through the throne room doors, heading toward his friends in the hall.

He fell into the pile of Rüstov guards he had fought on the way in. Jack scrambled to his feet, looking for something—anything—he could use to buy himself more time. Jack used his powers to reanimate the fallen imperial guards and march them at the Magus. The Rüstov emperor threw his arms out in a wide sweeping motion and shredded them before they got anywhere near him. He turned them into confetti without so much as a second thought. His effortless command of Stendeval's powers was frightening. Jack backpedaled, looking for a way out. There was nowhere to go. What was he going to do? He couldn't fight the Magus while Stendeval was fully charged with power, even if he could bring himself to attack him.

Next to Jack, Jazen was fighting Glave. Conscience had tied his hands as well. As a Mecha, Jazen's metal body was far stronger than Roka's human form, but Jazen didn't want to hurt him. Jack could see him trying to keep Glave at a distance while the Rüstov general went at him with his energy blades going full tilt. Across the hall, the Rüstov Allegra swung machete-shaped arms at Skerren with reckless abandon. Skerren was totally on defense, ducking, dodging, blocking, and flipping around every attack he could. He cried out as the edge of a silvery blade sliced across his back. He quickly turned to block the next attack and fell back to regroup. He did a double take when he saw Jack, clearly not encouraged by the state he was in. The Magus was coming out into the hall. "We can't keep on like this, Jack," Skerren shouted. "Can you beat him or not?"

Jack didn't answer Skerren. He was staring at the Magus, frozen to the spot.

Jazen tackled Glave to the ground and tried to hold him down. "Jack, if you're going to make a move, you better do it soon."

Jack didn't need to be told that but had no move to make. He couldn't think. He could barely stand. The Magus was pounding the life out of him inch by inch. The Rüstov emperor reached over and picked Jack up by the throat. Waves of power flowed out of his hands and into Jack's body. Jack shook with such force that the scrap-metal outer layer of his body flew off. As the Magus increased the volume and intensity of his assault, several mechanical components in Jack's neck and chest short-circuited. Jack struggled against the Magus's grip. He had to get free before the nullifier blew out right then and there.

Luckily, Skerren rolled away from the Rüstov Allegra and came up behind the Magus. He lunged at the Rüstov emperor with his swords. The Magus drew his head back just in time to keep it attached to his neck, but he screamed as Skerren's blade cut off the iron horn growing out from his temple. The Magus dropped Jack and staggered, clutching his head. Oil and coolant dripped down the side of his face. He wiped it away using his hand and the cuff of his sleeve. "You dare?" he said to Skerren.

Skerren spun his swords. "All that and more."

Jack propped himself up on all fours. He could only

watch as jagged crimson energy particles flew from the Magus's fingers and stabbed at Skerren like broken glass fired from a cannon. The blow drove Skerren back to the wall, but he didn't fall. He propped himself up against it and crossed his swords. "I think it's time the gloves came off."

As Skerren took on the Magus and the Rüstov Allegra at the same time, Jack crawled back into the throne room and collapsed. His body armor was glowing bright red like a sword pulled from a blacksmith's fire, and everything hurt. One of the throne room doors was hanging on its hinge. Through the opening Jack saw Jazen nail Glave with a hard punch to the jaw and run in after him.

"Jack, talk to me. How bad are you hurt?"

Jack coughed painfully. He couldn't move. The nullifier was about to go; he could feel it dying. Once Smart's device burned out, it was over. Jack shook his head. "I'm done, Jazen. This is it."

Before Jazen could say anything, Glave kicked in the broken door with a giant machine gun in his hand. Exploding shells ripped through Jazen's back, and he fell forward, hitting the ground next to Jack.

"Jazen!" Jack shouted. Before Jack could even process what had happened, his friend was hunched over with his cheek smooshed up against the floor and his mouth wide open. Jazen could take a lot of punishment, but Glave had brought heavy artillery to bear on him. He looked dead.

Glave strolled in grinning from ear to ear. "I'm sorry to bring a gun into this. It's impersonal, I know, but this is dragging on far too long."

Jack stared at Jazen's lifeless, unblinking eye a moment, and then looked up at Glave. "You ice-blooded, murdering bucket of—"

"Now, now," Glave said. "Wait your turn. This will all be over soon enough."

Glave slid a toe under Jazen's arm and went to flip him over with his foot. As Jazen's body turned, he shot upward and shocked Glave with an exposed power wire protruding out of his damaged right arm. Glave froze up in an awkward stance and dropped to the ground as if his bones had turned to jelly. Jazen grabbed the gun out of his hand and pointed the barrel under Glave's chin.

As soon as he was able, Glave smiled a blood-toothed grin. "Go ahead. Take your best shot." Jazen's finger pulled halfway back on the trigger and stopped. Glave laughed in his face. "This is why you lose . . . why you all lose! You don't have the stomach to fight yourselves."

Out in the hall, Jack could hear the Magus fighting Skerren. He heard swords clashing and angry shouts. Smoke drifted into the throne room lit up by bright red flashes of light coming from just beyond the door.

"Jack, get out of here," Jazen said. "Run."

Glave laughed even harder. "What for? There's nowhere for him to go. He's going to turn into Revile, and together with his father, he's going to bleed this world dry. You'll see. You'll all see."

Jack got a cold feeling in the pit of his stomach. The hard truth was that Glave was right. Once the nullifier was gone, he wouldn't be able to stop Khalix from taking over, but the Magus didn't know that. He thought his son was already gone. Jack looked up at the throne room's broken doorway. It was only a matter of time before the Rüstov emperor walked through it. "Glave's right, Jazen. There's nowhere else to go. I'm staying."

"Jack, no!"

"I said I would do whatever it takes, didn't I?" Jack

shook his head. "This is the only move I've got left." The good news was that Skerren wouldn't have to kill him to keep him from turning into Revile. The bad news was that the Magus was going to take care of that for him. Jack had failed. His friends were lost. Everybody the Rüstov had ever infected was lost, but at least he was taking Revile out of the equation. The Rüstov were going to lose their ultimate weapon. The Imagine Nation still had a chance, even if he wouldn't live to see it.

Jack got up onto a knee. He was going to face the Magus. He was going to make the ultimate sacrifice, just like Legend had done fourteen years ago. Then he heard a crash behind him, and a hand on his shoulder pushed him back down. He hit the floor once again and looked up in time to see Revile flying out to meet the Magus in his place.

"What the . . . ?"

Jack's other self crashed out through the doors and disappeared into the smoke. Jack, Jazen, and Glave all looked at each other in confusion. Jack struggled to get up and limped toward the door. He had made it only a few steps when hurricane-force winds sucked all the air out of the room and into the hallway. A blinding flash of light lit up the throne room, and for a half second, everything was quiet. Then a sonic boom sounded that left Jack's ears ringing. The shock wave knocked him over, and Revile came flying back in. At least part of him did.

Revile's upper body landed right front of Jack. One arm was missing, along with the rest of him. His red power core dangled out of his chest, barely hanging on with the help of a few loose wires and cables. A spiderweb crack covered the face of the crystal core. Energy leaked out of it like steam rising up off a boiling pot of water.

"Revile?" Jack asked, still trying to comprehend what had just happened. "Is that you?"

Revile pulled off his broken mask, and Jack's own face stared back at him. "Who else?"

Glave looked out into the hall with wide eyes. "Sire! That's not him! That's not your son's—"

Jazen put his hand over Glave's mouth, shutting him up. Outside, Jack could hear Skerren was alive and kicking. He was still fighting. Jack held Revile's head in his hands. "Where did you come from?"

Revile gasped for air and looked up at Jack. "You

354

were looking through my eyes this whole time. Does it really surprise you that I was looking through yours as well?"

Jack looked at Revile's broken body. He could feel him dying. "What did you do? I was going to end this."

Revile did his best to shrug. "I had to give you . . . every chance. Every possible chance. It's not over, Jack. Keep fighting. End it your way."

Jack shook his head. He was tearing up. "It's too late. I can't."

"You can," Revile grunted. "You're the only one who can. It's what you do, Jack. You're the hero, not me. You're the one."

Jack gripped Revile's hand. "But I don't know how. I don't know what to . . ." Jack trailed off as the light faded from Revile's eyes. His power core cracked inward, like an invisible foot had just stepped on it. He was gone. Jack was at a complete loss until the core fell out of Revile's chest, exposing his heart. That was when Jack saw it. The answer he was looking for. The exact thing he had been searching for ever since he gave in to the transformation in the first place—the root of his infection.

Jack picked up the heart and cradled it in his hands as if it were a baby bird. Finally he could see it with his own eyes. Khalix couldn't hide it from him if it was right there in front of his face. Suddenly everything was clear. The alpha and omega of Rüstov life. The bond between parasite and host. Jack understood at last.

Across the room, Skerren crashed through the doorway, knocking the other throne room door off its hinges as he ran. His shirt was cut up and his face was smeared with blood. He wasn't quite limping, but he was definitely moving slower as a result of his battle with the Magus. He was falling back when a red lightning bolt zigzagged through the doorway and struck him from behind. Both Skerren and his two swords went flying across the floor. He groaned and crawled toward the closest of the two, stopping only when he saw Jack.

Skerren's eyebrows tied themselves into knots. "You're alive? What's going on?" He looked at Jazen, but the Mecha said nothing. Jazen was just staring at Jack, whose eyes had lit up with wonder as he processed the information inside Revile's heart.

The Magus reentered the throne room with the

infected Allegra trailing a respectful half step behind him. He stopped short when he saw Jack, the fragments of Revile's body, and Glave held fast by Jazen.

"Impossible! How can you still be . . ." The Magus cut himself off and leaned in toward Jack. "Alive?" He put his hand to his ear. A moment later, his face lit up with delight. "You're alive!" The Magus pointed at Jack's chest. "My son lives!"

Skerren looked back at Jack, the Magus, and then at his sword. Jack was still staring at Revile's heart in silence. "I'm sorry, Jack. I promised you I wouldn't hesitate."

Skerren grabbed his sword and lunged at Jack. The tip of the blade was poised to stab through his power core.

"No!" shouted the Magus. He reached out a hand, but it was Jazen who tackled Skerren in midair. They fell in a tangled heap in front of Jack. Us usual, Skerren wasn't easily discouraged. He wrestled against Jazen's grip, trying to get at Jack, until the Magus locked them both up with one of Stendeval's energy fields.

"You fool!" Skerren shouted at Jazen. "Look what you've done. You've doomed us all!"

"Silence!" The Magus shouted. "I want to talk to my son."

Everyone turned to look at Jack. He stood up and dusted himself off. He was still in pain, but it would have been impossible to tell from the look on his face. "You want Khalix?" he asked the Magus. "Fine. You can have him, but it's going to cost you."

CHAPTER

25

The End of Infinity

Now that the Magus knew that his son was still alive, he seemed almost amused by Jack's defiant attitude. "You just don't know when to quit, do you, boy?"

Jack looked the Magus square in the eyes. "Nope. Came pretty close, but no. Your son knows that better than anyone. You could ask him, but you don't get to talk to Khalix until I say so."

The Magus snorted. "You're in no position to dictate terms. I see what you did now. You didn't defeat Khalix. You just tried to hide him from me." The Magus poked

Jack in the chest. "You put something in there . . . something to silence him. It won't last, will it? He's too strong." The Magus smiled. "I can feel him coming back. He's practically here."

Watching the Magus smile with Stendeval's lips made Jack's skin crawl. It was Stendeval there talking to him, only it wasn't. The lights were on, but somebody else was home.

"Khalix isn't coming," Jack said. "And he's not strong. The only real strength he ever had came from you."

The Magus tilted his head to one side. "Taking care of his children is a father's duty. He's going to be stronger than any of us. He's going to be Revile—*you're* going to be Revile. Be grateful for that. It's the only reason I haven't ripped him out of your chest."

"Funny you should put it that way," Jack said. "Ripping you guys out of our chests is something I'm finally ready to try. Check it out."

Jack nodded over at his two infected friends. His eye with the Rüstov scar lit up and they both froze in place. A golden glow surrounded them, and the parasites controlling them struggled in vain against Jack's will. Their eyes darted back and forth in confusion, which turned quickly into fear. Tiny particles rose up off the metal parts of their bodies like iron fillings being pulled by a magnet. The flakes of metal collected in the air above them, forming the shapes of the parasites' true selves. Allegra's body defaulted into its liquid state as her parasite was pulled from her. It looked like she was melting.

"No!" Glave cried out. "Please . . . don't!" The scrap-iron bug above his head neared completion. He begged for mercy, but Jack ignored him. He just kept his mind locked on the singular task of exorcising the Rüstov parasites from Roka's and Allegra's bodies. A few seconds later, the Rüstov marks faded from their eyes and they were free. Allegra's body reformed from the puddle she had dissolved into. She grabbed hold of Roka for support.

"What's going on?" she asked, cold and shivering. "What happened?"

The hostless parasites scrambled around on the ground, naked and defenseless. Jack made a fist, and their bodies crumpled up like tinfoil. As Jack put an end to their wretched lives, Roka put a hand to his eye, looking for the Rüstov mark. There was nothing there.

"I don't believe it," he said, looking around in a state of shock. "We're back. You did it."

The Magus shared Roka's sense of stunned disbelief. His hands fell to his sides, and all the anger and fury burning inside of him had drained out of his face. His mouth fell open and he looked more lost than anything else. "It can't be. That's not possible."

"The man whose body you're using right now has a different philosophy," Jack replied.

The Magus stared at Glave's broken body. "I don't understand . . . how?"

"Knowledge is power," Jack said, rubbing his wrists. "I already knew almost everything there is to know about Rüstov technology from working on your spyware virus last year. I thought that once I allowed myself to be taken over by the infection, I'd find out the one thing I didn't know—how and where you hooked into your hosts. If I wanted to undo that connection, I needed to understand it down to the last circuit. But I still couldn't see it well enough, even after I let the infection run its course. Khalix did manage to stop me from doing that much. Then I got a look at Revile's heart. Once I actually saw the root of infection with my own eyes, the rest was easy. The heart of a hero never stops, remember?"

The Magus let out a very faint, almost inaudible whimper. Jack heard it just the same. The tables had turned. The Magus was just now realizing that he was in very big trouble.

"Say good-bye to your army," Jack said. He fired a wide energy beam from his power core, blowing the rest of the roof off the throne room and taking out part of the exterior wall. The blast exposed the blue skies above and a view of the city below. Jack reached out his hands, and an amber-hued light ran through the fleet of Rüstov ships all around. A sea of iron particles floated up into the air as Jack pulled the parasites free of their victims. He used his powers to eject the pilots from their ships as soon as they were free. They flew out in jet packs and their parasites fell to their deaths as they were exorcised and cast off into the sea.

As the Magus turned his attention to his rapidly dwindling forces, the energy field around Skerren and Jazen faded away. They were free. Skerren ran to get a better look at the action outside. His eyes were the size of quarters.

"Jack, this is . . . this is amazing." He couldn't take his eyes off the window. "We have to let the people down there know what you're doing."

"Don't worry," Jack said. "They know." He accessed the media systems in the Magus's ship and opened up a series of holo-screens showing every borough in Empire City. "Everyone knows."

Jack's friends all gasped. The pictures on the screens showed nearly every hero and villain in the Imagine Nation attacking hostless parasites and stamping them out like vermin. Empire City lit up with a golden glow as Para-Soldiers everywhere were pulled kicking and screaming from their hosts.

The Magus watched it all happen. He was dumb-founded. Broken. He stood frozen in shock as his army was eliminated all around him. "This can't be. We saw the future. The future was ours."

"That was yesterday's future," Jack said. "We changed it. Revile changed it. This is a brand-new day, Magus. You've only got yourself to blame."

As the last of the hostless Rüstov were wiped out, Zhi, Trea, and Lorem Ipsum limped into the throne room.

They were wounded and weary, but Jack could tell there wasn't anywhere else in the world they would rather have been. The battle was over. There was no one left to fight except the Rüstov emperor.

"Your turn, Magus," Jack said. His friends watched as he tried to expel him from Stendeval's body.

Nothing happened.

The Magus tapped at his chest and studied his hands with mock surprise. His pompous arrogance returned behind a chilling snicker. "I'm sorry, I think you'll find that I'm put together somewhat differently than the others. The fact is, I've grown rather attached to this body." Now it was Jack's turn to be confused. The Magus started glowing with power once again. "You haven't won anything yet. You've only seen a fraction of what I'm capable of. This host body has more power than you can possibly imagine."

The Magus's confidence gave Jack pause. This wasn't right. The Magus was finished . . . wasn't he?

"You think you've beaten me?" the Magus asked. "Tell me, how do you defeat an enemy who can do anything? I can refresh this body every day, just like your leader

Stendeval does. I can use him as a host forever. I can and will rebuild my army, and I will have my son back as well! I'll have Revile! I just have to wait until that device in your chest burns out. I don't even have to waste my energy helping it along. The future still belongs to the Rüstov, and the first step toward tomorrow will be taking over your dead body."

Jack smiled. Now he understood the reason why the Magus was so optimistic. He just didn't know where he stood. "Is that what you're counting on? The nullifier?" Jack stifled a laugh. "Maybe you didn't hear me. I figured out how Khalix was bonding with my body. I figured out all his systems. It doesn't matter what you do now. Give him all the power you want. He's not beating me."

The Magus squinted at Jack. "What are you talking about? The nullifier—"

"The nullifier burned out two minutes ago, while I was wiping out your army. I don't need it anymore. I know how Khalix works. He's just another machine for me to control now."

The Magus's eyes went wide with shock. "No . . . no, that can't be true."

"You keep saying that. See for yourself. I won't fight you." Jack held out his hands. "Go on, have a look." Jack waited as the Magus tried to communicate with his son and heard only silence in reply. "Sorry, Magus. What was it that Khalix said to me?" Jack snapped his fingers. "Oh yeah, that's right. From this point on, he does nothing that I don't intend."

Shock dissolved from the Magus's face as his expression turned to a simmering rage. "I'll kill you for this."

"You could try," Jack said. "You might even have enough of Stendeval's power left to succeed, but you're not going to do that. Not while there's still a chance to save Khalix." The Magus didn't say anything, but Jack could see he had him hooked. "One chance, Magus. Here's the deal: You let Stendeval go, and I'll let Khalix live. I may not be able to push you out of Stendeval's body, but I can sure push Khalix out of mine. Surrender and I'll spare him."

The Magus was incredulous. "Surrender? I'd rather die."

"You're going to die either way," Skerren said. "At least this way your death will have meaning."

"It's a father's duty to care for his son, Magus," Jack said. "You may not care about your legions of foot soldiers, but I know you care about Khalix. His whole life, you were never there for him. You can still do right by him, but this is your last chance. The clock is ticking. What's it gonna be?"

The Magus scowled at Jack. "How can I be sure you'll keep your word?"

"You can't. But you can be sure that Skerren will kill your son right in front of you if you refuse."

The Magus mulled over Jack's offer. "And you'll let him live on how? Inside of you? Trapped in your body without a voice? That's no life."

"No one ever said life was fair," Jack replied.

"He wouldn't want to live that way. We'd rather die. Both of us."

"Are you sure about that? Why don't you ask him what he thinks about my offer? No tricks this time." Jack took a breath and let Khalix speak through him for the last time:

"Father . . . please. Save me."

The Magus turned away. He looked all around at the utter ruination of his forces. Jack could have sworn he saw tears well up in the Magus's eyes. That was just before they rolled back in his head. There was a *pop-hiss* sound, and the Magus released Stendeval. His body collapsed and was caught by Jazen. Down on the floor, the scrap-iron bug that was the Magus scurried away. It didn't get far. Skerren limped forward and stabbed the Magus in the back. He pulled the sword out and swung it down hard, chopping the body in half. Skerren spit on the dead emperor's body and kicked it away. The Rüstov emperor was gone.

Jazen deposited Stendeval in Jack's arms. Jack clutched him with tears in his eyes and held him close. Stendeval returned the embrace with equal vigor. "You never cease to amaze me, Jack," Stendeval said. He relaxed his grip and leaned back to look Jack in the eyes. "I don't know how to thank you."

Jack wiped away tears of happiness. "You never gave up on me. No way I was gonna give up on you." He let go of Stendeval and reached for Allegra. "Either of you."

Jack pulled Allegra in close and held her tight. He could see she was overwhelmed by what she'd just been through. "Jack, I don't know what to say."

"You don't have to say anything. You're safe, that's all that matters."

Allegra turned to Stendeval. "Is it over? The war's really over?"

Stendeval gave a warm smile and nodded. "We beat them, Allegra. It's over."

Jack breathed deep and looked up at the sky. He didn't need any additional confirmation to know that the Rüstov threat was gone, but hearing Stendeval say so made him smile. The words felt like warm sunshine washing over his body.

"I just have one question," Roka said. "What the heck happened to you, kid? You look terrible."

Jack looked himself over. Roka was joking around, but he wasn't wrong. Jack looked awful. His human body was gone. He was a patchwork assembly of machine parts now. "It's a long story."

"I'll bet," Roka said.

Allegra motioned to Jack's metal frame. "This is going to take some getting used to," she admitted.

"Oh, I don't know," Stendeval said. "I think the Magus

might have left me with enough power to do something about it."

Jack's head whipped around toward Stendeval. "You can change me back?"

Stendeval put his hand on Jack's chest. "Let's find out."

Jack spread his arms out, and his mechanical chest opened up like an iron gate. The red power core inside him lit up and slowly inched out of his body. Stendeval's eyes glowed with energy, and a tornado of crimson lightning twisted down from the sky. The tip of the funnel lodged itself in Jack's chest and churned about violently. Jack struggled to stand beneath its pressure. The cyclone felt strong enough to drill a hole straight through the floor of the ship. Jack's vision blurred. The roar of the electric vortex drowned out everything around him, but nothing was happening. He was afraid it might not work, until the red glass inside his power core cracked. It was a tiny crack, deep in the center, but it was followed by another. Then another. The core shattered, and a million shards of glass shot out and froze in place. There was no explosion or sound of any kind. There was only a blinding light from the exposed core, which turned everything white, like a giant magnesium flare. Jack disappeared within the radiant glare, and when the light eventually died down, he was flesh and blood once again. Stendeval had restored his body good as new . . . for the most part.

Allegra went to Jack, delighted by his transformation, but she drew in a sharp breath when she saw his face. "Jack, your eye. It's still . . ." Allegra put one hand on Jack's shoulder and morphed the other into a mirror. He looked and saw that a light, muted version of the Rüstov mark he had around his eye still remained.

Jack put his hand on Allegra's and squeezed. "It's okay. I made a deal. I'm going to have to live with it."

"Why is it still there?" Skerren asked.

"Because he's still there," Jack said. "Khalix is still with me, Skerren. He'll always be there."

Jack didn't know what Skerren would think of that. It didn't make sense to leave any Rüstov parasites alive, least of all the empire's crown prince. The armada was defeated and the Magus was dead, but as long as Khalix remained, there was a possibility, however remote, that the Rüstov Empire could one day rise again. Jack had the power to expel Khalix from his body, but he wouldn't do it. He'd given the Magus his word.

Stendeval rested a hand on Jack's other shoulder. "The heart of a hero," he said. "Like no one I've ever met."

Skerren thought about that for a moment. He reached down to the cinders and ashes on the ground and got his fingers dirty. "We're lucky for it." Skerren stood up and drew a Rüstov mark around his eye to match Jack's. "I'll always be there too, brother. You can count on it."

26

Fathers and Sons

Wars never truly end for the people who have lived through them. Every man, woman, and child touched by the hand of war carries with them scars of one kind or another. In this manner, the Imagine Nation's war with the Rüstov was just any other conflict that had ever been fought since the dawn of time. The fighting might have stopped, but the people involved would feel its effects long after the last shot was fired.

Over the next few days, people from every corner of Empire City banded together to try and undo the damage done by the Rüstov. The relief effort crossed every borough's border and was blind to labels such as "hero" or "villain." Everyone who fought the Rüstov was by definition a hero. Just as it had been in combat, the Imagine Nation remained united behind a single goal—saving lives. Superhuman healers went to work tending to the wounded. Superpowered rescue workers pulled survivors out of the rubble. Condemned buildings were torn down to prevent further injuries, and salvageable structures were reinforced to provide shelter for those in need. The city was in ruins, but it would be rebuilt. Unfortunately, some things were broken beyond repair.

Once Jack and the others had done everything required to care for the survivors, they turned their attention to the needs of those who weren't so lucky. No war ends without casualties, and the physical toll of the second Rüstov invasion was considerable. It took days, but eventually the bodies of all who had fallen were laid to rest. At least, those bodies that could be found. Many people were missing, and no amount of rebuilding or repairs could fill the void they'd left behind or make Empire City whole again. The Imagine Nation needed time to heal. Time to mourn the loss of friends and family. Most of all, the people needed time to celebrate their lives and the freedom their sacrifices had delivered. The war was over, and despite the pain that accompanied the loss of every life that the Rüstov had taken, there was still much to be thankful for.

Five days after the Magus surrendered, a ceremony was held in Hero Square to honor the fallen and rejoice in the end of the Rüstov war. That evening, Jack made his way to the center of the city to join in the festivities. He was among the heroes being honored for the role he had played in the battle. When he arrived, he saw a sea of people holding white candles and pictures of their lost loved ones. The crowd parted for him and the people thanked him as he made his way to the sphere. He was among the first heroes to arrive there. Chi and Prime greeted him as the other heroes being honored followed closely behind.

"Hail the conquering hero," Prime said, holding his fist against his heart in the Valorian salute.

"We're all heroes here, Prime," said Jack, returning the gesture. "Everyone who fought the Rüstov is."

"Some more than others," Chi said, bowing his head.

"Welcome, Jack. Your modesty is admirable, but your contribution was anything but modest. Your deeds replaced fear with hope when we needed it most. That saved us as much as anything else."

Jack looked past Chi and Prime to Legend's monument, which had been returned to its proper place. A far as he was concerned, a statue of Revile belonged right next to it. "I had help," Jack said. "I didn't do it on my own."

"But you made the difference," Virtua called out. Jack turned and saw the luminous Circlewoman of Machina arriving with Jazen. Blue was a few steps behind them. "Isn't that what my special assistant always says being a hero is all about? Making a difference?" When she said "special assistant," she and Jazen smiled at each other like it was some kind of inside joke.

"Go ahead and take the credit for once, Jack," Jazen said. "Enjoy this." He waved an arm out, motioning to the crowd. "You've earned it."

"He knows what he's talking about, Jack," Virtua said. "We're all grateful for what you've done."

Jack sighed. "Okay, maybe I have earned a little . . ." Virtua didn't seem to be listening to Jack's reply. She had taken Jazen's hand. The two of them looked into each other's eyes and smiled. Their faces were so close, Jack thought they might kiss. The looks in their eyes made him want to put money on it. "Wait a minute, are you two . . . ?"

"Yeah," Blue said. "They are." He snapped his fingers in front of Jazen's face. "Hey, loverboy, wake up. There's people here."

"Hnh?" Jazen said, his head snapping around. "Oh. Sorry," he said with a mischievous grin. Virtua's projection turned a subtle shade of red. It was a digital blush.

Jack held his hands up and shook his head with a mystified smile. "What gives? You're going out with Virtua and you don't say anything?"

"It was no big secret," Jazen said. "There just wasn't any good time to bring it up. I seem to remember us being kind of busy the last few days, don't you?"

Jack looked at Jazen and cocked his head sideways. "I guess you've got me there." He turned toward Virtua. "Now I understand why you were willing to go to war with Hightown over this guy."

Jazen smiled. "In the middle of a Rüstov invasion no less."

Virtua's eyes twinkled. "The things I do for love."

"Jazen, you dog," said Roka, who was sitting below the sphere, next to Stendeval. He clapped his hands together and laughed out loud. "I'm happy for you." He offered Jazen his hand and gave a slight bow to the Lady Virtua. "For both of you. Don't let anything come in between you two, or you'll regret it. Believe me, I know what I'm talking about."

"He's right," Hovarth said as he and Skerren entered the shadow of the sphere. "There's nothing more important than our family and loved ones. We're going to miss ours forever, just like all of the people here."

Jack looked out at the sea of mourners and white candles. Hovarth's words were something that every soul in Empire City could relate to. "We're lucky we didn't lose more," Jack said.

"There you go again," Blue told Jack. "It wasn't luck. It was you. You're the reason we're all here tonight, Jack."

Something about the way Blue said that seemed funny.

"I'm afraid we haven't been entirely honest with you," Stendeval explained. "You're not *one* of the heroes being honored here tonight. You're it."

"What?" Jack said. He looked out at the crowd of people holding a candlelight vigil. "What about the people we lost?"

"The only *living* hero," Jazen clarified. "Like I said, you've earned it. We didn't defeat the Rüstov by accident. You won this war for us, Jack. You did it."

Jack was trying to figure out what to say when Allegra, Trea, Lorem, and Zhi all arrived together. "You didn't tell him yet, did you?" Allegra asked. "Did we miss it?"

"They told me," Jack said. He shook his head and laughed, resigning himself at last to stand on the pedestal that his friends, and all of Empire City, seemed determined to put him on. He realized that for the first time, he didn't have to feel guilty about accepting their praise, or worry about their reaction to something he had yet to tell them. He wasn't hiding anything anymore. He was surrounded by friends, and his future was wide open. Nothing could have dampened his spirits at that moment.

Nothing except Jonas Smart.

"Hello, Jack," the former Circleman said. Jack tensed up when he heard his voice.

"Look who's here," Jazen said, moving to Jack's side.

"Come to pay your respects with the rest of us, Smart?"

Smart rolled his eyes. "I'm not staying. This ceremony is a travesty."

Jack scrunched up his face. He couldn't believe Smart still had it in for him, even now that the Rüstov were all gone. His friends all started talking at once, reproaching Smart for his total lack of respect. Blue looked like he wanted to let his fists do the talking. "Care to explain yourself, Smart guy?"

"I deserve just as much credit as Jack for this victory," Smart said, raising his voice to be heard over the group. "It was my SmarterNet that phased the Rüstov fleet and my nullifier that held back the Rüstov prince. I came here to give Jack the opportunity to do the right thing. To go out there and tell those people how we really won this war. You didn't beat the Rüstov by yourself."

Jack smirked at Smart. "I never said I did. You're right, Smart. Someone did help me. His name was Revile."

"Revile! Now, see here—"

"He laid down his life to save mine. If it were up to you, I would have been killed years ago. Revile's sacrifice is the reason I was able to figure out how to beat the Rüstov infection. *That's* how we won this war. You nearly cost us everything. You underestimated me, Smart. All you ever saw was the Rüstov. It's no surprise that you of all people didn't factor in what was in my heart."

Smart stood there chewing the inside of his cheek as Jack chewed him out. Jack could tell he was getting to him. Smart was doing his best not to show it, but Jack figured Smart had to know that everything he was saying was true. "I want you to know I apologize for nothing," Smart said. "I was only doing what I thought was right. What I thought was necessary to protect the Imagine Nation."

"Nothing personal, right?" Jack asked.

"Exactly," Smart replied. He and Jack eyed each other with an equal amount of contempt. There was no love lost between them, and never would be. "I have something for you," Smart said as he used his pocket holo-computer to generate a piece of SmartPaper. "Enjoy." Smart handed the paper to Jack and disappeared into the crowd.

Jack looked at the paper and gritted his teeth. Smart's parting shot had found its mark.

"What is it?" Allegra asked.

Jack held up the paper. "It's a backup copy of my

history file. Conclusive DNA proof that I'm part of the Noteworthy family."

Allegra stretched over to Jack's side. "Are you sure it's real?"

Jack nodded. "It's real. He's getting in one last dig at me, doing the right thing and telling the truth about my family, but only because he knows it won't make me happy. Have a look." He held up the record for Allegra to read. "You almost gotta respect the man's commitment to being an evil genius."

"Evil?" a voice called out. "Surely it's not evil to reunite a father with his son."

Jack looked across the plaza and saw Clarkston Noteworthy standing beneath the sphere.

"You've got to be kidding," said Solomon Roka.

Stendeval shushed Roka as Noteworthy came forward. The Circleman of Hightown looked humble. Contrite. "Too many families have been ripped apart by the Rüstov already, Jack. They may be gone, but if we let them add ours to the list, they still win."

Jack couldn't believe that Noteworthy was here. He looked around at his friends. They were all wide-eyed and silent. Other than Roka, it seemed none of them wanted to inject their opinion into a family matter. A *family matter*. The words felt all wrong to Jack. Jack squeezed Allegra's hand and let it go before taking a step toward the man he now knew to be his father. "Is that what we are now?" he asked. "A family?"

"You're a Noteworthy, Jack. That sheet of paper in your hand is proof."

Jack gripped the paper tight. "Sounds to me like someone's getting a jump on next year's election campaign."

Noteworthy took a breath. He put on a wounded look. "I deserve that. It's true. For a long time—too long, in fact—I couldn't see past that mark on your eye, but I see the truth now."

"And what's that?"

Noteworthy reached out a hand to Jack. "You're my son, Jack. You were always my son."

Jack recoiled from Noteworthy's touch. "But you were never my father. Where were you all this time? Every time Smart went after me . . . every time I needed someone to stand up for me, where were you? Where was the head of one of 'the most respected families in Empire City'?"

Noteworthy said nothing. "Did you suspect I was your son when I first got here?" Jack asked him.

"No!" Noteworthy said instantly. Jack gave him a skeptical look. "I may have thought there was a remote possibility, but—"

"But you didn't want to risk associating yourself with a Rüstov spy. An infected boy raised in the real world with a stain on his reputation that could never be washed off. Remember that?" Noteworthy clammed up. A year ago, Noteworthy had said those words about Jack in the Inner Circle's sphere. He had said them to his face. Jack had no intention of letting him play the doting father now.

"It's different now, Jack," Noteworthy said. "Now I know the truth. And you've defeated the Rüstov—you're a hero! We can write the next great chapter in the Noteworthy book, you and I. We can do it as a family."

Noteworthy offered his hand once more, pleading with Jack to take it. As Jack looked at his father's hand, he thought about what Hovarth had said. How nothing was more important than family. The more Jack thought about it, the more he was inclined to agree. The problem was, Noteworthy didn't know the first thing about family.

The Magus was a better father to his son than Noteworthy ever was to Jack.

"I already have a family," Jack said. "You've met them. It's made up of people who were there for me. People who backed me up when no one else would." Jack motioned to his friends. "You can keep the Noteworthy family name, *Dad*. My name is Jack Blank."

Jack turned away, not because he wanted to put his back to Noteworthy, but because he had a tear in his eye that he didn't want the man to see. Skerren saw it and so did Allegra. Skerren put a hand on Jack's shoulder and Allegra gave him a hug, shielding him as Noteworthy shrank away. "It's all right," Jack said, tossing his Smart-Paper history file aside. "I'm fine."

"No, Jack, it's not all right," Stendeval said, picking up the file. "You deserve better than this."

Jack wiped his eye and looked at Stendeval. "What do you mean?"

Stendeval examined Jack's history file. "As I understand it, this piece of SmartPaper verifies you to be a Noteworthy, as confirmed by a positive DNA match."

Jack leaned forward, impatient for Stendeval to get to

his point. "I know. That's the problem. It doesn't matter what I deserve. Blood doesn't lie."

Picking up on Jack's mood, Stendeval sped up his explanation. "No it doesn't. You're right about that. But if you're not satisfied with what this file is telling you about your blood, you need to ask it better questions. You need to get more specific."

Jack looked at Stendeval as if he were a death row inmate hoping for a pardon from the governor. Stendeval held up the paper one more time, looked at it in the light, and then handed it back to Jack. "I think you'll find this file confirms you are a match for Noteworthy *family* DNA, not Clarkston Noteworthy's DNA in particular."

Jack scanned the file again, looking at it like a child looks at a new toy. Stendeval was right. He'd just assumed the match meant Noteworthy was his dad, but there was no conclusive proof of that.

"I don't understand," Midknight said. "If Clarkston isn't Jack's father, who is?"

"I can answer that," Hypnova said, stepping out of the crowd.

"Hypnova," Oblivia called out from across the square.

She shook her head slowly, warning Hypnova to remain silent. "Secreteers do *not* share secrets."

"I know," Hypnova replied. "But since you expelled me from the order, I'm free to say whatever I want." She turned to address the crowd. "Jack's father is Clarkston's brother. The black sheep of the family, one Solomon Noteworthy. Or as he is known today . . . Solomon *Roka*."

Roka's head snapped up. "What?"

"What?" Jack said at the same time, spinning around to look at Roka. They locked eyes in a shocked stare, then both looked over to Hypnova, along with everyone else present below the sphere. Jack couldn't believe his ears. *Roka is a Noteworthy? And my father too? How is that even possible? Why didn't he say something sooner?*

Roka got right in Hypnova's face. "What is this? More Secreteer tricks?"

Hypnova put a hand up in a silent plea for patience. "I told you, I'm no Secreteer."

Roka balled up his fists. "You better tell me everything. Now."

Hypnova looked Roka right in the eyes. "Long ago, you were in love with a member of the Clandestine Order.

The Secreteers disapproved of your relationship and tried to make you forget her, but they couldn't do it. You loved her too much."

"I know all that," Roka said. "I told you, I remember Rasa. What about the rest? I'm no Noteworthy. I know who I am!"

"No, Solomon, you don't." Hypnova lowered her lips down to her palm and blew. A puff of purple powder went up into Roka's face. The tiny cloud hit him like a prizefighter's punch and he stumbled backward coughing. A sound that was equal parts surprise and concern ran through the crowd, but Roka caught his balance. He pressed his fingers to his temples and hunched over, rubbing his head.

Jack reached out a hand toward Roka. Hypnova turned to speak to him while Roka recovered. "Since Solomon could not be made to forget Rasa, the matriarch of our order decided to make him forget *himself*. She made everybody forget him. She gave him a new identity and sent him off into space alone. Sadly, your mother was lost in the first Rüstov invasion, Jack. Your father never knew about the son he left behind."

Roka stood up straight and looked around with wonder

in his eyes. Hypnova had given him his memory back. His awestruck expression quickly turned to anger as he lowered his gaze on Oblivia. "You monsters," he said. "How could you do this to me? To us?"

Oblivia's face betrayed no emotion. "You left me no choice. A Secreteer's duty is sacred. Our lives are pledged to the order. There can be nothing that distracts from that. Nothing."

"You could have let her go," Hypnova told Oblivia. "I don't remember you going to such lengths to keep me in the fold."

"Rasa was different," Oblivia said, dismissing Hypnova. "We hoped she would one day take my place as matriarch of our order. She was special."

"Finally, we agree on something," Roka said. "She *was* special. And now she's gone."

The head Secreteer's expression softened slightly and she looked away. "I will say this. At the time you were . . . sent away, we didn't know she was pregnant."

Roka shook his head. "That doesn't change anything. It doesn't matter what you knew. The only thing that matters is what you did."

Stendeval put a hand on Roka's shoulder. "If I may, there is one thing that matters more." Roka turned to Stendeval looking very much like a man not to be trifled with. Stendeval continued gently. "You have every right to be angry, but as you said, nothing can change what has happened. That is beyond all of us. At this moment, the most important question in your life is, what happens next? After all these years, the truth has finally come out. What happens now? That's up to you to decide."

Roka slitted his eyes, glowering at Oblivia. Jack watched him turn Stendeval's words over in his brain, simultaneously enraged and overwhelmed by the revelation of what had been done to him, who he was, and who Jack was to him. When he finally turned to Jack, he looked like a man lost in the forest. There was silence for a moment. Jack didn't know what to say. He didn't know what Roka thought about any of this.

"I don't believe it," Roka said at last.

Jack looked at the history file in his hand. He offered up the SmartPaper to Roka. "I guess we could do a blood test to make sure."

Roka took the SmartPaper from Jack.

He crumpled it up and threw it away.

"I don't need that," Roka said as he took a knee and put both of his hands on Jack's shoulders. "What I mean is, I don't believe I missed this. I spent years raiding Rüstov ships in the off chance that I might find her out there somewhere." Roka shook his head. His eyes were welling up with tears. "Then I come home and I can't even see her when she's staring me right in the face."

Jack looked behind himself. "What are you talking about? Where?"

Roka pushed Jack's hair back from his forehead. "Right here. Your mother's name was Rasa, Jack. Tabula Rasa. You've got her eyes." Roka wrapped Jack up in his arms with a grip so tight it would have put Blue's strongest bear hug to shame. It took a moment for the realization to sink in, but when it did, Jack hugged him back.

He hugged his father back.

Life on the Launchpad

The celebration lasted all night. The dead were honored, the heroes were hailed, and the people rejoiced as only people who have lived through war can. But not everyone in Empire City was joining in the festivities. In the midst of all the revelry, far away from the victory parades and festival goers, a ship was being prepped for takeoff. The pilot was Solomon Roka, and the ship was not his. He was "borrowing it" from the Calculan ambassador. Outside on the launchpad, Jack was talking with Jazen, Skerren, Allegra, and Blue while his father got the ship ready.

"So, how it's going with your dad?" Jazen asked him.

Jack had to shake his head at the mention of the word "dad." It felt so foreign, he didn't think he'd ever get used to it, and at the same time, he loved hearing it. "It's great," he said. "I still can't believe it. I mean, it's early. We've got a lot to catch up on. We still need to get to know each other, but that's what this trip's for, you know?"

"A little father-son quality time," Blue said. "I can dig it."

"He's telling me all about my mom, too," Jack volunteered. It was horrible what had happened to her. Jack was sad that he wouldn't get to meet his mother, but at least he would get to know her. Who she was as a person. Through Roka, he would know her, and that was something. After going through most of his life with nothing, he was going to take whatever he could get.

"Where are you guys going to go?" Skerren asked.

"Not sure yet. But we can go anywhere from here," Jack said, looking up at the ship. "Anywhere."

"Just make sure you come back," Allegra said, giving Jack a punch in the arm.

"Take it easy. I will, I promise."

"I mean it, Jack."

"Don't worry," Jack told Allegra. "I have to come back to school. Roka—" Jack stopped himself. "I mean *Dad* is big on that. I've already missed a whole year. This is just a vacation."

"A space-pirate who's big on school," Jazen said, scratching his head. "Who'd have thought that?"

"I told you . . . ," Roka said, exiting the ship.

Jazen laughed. "I know, I know . . . you prefer adventurer or entrepreneur. Fair enough. I think adventurer fits the both of you. Never a dull moment with this one," he said, pointing to Jack.

"A chip off the old block," Roka said. He patted Jack on the back. "What do you say, kid? Ready to hit it?"

Jack looked back and forth between Roka and his friends. He was ready, and at the same time, he wasn't.

"Go on," Skerren told him. "We'll be here when you get back."

Jack gave his friends each a hug and started toward the ship. "I hope you're not leaving without saying good-bye," a voice called out as a bright light flared up in the darkness. Jack held up a hand and blinked through the glare. Once the light faded away, he saw Stendeval standing in between him and the ship.

Jack shook his head with a smile. "No good-byes. That's not what this is."

Stendeval smiled back. "Fair enough. You won't object if I merely wish you Godspeed on your journey?"

"I think I can live with that." Jack felt Roka's hand on his shoulder.

"Take your time, Jack. I'll wait for you on the ship." Roka nodded toward Stendeval as he passed him en route to the launchpad. "Stendeval."

"Solomon," Stendeval said, returning the nod. He watched Roka disappear into the ship. "He's a good man, your father."

"Yeah, he is," Jack said. "Did you know he was my father when you sent him to break me out?"

Stendeval made a noncommittal noise. "Sometimes we need to simply let things run their course and trust they will turn out for the best. I find that when people like yourself are involved, they often do."

"Yeah, about that," Jack said. "You never gave me a real answer. All this time, you never once doubted me. Never. What made you so sure? How did you know?"

"Because I know you, Jack. I watched you a long time.

Longer than you know. I watched you grow up in that orphanage and saw a young man who refused to sink into despair, even as the world around him sank day by dreary day."

"Did you really have to put me in such an awful place?"

Stendeval shrugged. "I believe I did. To keep you safe and prepare you for the struggles that lay ahead, I did what I had to do. I know it was a hard life, but there are far worse places than St. Barnaby's Home for the Hopeless, Abandoned, Forgotten, and Lost. You spent the last year of your life in one of them." Jack couldn't deny that. Stendeval waved his hands, dismissing the matter. "Besides, I knew you could handle it. I had proof that you were capable of great things. In another life, some version of you fought the Rüstov, lost, and still battled his way across time to change everything. And succeeded, I might add! Everything that you survived, everything you were put through at such a young age, is what made you the person you are. That's what I placed my faith in."

A smile formed on Jack's lips. "I'm just glad it's over."

Stendeval shook his head. "Nothing is over, Jack. Enjoy this time. You deserve it. Just don't be gone too long. It's always been my experience that the world never stays 'saved' for very long."

Jack nodded. "I believe it. Don't worry. This place . . . this is home. I'll always come back." He took a few steps toward the ship but stopped a few feet from the main hatch.

"What is it?" Stendeval asked him. "Is something wrong?"

"No," Jack said. "It's just . . . I don't know. It's crazy. I haven't felt like this in so long. Not ever, really."

"Like what?"

"I don't know. Like I'm free. Right now I don't know what to do with myself. I finally got past the future, and for the first time in forever, I don't know what happens next."

Stendeval laughed. He put a hand on Jack's shoulder and nudged him toward the open door. "Don't worry, Jack. No one does. No one ever does."

ACKNOWLEDGMENTS

I keep putting the Jack Blank books next to each other and staring at them. Actually, that's not true. At the time of this writing, *The End of Infinity* has yet to come out, so I took an advance copy of its cover and wrapped it around a copy of book two so I could see what they all look like together. I'm staring at that. I can't help myself. It's hard to believe all three books are finished. I wrote the first one four years ago, entirely on spec (no book deal, no agent). Back then, getting even *part* of Jack's story published was a long shot. I was very careful to end things in a way that gave the reader closure, but still left the door open for more . . . just in case. I'm so grateful that things worked out the way they did and I was able to complete this trilogy. I hope you enjoyed the ride. There are a few people I need to thank for making the trip possible.

First off, there's my wife. My *beautiful* wife, who makes all my insane dreams a reality. The love and support she gives to me and to our family is one thing, but there's also the fact that, for whatever reason, I just can't seem to get good writing done when she's not around. She's my muse, and I love her for that and so much more.

I have to thank my mom and dad for the inspiration they gave me, probably without ever knowing it. Let's face it, using an orphan as your main character in a book like this is pretty common, but for me Jack's story is very personal because my dad was an orphan. He was raised by his foster family, which was not a term that was ever used in my house. He was raised by his *family*. My mom and dad taught me what that word really meant, and I learned early on that it was about a lot more than blood. On top of that, I have to say that my dad is a lot like Jack in that he has zero "quit" in him. Jack was named for my son, but there is a lot of my dad in there too.

Speaking of my kids, I want to thank my two boys for keeping me young, keeping me crazy, and keeping me laughing every day.

No acknowledgments page would be complete without mention of my agent, Chris Richman, who was the first person to take a chance on Jack Blank. Thanks again, Chris.

Then there is my brilliant editor, Liesa Abrams, whose faith and support allowed me to tell this whole story, and whose keen insights helped me make it the best it could be. Thank you, Liesa!

Additional thanks is owed to Annie Berger, whose input on the later drafts of this book was invaluable. Thank you to Stephanie Evans Biggins, the tireless copyeditor who catches all my mistakes and makes my words talk real good. Also to Karin Paprocki, the talented art director, and Owen Richardson, the amazing artist responsible for this book's cover. Thanks to Bethany Buck, Mara Anastas, Paul Crichton, Anna McKean, and everyone at Aladdin. Please forgive me if I'm leaving anyone out! (I'm sure that I am.)

Finally, I want to thank you, the reader, one more time. Thanks for buying into Jack's story and sticking around to see how it turned out. I hope you were satisfied with the end . . . for now, anyway. You're all invited to join me on the next adventure. When that will be, I can't say, but some time in the near future. Like Stendeval always tells Jack, "The future isn't written."

Don't worry, I'm writing as fast as I can.

MATT MYKLUSCH

has been obsessed with comic books and superheroes since he was five years old. He lives in New Jersey with his wife and family, where he is hard at work on his next book.